"IT'S NOT GOING TO BE ANYTHING LIKE RAPE," SEGRETTI SAID.

"Mindplay. Not the piddly little stuff you've been fooling around with. Not even the stuff that most people fool around with, buying neuroses and thrills and having their dreams fed. The real mindplay. What I'm going to do is show you a few things. After that, you'll be given some options."

I didn't like the sound of any of it. The thing was, I was scared. Not just of him or the Brain Police, but of all mindplay. The idea of going naked mind to naked mind with someone—

Leaning on one elbow, I twisted around and looked at the head hole. In the soft light of his office, I couldn't see anything inside.

"Lie down now," he said, patting my hand. "There's nothing to worry about. I want you to understand—I won't be joining you inside your mind. I mean it. Our minds will meet within the system. I just want to make sure you're clear on that."

"Okay. But I'm unwilling. I just want to make sure *you're* clear on *that.*"

Segretti touched something on the side of the slab and it glided back to the system and inserted my head in the hole. . . .

PAT CADIGAN

M
IND
PLAY
E
RS

BANTAM BOOKS

TORONTO • NEW YORK • LONDON • SYDNEY • AUCKLAND

MINDPLAYERS

A Bantam Spectra Book / August 1987

ISBN 0-553-26585-7

Published simultaneously in the United States and Canada

PRINTED IN THE UNITED STATES OF AMERICA
KR   0 9 8 7 6 5 4 3 2 1

This is for my husband,
Arnie Fenner
for love and loyalty
above and beyond

and

In loving memory of
Tom Reamy
Won't forget, Tom

I wish to express my thanks to the following people, for their considerable help and encouragement:

Gardner Dozois, Terry Matz, Lisa Tallarico, Ellen Datlow, Merrilee Heifetz, Victoria Schochet, Susan Casper, Tom Abellera, Jim Loehr, Ken Keller, Kathye McAndrew, Parke Godwin, Barry Malzberg, Jeannie Hund-Stuart, Robert Haas, James Gunn, Renée Duvall, Carolyn Hoppe, Cheryl Hawkinson, Mr. and Mrs. Robert A. Heinlein, Mr. and Mrs. George W. Fenner, and not least of all to my mother, Mrs. Helen S. Kearney, whose contributions would fill a book on their own.

And of course, many thanks to Shawna McCarthy, caring editor, great friend.

PART ONE

ALTERED STATES OF CONSCIOUSNESS

THE MADCAP

I did it on a dare. The type of thing where you know it's a mistake but you do it anyway because it seems to be Mistake Time.

Of course, any time I did something with Jerry Wirerammer was Mistake Time. That seemed to be Jerry Wirerammer's purpose in life. He was a cheery-looking type, very fair, all good teeth and clean hair and new clothes. He was also very crazy. His angle was skewed with respect to the rest of reality; one of those localized anomalies in human skin who always wants to make things interesting.

He came to me with the madcap, I didn't go looking for him, which proves that when it's Mistake Time, it won't do you any good to hide out in your efficiency, wondering how overdrawn you can get with the kitchen before the meal dial locks up.

Even so, I suppose I should have known better than to let him in, but I figured, what the hell—he'd gone to all the trouble of fooling the entrance security program, I might as well see what he was up to now.

The madcap was surprising. Jerry's trade ran mainly to bootlegged pharmaceuticals—hypnotics, limbos, meditative facilitators, hallucinogens. Hardware was usually beyond him unless he stole it, and he didn't like to steal. Stealing was too physical, he'd told me once.

"But this is just borrowed," he said, handing the madcap to me. I held it up and examined it as he made himself at home on my futon. It seemed to be a professional make, not jerry-rigged (or Jerry-rigged)—cushioned helmet, wraparound eye-shield, built-in reservoirs for premeasured doses of anesthetic, sedative, and madness. "Go ahead, Allie. I brought it over for you. Put it on. Dare yourself."

Psychosis is an acquired taste and I wasn't sure I'd acquired it. But I was game. After all, game was the name of the game. I slipped it on. The inner cushion molded itself to my head with a snugness so comfortable I forgot I was standing up and almost toppled over.

"Whoops. Careful," Jerry giggled, lowering me to a sitting position on the futon. "You'll be okay in a minute."

Less than a minute. Behind the eye-shield, I was already getting a local anesthetic. Then the connections snaked under my eyelids and around my eyeballs to the optic nerve. Big splashy color explosions when they made contact. Where had *Jerry* gotten something this good? I was aware that my eyes were partly out of their sockets but the shield held them so securely I couldn't really feel them. Then the psychosis kicked in.

Very slick—the transition from sanity to insanity was smooth. All the neurons involved were hit at once, so there was no bad-splice sensation. The right things were inhibited just as other things were stimulated, producing a change in brain chemistry that felt as natural as changing your mind. Not a bit of dizziness or pain. I got crazy.

The actual psychosis itself was quite conventional, paranoid delusions that built up quickly, one drawing on another for substance. Jerry had been wearing a white shirt, so that meant if I heard anyone, including myself, cough within the next few minutes (I did), I could be sure that there was a machine on the roof beaming thoughts at me. Exactly whose thoughts wasn't clear, but I had to receive them: I was the One Chosen, and only moments after I realized that, I heard a voice in my ear confirm it.

You are the One Chosen, said a pleasant male voice. *Don't let on to Jerry, though. You know what a mistake that would be.*

I sure did. I let the thoughts flow into me and watched a few mildly interesting hallucinations for a while and then the alarm signaled the end. The madcap separated the chemistry it had added from my own, cleaned it out, sedated me and disconnected, replacing my eyes in one smooth stroke.

Jerry struggled the cap off my head for me. "Good, huh?"

"Not bad at all. How'd you get it?"

He shrugged cheerfully. "Told you. Borrowed it."

"Yah, but who do *you* know that would loan it to you?"

He shrugged again. "I didn't ask."

"Probably the same people who put the machine on the roof."

"What?" said Jerry, still cheerful.

"The machine on the roof. The one that—"

I told you *not to say anything*, said that male voice, now coming from a point slightly above me and to the right. I looked up in its direction. Jerry caught it and his cheerfulness faded a bit.

"Uh-oh," he said.

"What do you mean, 'uh-oh'?"

"Nothing."

"No, you meant something by it and I want to know what."

"Nothing, Allie, I swear. It's just an expression."

"Right."

"It is. Honest. It's just something I say once in a while. Uh-oh. See?"

I tried to look knowing. "Okay, Jerry. Have it your way. But I'm in on it."

"You are?"

"You bet. And there's nothing anyone can do about it."

Well, I was wrong on that count. Jerry just waited until the sedative kicked in a little more and then left me off at a dry-cleaner emergency room where, after I was sane again, the Brain Police took me into custody.

Of course, they traced the psychosis to Jerry and his borrowed madcap and got him, too. Jerry was hardly a licensed psychosis peddler, and the madcap turned out to be an experimental model he'd lifted out of someone's back room.

I didn't find out for a long time what they did with Jerry. But what they did with me was pretty interesting.

THE REALITY
AFFIXER

You lose consciousness when you're dry-cleaned; afterward, you dream or you drift. When the fog cleared, I was lying naked on a slab in a boxy gray room while the Brain Police photographed everything inside and out. I could see the mug-holo taking shape in the tank on the ceiling. Unbelievable. My first offense and they were taking a mug-holo as though I were a hardcore mind criminal, and for what was basically a victimless crime at that. Was this someone's election year? I wondered. Or maybe I was still at the dry-cleaner's waiting for treatment and this was a psychotic dream.

"Haas, Alexandra Victoria," said a female voice. Not a paranoid delusion but real, belonging to the Brain Police officer looking through the thick observation window at me.

"Yes?" I said, trying to sound casual and matter-of-fact all at once.

"You can dress now," she said.

I sat up. A set of prison jumpjohns was lying over the foot of the slab. I put them on a leg at a time, trying to get my thoughts together.

I didn't know much about the Brain Police—not many people do unless they get into trouble with them, and those people don't talk much about it later—but at that moment, I'd rather have been facing the IRS. At least the IRS couldn't audit your thoughts. The woman on the other side of the window didn't look like gestapo; she was plain to the point of dowdy with her straight sandy hair and bare face. The uniform was more the kind of thing you'd put on if you were going to paint something yourself. She was gazing expressionlessly in my direction without looking directly at me. When I finished dressing, a door opposite the slab whispered open and I stepped through into another boxy room.

"Have a seat," the officer said, pointing at a table and

two chairs in the center of the room. She remained at the window and the desk beneath it. I could see a smaller duplicate of my mug-holo revolving in one of the two monitors set between the array of system controls.

I sat. "Now what happens?"

Another door across the room opened and a round man in a beige sacsuit came in. The officer turned away and made herself busy at the desk. The man looked harmless enough; he wasn't any taller than I but a good deal heavier. He barely nodded to me as he went over to her. They whispered to each other for a few minutes. I stared at my hands on the tabletop, trying to catch a few words, but I couldn't hear a thing.

Abruptly, the woman crossed the room and left. I watched her go and then looked questioningly at the man, but he was busy studying the monitors. I waited a while and then cleared my throat.

"Could you at least tell me if there's anything good on tonight?"

He peered at me over his left shoulder. He said his name was Paolo Segretti and he'd been assigned to my case. "I see you still have your own eyes," he said, after a pause. His eyes were carnelian biogems. "Unusual for someone in your position."

"What position is that?"

"Mind criminal."

"Oh, for— I put on a madcap for maybe two minutes. *Two minutes*. I didn't go out and urge children under twelve to do likewise and I didn't threaten anyone with bodily harm. The madcap was stolen but *I* didn't steal it. This is my first offense!"

"This is the first time you've been caught," the man corrected me. "But that's better."

"What's better?"

"That wailing note in your voice. Now you sound more like what you are, which is a woman only a few years over the age of consent—an age I personally think is too low, but I'm sure that doesn't interest you—who took a wrong turn." He smiled. "You're very lucky. I mean it."

"I know," I said, somewhat defensively. "I had no idea a madcap could leave you altered after it cleaned out the psychomimetics. I thought when it was over, it was over."

"The particular madcap Wirerammer 'borrowed' was incomplete; it didn't have a restore setting, which you need even with the clean-out sequence. Once you put it on, you're crazy until you go for the cure. Is that his real name—Wirerammer?"

"I don't know. I never asked." I took a deep breath and sat up a little straighter. "You can probably find o‿t easier than I could. Take a look at his specs."

Segretti glanced down at the monitors again. "Can't. He's not my case. I can't just go barging into anyone's head as the whim takes me. I was just curious. 'Wireramer.'" He pronounced it carefully. "Nah. Couldn't be, it's too good."

I got up and went over to look at the monitors. There was some kind of program full of numerical gibberish running on one; on the other, my nude form was still revolving slowly next to a list of distinguishing characteristics—two moles on left shoulder, nose broken once, and so forth. I frowned at the display of my rather padded form, with my hair showing a little more auburn than it actually was, rippling down to my shoulders as though I were underwater.

"What's the matter, One Haas? Don't like what you see?"

"On the contrary. I didn't think I looked that good."

Segretti restrained himself from chuckling. "Have you ever heard the expression 'Nobody loves a smartass'?"

"Yes, and I don't think it's necessarily true."

"Well, it's truer than some smartasses might care to admit. When I said a little while ago that you were lucky, I didn't mean only that you were lucky Wirerammer had enough decency to leave you off at a dry-cleaner's when he realized you were in trouble. I meant you were lucky they caught you."

"'They'? Shouldn't that be 'we'? As in 'you'?"

He shook his round head. "I'm not Brain Police. I'm your attorney. And your reality affixer." He glanced at the watch on his shirt cuff. "Ah, it's time."

"For what?" I was still trying to absorb the fact that I had an attorney who was a reality affixer, or vice versa.

"For a little trip. We're going over to my office to get your reality affixed."

I stepped back. "Wait a minute. What if I don't *want* my reality affixed?"

"Sorry. It's mandatory after an emergency dry-cleaning for an illegal psychosis."

Great. I wasn't sure who to curse, Jerry Wirerammer, Segretti, or myself. "No, *you* don't go barging into everyone's mind as the whim takes you, not *you*. You're a real respecter of privacy, *you* are."

"You're my case," he said brightly. "I won't take you out restrained and I'll even treat you to dinner."

Yippee, I thought sourly.

Restraints were hardly necessary. With my mug-holo in the active file, I couldn't have used any credit and I couldn't even have gotten into my own apartment building without alerting the authorities. I was no Jerry Wirerammer, I didn't know how to hackety-hack the security program. I was beginning to see how ill prepared I was for a life of crime, even petty crime like being crazy without a license. But then, Jerry Wirerammer *had* been prepared and they'd gotten him, too.

Segretti took me out a side entrance, signing me out in his custody by pressing my left hand to a screen and superimposing his own print. The big Brain Police officer on the door didn't look like the type who knew much about anyone's brain; he was built more like an assassin. He also had that same lack of expression that I'd seen on the woman officer.

"Glad to be out of there," I said as we stepped out into the deepening late afternoon sunlight. "Are they always so emotional?"

Segretti looked at me as though he couldn't decide whether he should be amused or not. "They get that way, dealing with mind crimes. Stuff like mindsuck, mindrape. Even the petty stuff like unlicensed psychosis. Defensive suppression of emotions, what with all the mental stuff they sort through." He took my elbow and guided me up the sidewalk to the corner.

The city was just starting to get its second wind for the onset of evening. Overhead, airborne traffic was accumulating as it headed for Commerce Canyon; a looped holo on the belly of a crosstown express urged anyone looking for a new lease on life to visit any of Power People's 57 local outlets "and browse our selection of over 1000 franchised personas! Rates are reasonable but reservations are *required!*" I shuddered slightly as the goose walked over my grave; franchised people gave me the creeps worse than the Brain Police. Segretti noticed, but he didn't comment.

"Ground traffic's lightened up a lot," he said. "We'll walk. It's only eight blocks and walking's good for the brain. Ever notice how after you take even just a short walk, you get a new idea? Or do all your new ideas come out of madcaps?"

I tried to duplicate the Brain Police officers' no-expression look. Segretti laughed, his chubby body jiggling in his sacsuit. "Remarkable," he said. "You could be taken for one of them. I mean it." I must have looked alarmed then because he laughed a little harder.

We started walking in the general direction of Commerce Canyon; through the gaps in the air traffic, I could just see the haze-covered lines of the buildings that rose up in man-made walls on either side of the central urban air and ground artery. In eight blocks, we wouldn't get anywhere near it, which was fine with me: the filtration systems in Commerce Canyon left a lot to be desired. I didn't care much for breathing air I could see.

"Did anyone ever tell you your brain organization is unique?" Segretti asked, still keeping a firm hold on my elbow as we walked. A woman in a red plastic workerall gave my prisoner jumpjohns a disdainful look but she gave Segretti an equally disdainful look.

"Everyone's brain organization is unique," I said, glancing over my shoulder at the woman as she passed us. "Even people who think alike think differently."

"Well, I was looking at your activity readings and it seems you store a lot of information in places where most people tend to store only those things they've experienced in real time. You lead an awfully mental life. I'm surprised no one's ever approached you about it."

"'Approached' me? What do you mean, 'approached' me?"

"Talked to you about it after mindplay."

"I don't mindplay." A pair of onionheads linked together by a three-foot chain gave us a wide berth, ignoring us as hard as they could. Onionhead marriage is about as weird as you can get without drugs. "Wait a minute. I thought you were supposed to be able to tell whether somebody mindplayed or not."

"Yah."

"Well? Wasn't it in my readings?"

Segretti gave me the look I was beginning to think of as his Standard Cheerful. "Nope. You've got the brain chemistry of someone who has mindplayed regularly, entered into altered states of consciousness."

"That's from the madcap."

"No, it isn't. The madcap left an entirely different sort of trace. And a madcap, by the way, is technically a form of mindplay, though not the kind we both know I'm talking about."

We passed a dreamland where a freestanding holo of some sort of silvery bird-person was beckoning with a feathery arm. A melodious recorded voice assured us that if we could imagine it, we could dream it, and with their enhanced dreaming technique, we'd never know the difference between it and a real experience. Big deal; I never knew when I was dreaming even without enhancement. Anyway, the claim wasn't true. The human mind won't accept a script in the rem state. I'd tried it.

"Mindplay is a hell of a lot safer than madcaps or drugs, you know," Segretti said, oblivious to the dreamland come-on.

"And a hell of a lot less private."

"You'd be surprised. How private is it to end up at some dry-cleaner emergency room babbling every thought that runs through your head at the top of your lungs?"

"That's never happened to me before. Maybe because of my unique brain organization."

"If it happens enough, you could lose that unique brain organization. And a lot of other stuff. Having unique brain organization doesn't automatically make you smart."

I shrugged. "Being smart doesn't make you smart."

"But it does make you a smartass."

There was a neurosis peddler on the next corner, spitting glittery little stars into the air from a pouch in his cheek as he solicited passersby. "Are you paranoid enough? Are you sure? Paranoia's the wave of the future. Get alert, get paranoid!" He spotted Segretti and made a fast getaway down the cross street without looking back.

Segretti smiled benignly at me. "I used to know him. Such a shame. His license was revoked a while back and what he's selling are basically his own fears and insecurities. So sad when talent goes bad."

"Why was his license revoked?"

"Because he was selling his own fears and insecurities. Bad ethics. You use the client's own raw material, you don't impose your mental state on someone else."

"How can you avoid it?"

"There are ways. Training."

For some reason, I thought of the Brain Police and their blank faces.

In the middle of the third block, one of Power People's franchise outlets was having a grand opening, with a freestanding holo of a party in progress on the sidewalk in front of the store. There were hardly over 1000 personas displayed; probably just some of their best-sellers mixed in with the slower-moving types. A deliriously-in-love Nordic couple with matching gold hair and sculpted noses were discussing something with a grandfatherly man holding a bowl of pretzels. Next to him, a licensed likeness of this month's hottest holo star was laughing with the licensed likeness of last month's hottest holo star, while a tall, slender woman with large sad emerald eyes wandered among some of the other images. Very slick arrangement—it was cued to have them all turn and greet anyone stepping into the display field. Silently, though; there was no sound track. It wasn't that slick.

The grandfatherly type held out the bowl of pretzels. It passed through my shoulder and I looked the other way just in time to see I was marching through a bouncy brown-haired woman with her arms wide open in welcome. Of course, I didn't feel anything, but it still made me uncomfortable.

"It was an inevitable outgrowth of the chain method of merchandising goods," Segretti said, smiling at me. "It lets people be the way they'd like to be with each other, and when they'd like to be different, they can change without a lot of emotional problems."

"Yeah, everybody wants to be somebody but nobody wants to be just *anybody*."

"Would you deny them a little pleasure just because they're so dissatisfied with themselves they'd rather exist with an imposed persona? It's really just another form of acting."

"Actors don't rent personas so they can act."

Segretti walked us a little faster as the afternoon began to fade. "No, but a lot of them are licensing themselves. Acting being what it is. What it's always been. It's no different than selling their faces to endorse jumpjohns, say, or flyers or drugs."

"If you say so. But that doesn't mean *I* have to think it's wonderful." I remembered when they'd finally legalized franchises. My parents had gone out and put their applications in the same day. The last time I'd seen them, I still hadn't known who they were. "Listen, I don't feel like a big sell on how wonderful it is to be alive in this age of mental marvels. Just affix my reality and let me pay my fine and I promise never to get loony without a license again."

"I don't believe you," Segretti said flatly but no less cheerfully.

Well, he was on target there, but I didn't say anything. The streets were becoming a little more crowded as the lights came on; apparently there were plenty of parties somewhere tonight. We went in silence the rest of the way to his office.

* * *

Segretti's office was schizy; half of it was crowded with screens of various sizes and cassette library cases piled floor to nearly ceiling. You could hardly see out of some of the windows for the stacks of books and program boxes on the sills. He had two desks, back to back, and there was less than a square foot of clear space on both of them with all the slates and styluses and even more books he had scattered all over them.

The other side of the room was completely separate, as though a tangible, if unseen, barrier ran right through the center. That side was reserved for his system. It was fair-sized, maybe seven feet by ten, with two cushioned slabs and two holes the size of small ovens, where we'd be sticking our heads. The outside of the system didn't show much, except for six monitor screens and the lighted control panel between the headholes.

"Hungry?" Segretti asked brightly.

I just looked at him.

"I've got a nice lasagna dinner on the dial. Algae instead of spinach but it tastes great, I mean it. Come on." He led me around a corner on the cluttered side of the room and into a small, tidy alcove where an old-fashioned breakfast nook stood under a delivery box and a dial.

When the delivery box chimed and the door slid up and I smelled the lasagna, hunger hit me all at once. Segretti served us healthy portions from the dish without making much of a dent in what was left. "Plenty of cheese," he said, putting a fork in my hand. "You're a bit depleted in the neurotransmitter department, so eat up. We're going in."

"On this?"

"Oh, it's all fortified."

"You could have just shot me."

"The brain likes to take its nourishment conventionally, through the stomach. Shooting you full of concentrate is a strain in the long run, something you should be more concerned about. You don't go cranking up the thought

machine indiscriminately or someday you'll wake up
with Swiss cheese behind your eyes, I mean it. *I* eat."

"Obviously."

He didn't take offense. "If I wanted to look different, I
would. Anyone can."

The lasagna tasted wonderful, lacking the mediciney
undertaste fortified food usually had. Segretti let me
diminish a fair amount of it in peace, beaming at me as
though he'd cooked it himself. I could feel myself
starting to relax after a bit, at least physically. No
tranquilizers, just the right combination of carbohy-
drates in the right dosage. But I didn't want to relax.

"I've never had my reality affixed," I said, after he'd
served me another helping. "I don't see why I have to."

"It's the law." He frowned at the dish, then shrugged
and helped himself to more.

"But why? I mean, I know what reality I'm in now."

"Then, you'll still be in the same reality afterwards.
Nothing to worry about."

My appetite died suddenly. I sat back against the
booth and pushed my plate away.

"Uh-uh," Segretti said, gesturing with his fork and the
long dangle of mozzarella cheese hanging from one of the
tines. "Keep eating."

"I thought you referred to mindrape as a crime."

Now I got a reaction out of him. He put down his fork
and stared at me, the carnelian eyes scanning my face.
"I'm not going to mindrape you."

"You're not? Tell my mind that. It doesn't seem to
believe you. My mind has a mind of its own. As it were."

"*You* committed the crime. I can't believe you didn't
know you'd have to go through some kind of probe."

"What I didn't know was that I'd get caught," I
mumbled, staring at the half-finished lasagna on my
plate.

"The Brain Police put together an approximate picture
of your history without having to access your mind.
Everything you do leaves its mark on your brain
chemistry, you know. Though I must say this is the first
time I know of that anyone's brain chemistry deceived
their analysis. I'll have to enter a note in your record that

you've never mindplayed. Real mindplay is harder to pinpoint specifically than things like madcaps or drugs. Because it's so global, you know.

"Anyway, this was the fifth madcap you've taken, the third in about the last twelve months. A fair amount of hypnotics and meditation drugs. You've also limboed quite a bit with catalysts and you've tried enhanced dreaming two or three times—it was hard to tell because it apparently affected your normal dreaming for some time afterwards. You'd do better to visit a dreamfeeder but instead you put on illegal madcaps that could do serious damage. Makes sense." He pointed at my plate. "Eat. I mean it."

I pulled the plate over and twiddled my fork in the sauce.

"Once you have commerce in things mental," he went on, "you give up your right to be free of an apropos legal system. Mindplay's been around a lot longer than you have. Blame it on society. Perhaps you'd prefer to go to an enclave and live happily ever after, sans madcaps, sans Brain Police, sans any kind of mindplay at all."

"It sounds more attractive all the time."

"You wouldn't like it. I can tell." He leaned his elbows on the table and looked at me with his round face all puckered up earnestly. "It's not going to be anything like rape."

"But you'll be in there!"

"No, I won't. We'll both be in the system, where we'll meet in mind-to-mind contact. But I won't be *in* your mind. There's only room enough for you in there. Part of you would have to be excised for both of us to fit. I'm not going to do that."

"How would I know if you did?"

"A record of your brain activity is being kept at three separate locations. When we're through here, you'll be tested at each location and the results compared. Any sign of tampering and *I'm* under arrest and you get restored. With a large cash settlement. But you have to know."

"Know what?"

"Mindplay. Not the piddly little stuff you've been

fooling around with. Not even the stuff that most people fool around with, buying neuroses and thrills and having their dreams fed. The real mindplay—that isn't even the word for it. 'Mindplay.' It's always sounded trivial. But it isn't. What I'm going to do is show you a few things. After that you'll be arraigned, and what happens after your arraignment depends. You'll be given some options. Because of your unique brain organization."

I didn't like the sound of any of it but I forced myself to start eating again. If we were going to run around inside my head, or whatever, and I really was low on neurotransmitter, I'd be no match for him.

The thing was, I was scared. Not just of him or the Brain Police, but of all mindplay. I didn't mind, as it were, an altered state of consciousness, but the idea of going naked mind to naked mind with someone . . .

And people did it every day, as though they were just meeting each other on the street instead of mind to mind. How did they keep themselves from leaking into each other, or from disintegrating completely into one big blob of mixed-up consciousness?

It worried me. Everything worried me. Segretti said the Brain Police hadn't accessed my mind—what a way to put it—while I'd been down, but how would I know the difference? Like a perfect crime— the locked room, no way in or out, but, somehow, someone gets in anyway, looks at every single thing in the room and gets out again, and (let's just optimistically assume) doesn't disturb so much as a speck. No on knows, no one will ever know. So, did it happen? Was the room really entered? The only person it would make a difference to would be the person who'd gotten in. Would that mean it happened only in his or her reality, and as far as anyone else was concerned—even the owner of the room—nothing happened? Or would it be like quantum, where something might change just by virtue of the fact that it's been observed? And how would you tell it's been changed? *Could* you tell?

It worried me. It worried me all the way up to the time Segretti was satisfied I'd eaten enough and put me on one of the slabs.

"The system will administer a local anesthetic and displace your eyes," he said, very businesslike, as his fingers danced over the control panel. "You shouldn't feel any discomfort, though it would be a lot easier on you if you didn't still have your own eyes."

Leaning on one elbow, I twisted around and looked at the headhole. In the soft light of his office, I couldn't see anything inside.

"Lie down, now. There's nothing to worry about." He patted my hand.

"Do I look worried?" I said, forcing myself to lie down.

"No. The first thing the system will do is play a little game with you, just by way of getting acquainted and helping you relax. I've set it for a simple color exercise. You can just watch or participate as you choose. Once the system senses you're relaxed enough, we'll make contact."

"What if I never get relaxed enough?"

Segretti did something to the slab and I felt it rearranging itself slightly under me, molding to the contours of my body.

"Comfortable, isn't it. Listen, I want you to understand—I won't be joining you inside your mind. I mean it. Our minds will meet within the system."

"So you said."

"I just want to make sure you're clear on that."

"Okay. But I'm not willing. I just want to make sure *you're* clear on *that.*"

Segretti touched something else on the side of the slab and it glided back to the system and inserted my head in the hole.

The inside of the headhole was dark and pleasant smelling, like a field after a light spring rain. The smell grew stronger with every breath I took and I was just starting to feel almost calm when I felt something soft close around my neck and panic kicked in like an electroconvulsant.

Dark! And small! And close! And something had me by the neck and that smell, that smell, smothering me in pleasantness and I had to get out, get *out*—

Then the system was injecting the local anesthetic and before I could even register that my eyes were partway out of their sockets, the connections had reached my optic nerves and it was no longer dark and small and close. The fresh-field smell seemed to be coming from me now, spreading through my awareness like haze. I was floating along with it, alert but calm, no longer burdened with a physical body.

It felt pretty good. Not ecstasy but all right, the kind of well-being you'd choose over ecstasy when you were having a bad day—and this, I thought, definitely qualified as a bad day. I had a sense of being somewhere, in some sort of location, and I thought of looking around, even though I didn't really have anything to look with.

As soon as the idea occurred to me, the colors came up. It wasn't like light coming up, though you'd have thought it would be. For some reason, it made me think of music rather than light, like music I'd been hearing for a while but had only just become aware of.

Blue came first, deep, dark, fading in from the edge of my perception. As I watched, it changed, becoming lighter. It evolved into a soft green and I automatically thought of the fresh-field aroma. I smelled the memory and knew that it was the memory, not the aroma itself. Very trippy.

A small spot of yellow blossomed at the center of my perception and sent out tendrils. Well, it was *like* that, but that wasn't precisely what I saw. I couldn't really resolve what type of movement it was, unless I changed my perspective so that I was perceiving it directly, and then I *almost* got it. *Almost.* Exactly what was going on eluded me, as though I were trying to grab hold of mercury. I stopped trying to force the colors into a coherent pattern and they sort of settled around me, the yellow changing to gold and then to orange.

No pictures, I thought, watching the colors move and change. No pictures and no sense of environment or dimension. It was a few steps away from watching patterns on the backs of your eyelids, which was a perfectly respectable way of achieving entry to certain mental states. I used that a lot myself. I'd tried all the techniques for reaching altered states of consciousness— unaided, that is, without drugs or involving another person like a mindplayer. The colors thing felt like the best solo stuff but even better, because I didn't have to concentrate so hard to keep my mind from wandering off on tangents.

The colors became a little more complex in their shadings, acquiring nuances—turquoise with a hint of stronger yellow, gold with an emphatic red underlay, red falling into purple that flickered back and forth on the border of midnight blue.

He was there, in the blue, his presence coming up the way a diver might slowly approach the surface of a dark lake.

See? No shock, no intrusion. How are you doing?

The sensation of his presence made me think of bubbles touching. There was the surface tension of his personality, his *Segretti-ness*, all the things that revolved around his actively being who he was, meeting my *Allie-ness*, the container that was me and the me the container contained, and which materials went into the container and which into the thing contained—it was the most powerful sense of identity I'd ever had in my life.

There was a feeling of barriers going. Somewhere panic jumped in me again, but the sensation leveled off and I perceived that there hadn't been a total breakdown in my border condition or in his either. We were still separate, but we were in contact.

Suddenly, and yet somehow not abruptly, I had an orientation; the colors were rising, or I was falling, or both. Like veils drawn upward as I descended, the colors were lifting and something else was coming into focus around me.

Here we are, Segretti said.

Here was the edge of a broad field bounded by a low, flimsy wire fence; a roughly made sign on a post in front of me read WATCH THIS SPACE.

I didn't realize I was so suggestible, I said, feeling rather amused.

Suggestible? How so? asked Segretti. He had come into being (if that's the way to put it) sitting on the grass near the sign but a respectful distance from the fence.

That fresh-field smell in the system. It must have triggered this image.

Segretti smiled up at me. I looked around. Perfectly ordinary blue sky (maybe with a hint of the depth of that midnight blue behind the light day color); the field went as far as I could see in front of me. Behind me was more countryside but it was different, unbounded, grass grown up freely, the land rolling, the horizon obscured by haze.

This is what your mind looks like from this angle, Segretti said, still smiling.

What angle is this?

Your point of departure.

I shook my head, or rather, I did the mental equivalent of shaking my head and discovered I'd visualized/ materialized a complete body for myself. I studied my hands for a moment; they were my hands as I'd always known them, no surprises there. I reached up to feel for my face.

Big surprise. No face. No head, even. Nothing but air.

You're all right, Segretti said, looking both amused and concerned.

I'd be better if I could find my face and everything that goes with it, I said, my fingers groping in the empty air where I judged my mouth should be.

From your perspective, you'll have a head only when you really need to feel one. To shake, for instance. From my perspective, you look quite normal. Remarkably normal, in fact, very much the way you look out there. You have a very strong physical image of yourself. How you look is, uh, how you look. Most people's inner image is a little more idealized, at the very least, and there are plenty who don't look much like their outer selves at all.

I was still feeling for my head, trying to concentrate hard enough to bring one into existence. *Suppose I want to put on a hat? Or maybe a madcap?*

Segretti's amusement took on an edge. *If you really need to do that, you'll find something there when the time comes. But if you spend all your time trying to feel for your own head when you're already inside the contents, you're not going to find out much about yourself or anything else.*

He had a point. I looked back at the open country again, straining to see through the haze in the distance. *Well, I find it strange that my mind looks the way it does from this angle or any other, even taking my suggestibility into account,* I said. *I'm not queer for the country. That I know of.*

Segretti got up, brushing a little dirt and grass from his pants. I felt as though I should have had some kind of sensation or reaction from that—he was brushing at my visualization on himself. But I didn't feel any differently than if we'd been out in the real country in real reality and he'd brushed some dirt off himself.

Well, I'm not going to tell you about your mind, he said, *or perform a thoroughgoing analysis of your imaging. But I would guess it grows out of some kind of personal metaphor you're so accustomed to that you're not even aware of it anymore. And metaphors do tend to propagate, if you don't keep an eye on them. Since they have no discrimination, they'll go on into the unimaginably absurd.*

Good thing I couldn't see any trees; I'd have been afraid to think what they meant.

But you have to remember, Segretti went on, *that this is only what we're seeing from this angle. Your point of departure.*

So how do we get somewhere else and see something a

little more interesting? I looked at the sign. *I don't really want to hang around here watching this space.*

Segretti shrugged. *This is your mind, as I keep telling you. And as I also kept telling you, I'm not going to force you to do anything.*

It may be my mind but you're making yourself at home in it.

Not quite true.

True in the sense I mean and we both know it.

For the first time, he showed real irritation; it manifested as a small swarm of noisy little insects buzzing around both of us. *All right, yes, in that sense. But if you think I'm going to go leading you around in your own mind, think again. And I do mean think. It will be quite a change for you.* The insects' buzzing grew louder. *Up till now, you've been perfectly happy to pour all sorts of junk into your head to jerk your own consciousness around, supposedly in the name of thought. Madcaps aren't thinking; limbo isn't thinking; you don't engage anything, you just lie there and have it done to you. Altered state of consciousness. You might as well alter your ear for all the good it's done your consciousness.*

I batted at the insects; now I had a head just so they could annoy it. *Okay, okay,* I said, *I'm a mental suckling, have it your way. But you're the one who dragged me in here and now you're expecting me to behave like a seasoned tripster. I just wanted to know what to do, I didn't ask you to do it for me.*

The insects faded away, along with my head.

You're right, I'm wrong, said Segretti. *Come to that, you really are taking this awfully well.*

Yah, I said, looking around again. *It's not the way I thought it would be in here with someone else. I mean, you're here but you're not invading. You're still— outside. And I like it here. I'm—* I groped for a word and found one I hadn't quite expected. *Home.*

I was, too. It was more than just getting used to it. I really wasn't enthralled with the country, and if I'd come to an identical spot out there in real reality, I'd have thought it was pretty enough but I wouldn't have fallen in love with it at first sight or anything. But in here—in my mind, I kept reminding myself—I could feel the rightness, the *appropriateness* of it. The faded grass at my feet, bending over my shoes—shoes? I wore *shoes* when I ran through my own mind? Guess so, they persisted—I might have spent my whole life standing around in that grass (in those shoes), I felt so at home. And of course, I *had* spent my whole life standing around in it (after I'd grown it . . . watered it? cut it? Stop. Segretti was right, metaphors propagated too damned crazily). Just as I'd spent my whole life walking around under *this* sky, the sky I'd always assumed to be over me when I didn't take note of the one out there. Yah, and that was my haze in the distance. The longer I was there, the more at home I felt. It was, as it were, *me*.

My attention wandered back to Segretti, who was staring up at the sky with a pleased expression. I looked up to see what was making him so happy, but suddenly the sun (or whatever) was too bright.

What are you looking at? I asked.

Symbols.

Where?

They happen to be overhead at the moment, probably because you're elated. Kind of a getting-acquainted euphoria. A high, as it were, and the mind's symbolism is often simplistically literal when it can get away with it. The symbols tell me that you're glad you're in here and you feel very comfortable among all your mental trappings.

I tried to look up at these too-revealing symbols again but the light was still blinding.

Don't bother, you can't see them. Not at your level, anyway. That's a very sophisticated mental trick you couldn't perform without training, I mean it, and even then lots of people never manage to get a deliberate look at their own symbols.

That's nonsense, I said. *All of this is made up of symbols.*

All of this is your visualization. It carries a certain symbolism, yes, but it's not the same as what I was looking at. It would be like your trying to see one of your own spontaneous facial expressions by staring into a mirror.

You can if you're caught off-guard, I said.

Yes, you can, Segretti said smoothly. *And when was the last time you were deliberately caught off-guard?*

I couldn't help squirming. The grass rustled with me.

That noise you hear is the sound of a mind beginning to work for a living.

It's grass rustling.

So, are you game to take the tour? he asked.

Definitely the right thing to say to me. Sure I was game. Much later, of course, I realized that Segretti wasn't always so obvious about reading symbols.

All I had to do was move around a little. But in the beginning, I was moving around a lot, just to watch the way things changed. I couldn't tell how it was going to happen—quickly, gradually, with a shimmer and a sigh or a blink and a flash—but there was high entertainment value in it, at least for someone who'd never done it before. I didn't ask Segretti any questions; somewhere between the open country and the cathedral, he'd tied a gag over his mouth.

The cathedral—now, *there* was a surprise. I'd never imagined that *I* would have a church in *my* head, but there it was, taking up a healthy portion of space in whatever area of my mind I was in. I looked around for anything that might have been a mental landmark but the only thing I found was another sign near the cathedral's front steps, so inconspicuous I might have missed it, bearing the legend: YOU ARE HERE. And below, in smaller letters: WHERE DID YOU THINK YOU WERE?

Segretti stayed right with me, handy but unobtrusive and still voluntarily gagged. I walked from side to side in front of the cathedral, trying to get some idea of what kind of church I'd been keeping all these years. I didn't know exactly how many years but it had obviously been around for a long time. In spots, the architecture (architecture in the mind—I wavered between accept-

ance and disbelief) seemed traditionally Gothic from one
angle, but then from another it looked different, all clean
lines and windowless, and from still another, it had a
rough-hewn appearance, like a log cabin or something. I
kept finding odd spots here and there that I couldn't see
clearly, a hole or a patch where a hole had been or a
place where the stone had changed to wood or glass or
something softer, like leather (Leather? Me?).

I was hesitant to go inside. After all, I hadn't expected
to find anything like that in my own mind; I wasn't sure I
was prepared for what I'd been keeping in it. But after a
while, I'd seen just about all I could of the front, and for
some reason, I seemed to have some kind of block about
going around to the back. Eventually, I went up the
steps to face the front door.

It was a big wooden door with a lot of carving on it. I
couldn't quite make out what the carving was—it kept
shifting and changing. When I put my hand on it, it
rippled under my fingers, sometimes changing texture
so that it felt like velvet or fur or, disturbingly, flesh.

There was a doorknob instead of a chip slot. I was
reaching for it when the door swung open and I was
inside without having taken a step.

The room was nothing like the interior of a cathedral.
It was bright with serene golden lamplight and filled
with more things inch for inch than Segretti's office, all of
them things that I especially liked, things I'd owned or
wished I had, souvenirs of things I'd done or seen. A pile
of rock crystals I'd seen in a geology exhibit when I'd
been a kid were sitting in an old felt hat I'd found in a
clothes bin in a secondhand shop. There was an old
jacket of my father's that I'd coveted lying next to a static
holo of myself on the street in front of a dream-
enhancement parlor with someone I didn't usually let
myself think about (unrequited love makes you feel like
such a jerk). I tried to see it all and couldn't. But directly
in front of me, high on a wall covered with red brocade,
was a large portrait of my great-grandmother.

A goofy kind of happiness spread through me at the
sight of her. It wasn't a holo but an oil painting, like the

ones she'd owned. She was sitting on some kind of antique chair with a high back, dressed in a white silk kimono embroidered with delicate butterflies. I remembered her showing me a picture of it in one of her old big books (the book itself, I noticed, was on a glass-topped table, open to that page).

My great-grandmother had been incredibly old, having, by some feat of endurance, outlived even my grandmother. I'd never known her when she hadn't been bedridden, often with tubes running in and out of her. Some institute had maintained her for years, just for research because she'd been so stubbornly *not dead.* But she'd been more than that to me—she'd been so stubbornly *alive,* signing for me when my parents had gone franchise (my mother had opted for a party-animal model while my father chose the soldier of fortune, complete with memories of the Malaysian war he'd never been in).

Having outlived her time, my great-grandmother hadn't approved of mindplay or anything else that couldn't be slept off. *If you have to get messed up,* she would tell me, *get drunk. You can sober up from that, and for free. And it'll probably make you sick, which will keep you from doing it too often. If you're smart, anyway.* The institute hadn't approved of her attitude, but she'd told them that if they took away her vodka she'd withdraw from their maintenance and they could go hunt up someone else over the age of 110 to study. Nor had she given them permission even to delve her memories, in spite of the fact that her eyes had been replaced decades before and it would have been a fairly easy procedure.

Eventually, she'd begun to fail. The organism was simply wearing out, as the institute had put it. Near the end, she suddenly chose dream therapy, and went out hooked into a dream enhancer. The dent her death had left wore smooth after a while, but it was still there. Obviously. Here she was, enshrined in my personal cathedral. I was beginning to catch on.

The portrait showed her a little better than I remembered her ever looking when I'd known her, but otherwise it seemed to be fairly true to her appearance. There was the same wiry, colorless hair, the square forehead and gray eyes, aquiline nose, the long jaw, her lips set in some private, probably reactionary thought; I might have been looking at my own face a hundred years on.

And maybe I was. I couldn't figure out how much really was accurate memory and how much I was filling in myself . . . *with* myself.

The woman in the portrait turned her head and looked down at me. *Now you're really catching on,* she said.

I stepped back in shock; around me, the cathedral shuddered in sympathy.

Gran? I said. *Are you—I mean—* I floundered, unable to find the right question.

How would I know anything? she said. *This is* your *place. I just stay here. Never expected to see you here like this. You're not drunk, are you?*

No, Gran, I'm not.

You're a lot more messed up than that, aren't you?

Yah. I sure am. I paused. *Can you come down out of there?*

I doubt it. The portrait frowned. *I told you, I don't know anything.*

There was a strange high whistle from somewhere. *What's that?* I asked.

Something I do know. Telephone. Voice only. I hung onto that thing until your mother finally wired it into the regular phone for me because I liked the sound better than that beep-beep-beep. You put it in here with me. You never call, though.

The phone whistled again. I found the long flat receiver on the desk next to a large crystal bowl filled with silk lotuses and picked it up.

So, how are you doing? said Segretti.

There's a picture of my great-grandmother in here. I'm talking to it. To her, I amended, glancing up at the portrait.

Are you learning anything?

Well, she says she doesn't know anything.

She doesn't know anything you don't know is what she means.

That figures.

Don't take too much longer in there, all right? We have other things to think about.

Okay. Just let me take a look around and I'll be out in a minute. Or something. I put the receiver down and looked up at my great-grandmother's portrait again.

I have to be going soon, I told her, *but I'd like to see what's here, if that's all right with you.*

She shrugged. *It's your place.*

I could have spent something equivalent to the rest of my life rooting around in there. In a short space of time, I came across a copy of *The Love Song of J. Alfred Prufrock* (which my great-grandmother had first read to me), several musical recordings, a picture of a friendship that hadn't been active in years, and, to my great surprise, a very small holo, smaller than the palm of my hand, of Jerry Wirerammer.

He grinned up at me. *Heya, Allie,* he said.

Quickly I put the holo down on the desk where I'd found it.

I never met him, said my great-grandmother, *but I don't think he's any good for you.*

Yes and no, Gran, I said. *I have to leave. I don't know when I'll be back.*

I'll be here, she said. That had been something she used to say back when she was rooted to her bed with the tubes. *I'll be here.* I felt mildly melancholy as I left.

Outside, Segretti still had his gag on.

You can make phone calls through that thing? I said.

He shrugged.

You're not helping me.

He pulled the gag down from his mouth. *Sorry. I can only help so much. Come on.* We walked around the side of the cathedral and into an apartment.

It was my apartment—not the overpriced efficiency I was leasing, but the apartment I'd idealized for myself out of wish fulfillment and the best parts of other places I'd lived or visited. There were windows all over the place, looking out on the ocean to the east and on a city skyline from high up on the west. The differing views were almost the only things I could see coherently; the rest was jumbled up, sometimes the overstuffed leather sofa (okay, that was where the leather had come from) taking up my vision, sometimes the gleaming fully-equipped lavabo crowding everything else out.

Just decide on something and get comfortable, Segretti told me.

I concentrated, clearing away a big area and laying a futon down in the middle of it. After holding that for a while to make sure it wouldn't melt away on me, I added the right amount of humidity and a hint of joss-stick fragrance.

Okay, I said, stretching out on the futon. *No, wait.* I glanced at either side of the futon; it tripled in width. *Now it's okay.*

Segretti sat down near my head (I could feel it again, for the sake of comfort, I guess). *Relax.*

I'm relaxed.

Really *relax. Stop thinking about being relaxed. Stop talking to me, or you won't be able to hear it.*

I almost asked, but for once I managed to do what I was told. I had to lie there for a long time, but at last it started coming through to me. It was like singing, or white noise, but not really like either one of them; like the murmur of the voices of people you like who are close enough to hear but too far away really to listen to; like the sound of the voice that comes sometimes in dreams, telling you the secret of life and shutting off just as you snap to awareness of what it's saying; like something you almost see but miss; like something you almost remember; like being almost asleep and almost awake; like thinking you're awake and finding out you're asleep; like thinking you're asleep and finding out you're awake; like holding a familiar object just before you identify it; like a face you know but without a name; like teetering before you fall; like a shadow you can describe only by what it is not; like a figure that is in reality the ground; like the ground that comes forward as a figure; like . . .

After a while, I sensed Segretti shifting position and I was alert, just like that.

Here, he said, and handed me a folded sheet of paper.

What is it?

Letter from your great-grandmother. Read it. Then we have to go.

I unfolded the paper, feeling rather strange. It was really a letter from another part of myself, sort of.

You find this peculiar, getting a letter from your great-grandmother while visiting inside your own head. It's peculiar having you here. Mostly you live out there, in what you call "real reality," in spite of the fact that this reality is just as real.

I've been here a long, long time, not just since your great-grandmother's death. For years, I kept pace with that woman in "real reality." When you indulged your thoughts and memories of her, it was me you were activating. Visiting me the way you just did activated me even more; I'm becoming somewhat of an entity in my own right. Because of the way you relate to me, as we used to say in my day, and because of this terribly mental life you lead.

If you think this is something, wait till you see the rest of your head. If you live that long.

I looked at Segretti. *How did you do this?*

You did it. I just helped you attain the proper mental state.

Passing the letter from one hand to the other, I could feel the paper quite vividly. It was that strange, non-tear stuff people mostly use for formal invitations. *You really didn't have anything to do with this?* I asked Segretti.

No.

How do I know that?

You'd know the difference right away. He yawned. *Listen, I'm worn out after that trick, I mean it. You can come back later if you want but I'm about to go to sleep.*

That made me nervous all over again. *What would happen if you went to sleep in here with me?*

We'd wake up unable to tell ourselves apart. The sarcasm was mild.

I'm just asking.

If it were unintentional, the system would automati-

cally break our contact as soon as it felt the loss of consciousness.

Oh, I said. *But—unintentional? Why would it be intentional?*

Sometimes the dream state can be very useful. Or just plain unconsciousness, for that matter. Never mind. Let's go back outside.

How?

You could click your heels together three times and say, "There's no place like home."

Say again?

I felt his laughter. *Never mind. Find a blank wall and stare at it.*

I found one but it wasn't blank for long. The colors came back, possibly in the reverse order in which they'd appeared; I couldn't remember well enough. A calm spread over me again and I had a sense of the colors receding, something like a tide ebbing. Very pleasant sensation. I kept watching them forever, it seemed like, and then they faded, blurred, and resolved themselves into Paolo Segretti's face.

He let me go home. He had to: I made bail. Of course, I wasn't about to jump. I couldn't afford to lose any money or start over as a fugitive from a stupid offense like being psychotic without a license. I had to go right back the next afternoon, anyway. It seemed the disposition of my case might go differently than the usual thirty days and thirty dollars or whatever the penalty was. Usually a fine for the first offense, but not always. The law was not that crazy about people being psychotic without a license. I could hope for leniency—which was better than Jerry Wirerammer could hope for. This couldn't have been *his* first offense. I wondered what they'd done with him.

I mooned around my efficiency—no spectacular views from any of the three windows. There was a futon but not as wide as I'd have liked, and I was still on the verge of being overdrawn with the kitchen. I was homesick for the apartment in my head, just as though it were a true, separate place I'd visited. Maybe in some way it was.

In the midst of all the mooning and sulking and wondering, I found that Segretti had been right—I really could feel the difference of having been in mind-to-mind contact with someone. He'd left a sort of aftertaste in my thoughts, a sense of intense familiarity, as if I'd seen him every day for years or something. It was a purely mental phenomenon, what some people call the "pressure of presence." He felt even more real to me than my great-grandmother. Maybe I had a picture of him in the cathedral now.

No, I thought, it wouldn't be there, not in the cathedral. There had to be another place where I'd keep people like Segretti. I didn't feel like trying to figure out where at the moment, though he clung to the top of my mind like a tune I couldn't stop humming. Just to distract myself, I went into the kitchen and calculated how much I could get out of the dial.

It was a little more than I'd originally thought, which

elated me all out of proportion. In the throes of delight, I ordered up the budget protein-algae casserole and ate it out of the wrapper on the counter. There was even enough credit left for a drink and a quarter, or for a moderate-to-weak shot of something moderate-to-inferior. My great-grandmother wouldn't have approved. If you had to get drunk, she'd said, make sure it's something worth getting sick on.

Maybe I had a soporific in my also-depleted goody bag, in which case I could try to sleep everything off. I checked the head of my futon; the bag was still there, and I laid everything out on the smooth black cushion.

One soporific, from Jerry Wirerammer, of course; one limbo spansule, two meditative facilitators, also from Jerry Wirerammer; a sleeping capsule in drop-dead strength, courtesy of the Wirerammer larder; one of the new minor hypnotics, Jerry Wirerammer stock; and a breath mint. Probably also from Jerry Wirerammer.

I popped the breath mint and stretched out next to my pharmacy, trying to decide which, if any, would get me through the next twelve hours, or at least give me a running start on them.

Somehow you always ended up doing that sort of thing alone. Where had my life gone, I wondered—into a lot of funny pills and spansules? What happened, and when? I hadn't always lived like this.

Well, there had been the separation from my parents, when I'd moved to live closer to my great-grandmother. I'd spent some time with her but the institute people hadn't cared for me hanging around slipping vodka to her, and since she'd been bedridden, we couldn't exactly go out doing the town or even a small portion of it. Friends—yah, there'd been friends, but they'd all drifted away when they'd started mindplaying. I could see why. What would I have to say to someone like myself now? I was just talking to my great-grandmother the other day—she lives in the cathedral upstairs. Sure. Saying it out loud would make it seem lame. Even just thinking it out that way made it seem lame.

So much for friendship, or anything deeper. There was a little of that, mostly superficial contacts, outside of the

Unrequited. I could have lined all of them up next to the drugs and they'd have come out one for one except for the Unrequited because I'd eaten the breath mint.

I rolled over onto my back and stared at the meditation mandala on the ceiling. The colors reminded me of the colors from the relaxation exercise Segretti had hooked me into. The program had probably drawn on them, I realized, and for some reason, the idea was rather comforting.

So the course of action seemed to suggest itself. I looked at the meditation facilitators. Jerry Wirerammer Vat No. 44. They were actually mild hallucinogens I used them regularly. Meditation was such a loose term; you can do almost anything mentally and call it meditation. Maybe, I thought, I should have told Segretti and the Brain Police I meditated by ingesting bouts of paranoid schizophrenia, and seen if I could have gotten around the freedom-of-meditation statute, which didn't cover psychosis.

What the hell. I slapped both patches onto the side of my neck directly over the blood vessel and stared up at the mandala, thinking about the cathedral and my great-grandmother.

After a while, the mandala began to shimmer, the colors loosening their boundaries. I looked past them, trying to recreate the whole scene of the outside of the church in my mind's eye. The extra neurotransmitter in the hallucinogens kicked in, giving me a boost that enabled me to picture it in more detail than I'd have been able to manage unaided, but I never achieved the detail I'd had with Segretti.

Segretti—his aftertaste was stronger than ever under the influence of the facilitators. I couldn't picture the cathedral without him standing outside with his gag on, frozen in place but very present. I let him stay there and concentrated on getting a firm visual hold on the front steps.

I went up those steps four times, and every time I got to the door it dissolved into the mandala. On the fifth try, I almost lost it. The colors threatened and then suddenly I found myself inside the cathedral.

There was hardly any light at all this time. All I could see was my great-grandmother's portrait and not very well at that. There was no possibility of getting it to speak to me. Nonetheless, I concentrated on it for a long time, trying to move a little closer to it.

What light there was faded away. I didn't even get the mandala back; I just fell asleep.

CONSCIOUS CHOICES

Segretti laughed. "Well, what did you expect?"

"I tried not to expect anything," I said, not entirely truthfully. "I thought maybe once I'd been in, I could go back whenever I wanted."

"Someday you might be able to do that, but you don't have the brain paths right now." I stared down at the thick protein drink he'd given me. We were back in the boxy gray room at Brain Police headquarters where I'd first met him, sitting across from each other at the spare little table. Two expressionless Brain Police officers had escorted me through the maze of corridors, placed me here, and left without bothering to speak a word. Maybe they'd thought I was some sleazoid mindrapist. Or maybe they hadn't thought anything at all. It was hard to tell. They seemed more cut off from everything than I'd ever been.

When Segretti had come in, bearing the protein drink like some kind of priceless gift, I'd had to force myself not to jump out of the chair and run over to him. The sight of his round face and pudgy little body reactivated his mental aftertaste, turning it into a small storm of associations I hadn't been aware of. Somehow I knew he was probably feeling tired because it was morning and he didn't hit his stride until afternoon, and that he was already hungry for lunch, which he wanted to eat in his office. He'd also just finished discussing me with someone, probably one of those deadpan Brain Police officers. I had no idea how I knew something like that; it was just that *familiarity*. I wondered if I felt as familiar to him as he did to me and, if so, what he did about it.

"News on your case," he said to me. "Care to hear it?"

"I think I can guess. Plead guilty to a lesser charge of going crazy without a license or plead not guilty and be tried for one count of failing to report a stolen madcap,

one count of receiving a stolen psychosis, and one count
of second-degree insanity without a license."

He was impressed in spite of himself; I could tell by
the way his mouth curled at one corner. "Or you can shut
up and listen to the third option."

Chastened, I gulped my protein. The fishy flavor was
unpleasant but it was breakfast.

"Your third choice," he said, when he was sure I would
stay shut up, "is to do something."

"Community service," I guessed, not without a hint of
weariness in my voice.

"In a way. You can become a mindplayer."

I blinked at him. "Me? What kind?"

"Any kind you want. Thrillseeker, belljarrer, dreamfeeder, pathosfinder, neurosis peddler." He grinned.
"Reality affixer."

"Justice goes poetic, huh?"

"Your brainwave and activity patterns along with the
results of yesterday's reality-affixing have been pre-
viewed by the presiding judge and a consulting panel. In
light of the potential demonstrated by your brain
organization and native mental abilities, the judge and
panel both feel that justice would be better served if you
entered mindplay training with the goal of becoming a
professional of some kind. Your criminal record would be
erased a year after your certification." His grin flattened.
"Or you can just go to jail."

The bottom dropped out of my stomach. "Really?"

"Well, not right away. You'd be fined and go to jail for
your second offense, which you will inevitably commit.
It's your decision. What's going to happen?"

I set the fish-shake aside and leaned forward, resting
my elbows on the table. "You probably know me better
than anyone. What's going to happen?"

Segretti looked troubled. "I don't know. I mean it. If
you want, I could draw you a decision tree. But just
making a guesstimate on the different outcomes, I'd say
most of the other courses have you ending up subsisting
from offense to offense, possibly incarcerated as a career
mind criminal, though that sounds extreme to me. More

likely you'd get burned out from one thing or another. Or one thing *and* another."

"I didn't ask you that."

"I know." He smiled again. "But no matter how well you know someone, you can't predict the future."

I pushed the fish-shake further away. "You know—and you *know I know you know*—that I'm going to go for the mindplay thing, if for no other reason than to lose the criminal record. Once you're a convicted mind criminal, you're locked out of anything but menial work, even if it was a victimless crime, because nobody trusts you not to tamper with reality in some way, your own or someone else's. I don't want to spend the rest of my life swabbing out some neurotic's vomitorium." I sat back in the chair. "You also know that I'm hooked. Once you've taken the trip, you're never the same afterwards.

"But I want you to know that I still feel like I'm forced on this. The choice is really no choice at all. And how do you know, once I get to some mindplay institute, they won't find something in my head that will weed me out as a crank?" I paused. "Or do you keep your finder's fee anyway?"

Segretti just looked at me without anger or recrimination, but he looked at me for so long that I thought I'd squirm completely out of my skin.

"Someday," he said slowly and quietly, "I hope you'll know the rewards of finding something of value and quality in the most unlikely situation. And how that doesn't require the extra incentive of material gain. 'Surprised by joy,' as it were."

I sat there studying the tabletop. There wasn't much to study, but I memorized every featureless inch in front of me.

"The best place," he went on, "is J. Walter Tech, up north. They've been the best for the last sixty years, almost from the beginning. Started out in another line of work entirely, became one of the pioneering mindplay institutions on the basis of thorough studies of human nature."

"Where you went," I said.

"Where I went."

I jerked my head at the desk under the observation window. "You can punch me up an application anytime."

"Not necessary," Segretti said cheerfully. "They've already accepted you. I mean it."

Oh.

So it was all over but the court appearance, which had been reduced to a formality. The judge gave me a speech about how failure to find my niche in life (unquote) was a mitigating circumstance, and that my mental abilities warranted all-out effort at rehabilitation, with the added warning that if I dropped out, they'd snap me back into court with all charges reinstated. Next case.

Which happened to be Jerry Wirerammer. They wouldn't let me stay and hear the outcome but the recommendation had been for an Exploratory—the Mental Strip Search. Or, as Segretti put it, death by embarrassment.

It wouldn't actually kill him. You could survive someone knowing every single thing about you—every single thing you'd ever did, said, seen, or thought, not just exposed but examined and analyzed. You could survive that. Therapy helped.

Jerry Wirerammer in treatment. I couldn't picture it. I didn't much like it, either. I thought about what Segretti had said: once you have commerce in things mental, you give up your right to be free of an apropos legal system. How apropos was the Mental Strip Search, really?

And I was going head first, as it were, into the whole thing, legal system included. (Head first made me think of the headhole in Segretti's office; the thought of that small dark place was enough to give me reminiscent horrors.) As if I were condoning this ultimate invasion of Jerry Wirerammer's privacy, or of anyone's, career mind criminal notwithstanding.

There were some things about mindplay that just weren't very nice, Segretti told me the day he saw me off on the underground tube. He treated me to another of his lasagna dinners in his office. I sat with my back to his system so I wouldn't have to look at the headhole but it seemed as though I could feel it gaping at me the whole time.

"Appeal is automatic. And at least they aren't going to incarcerate him," he said, digging into his portion heartily. "They're not going to offer him the same chance they did you. Most likely they'd simply let him loose afterwards to put himself together however he can."

"That's a hell of a thing to wish on anyone."

"He's not an innocent. I've seen his record. Wirerammer, indeed. The boy's a burglar. You're lucky you never went mind-to-mind with him. Jerry had the rather tacky practice of cloning memories and fencing them. Half your life would have been all over town, I mean it. How's *that* for invasion of privacy?"

"My life isn't interesting enough to fence."

"That's what you think. Suppose you found out some burnout case was having your great-grandmother? Or reliving one of your love affairs?"

The idea and the headhole behind me combined to kill my appetite. Again. "Okay. I hate it. But I hate the Mental Strip Search, too. Getting a taste of your own medicine isn't medicine."

"What would you suggest they do, dry-clean his criminal tendencies out of him? That would be much worse, wouldn't you say? I would, I mean it. And dry-cleaning wouldn't work, anyway. They'd have to go to a full wash, maybe even with surgery, a procedure that was outlawed generations ago before mindplay was hardly more than an experiment. To prevent the government from correcting people into obedient robots. Mindplay was never meant to be mind control."

I leaned my elbows on the table and cupped my chin in my hands. "It's just as bad. Choosing between having every detail of your mind exposed or being *corrected* isn't much of a choice. The Mental Strip Search is just one step removed from brainwashing. If authorities are allowed just to look at anything they want, the next logical thing to do is to allow them to mess around with the arrangement."

Segretti nodded at me. "You're not the only one who

thinks so. There's a move on now to ban the Mental Strip Search as cruel and unusual."

"Is that the way you feel about it?" I asked.

"I'm a lawyer. I deal with the law as it is, not how I feel about it."

"Yah, but you're a person, too. You have to have some feelings about it. *I know.*"

"Yes, I know you do." Segretti's smile was gentle.

I sat up straight and stared at him. "And that's not all you have feelings about, either."

"Pardon?" The smile vanished and he took on that Brain Police kind of expressionlessness.

"After that first night you brought me here, I had this—aftertaste in my brain—"

"In your mind."

"Yah, that, too. This aftertaste. Of you. Like, I don't know. Like you were the only person who'd ever gotten to know me so well. And you affix realities for—god, I don't know how many people you've gone mind-to-mind with. And they all leave that mark on you, don't they? That aftertaste. How do you handle it? How does *any* mindplayer handle it?"

Segretti glanced down at his plate for a moment. "How do you handle what *is?*"

I squinted at him. "What's *that* supposed to mean?"

"The aftertaste, as you put it, comes with the territory. You learn that *any* contact, face-to-face or mind-to-mind, leaves its mark on you. In mindplay, it's a bit more profound—"

"*That's* an understatement."

"—it's a bit more profound, but no less impermanent, really. The mind is a dynamic system. More information comes in, rearranges everything. Impressions fade. Unless, of course, you reinforce them with continued contact. Just like anything else."

I thought it over. "I don't think I can deal with that."

"It's just a matter of training, I—"

"—mean it," we said together.

Segretti burst into hearty laughter. "It really is, though," he said. "And there's nothing wrong with any of it. What are you so afraid of?"

I opened my mouth and then hesitated. "It would take too long to tell you."

"I know. Finish up, now. You've only got half an hour till the northbound tube departs and you should board at least ten minutes before."

"Paolo—"

"What?"

"Are you really trained just to forget me?"

"Oh, not forget." He laughed a little. "*Recover from* would be the more appropriate term, I think." He shook his head. "As long as it's alive, the mind is a most resilient thing. You'll see. Mindplay makes it work a lot harder than it's ever had to, but what's wrong with pushing the limit—of anything?"

"But if you get pushed over the limit instead . . ." I shrugged. "Forget it. I guess I'll recover from you, too."

"It's better to recover from something than to have been numb to it. I mean it."

"I know you do," I said.

When he left me at the tube station, it was like watching my mother walk away. Not the mother who'd bought herself a franchise personality, not her. I wondered if other people were hit so hard by their first mindplay experience, or if it was just because I was so much older and had that much more resilience to learn.

The Mental Strip Search was declared unconstitutional before they got a chance to do it to Jerry, even though it made me wonder what they'd find to do to him instead. By then, I'd been at J. Walter Tech for over a month, and they were doing plenty to me.

"**P**yotr Frankis wants to see you."

I sat up on Jascha's bed, wincing at the give of the mattress. "I'm going to ache like hell in an hour. Why can't we use *my* bed?"

"Because I paid a fortune for this one and all the equipment's built into it," Jascha said, his mustache twitching. It was gilded today, as were his eyebrows. "I've already fixed up special connections so you won't have to stick your head into the cavity." He straightened the wide neck of his sweater for the millionth time. A few more yanks and it would be an off-the-shoulder number, which wouldn't have been so bad. Jascha was an attractive man. It wasn't exactly protocol to think of your dreamfeeder in terms of his desirability, but I did it anyway. I couldn't really help it. The familiarity reinforced by repeated mindplay didn't discourage me, either.

Jascha remained professional about it, neither emphasizing nor glossing over the pertinent elements that turned up from time to time in my dreams. His matter-of-factness made me marvel; he fed elements into my dreams nearly every day and watched the outcome as I made my way through the various events and images and symbols. Having your dreams fed was a lot better than enhanced dreaming. Jascha's judgment was unerring as to what elements should be added to a dream to make it stronger or stranger or more complex, whatever the therapy seemed to call for, which also made me marvel. But it didn't make me want to be a dreamfeeder.

I swung my legs over the side of the bed and rubbed the small of my back. An hour, hell; I was starting to ache now. Jascha shook his head at me.

"I suppose I could put in a bedboard for you."

"I'd appreciate it."

"I'm sure you would. I'm just not so sure it'll help."

"Neither am I. But I told you the first time you plugged me in, I've never dreamed lucidly and I never will. I'm incapable of it. No matter how bizarre it gets, I just can't tell when I'm dreaming, even if you signal me with the most obvious symbols. If you can't tell when you're dreaming, it's impossible to take control and start steering things around."

"A lot of impossible cases have lain on that bed—"

"No kidding."

"—and they were all dreaming lucidly by the last time they disconnected and got up." His gold-flake eyes narrowed. "If I put in a bedboard, will you stop saying it's impossible?"

"I'll stop *saying* it. But you'll still have to turn in the readings to Pyotr Frankis." I paused. "When does he want to see me?"

"As soon as you're feeling alert. I'd give it at least two hours if I were you. You were dreaming pretty hard, especially toward the end."

"You put that stuff in." I yawned and rubbed my eyes.

Jascha pulled my hands away from my face. "Not all of it. And I told you not to do that."

"Old habits die hard." I got down off the bed and left him puttering around with his system, getting it ready for his next appointment.

By the time I got back to my apartment, five levels below Jascha's office in the peculiar maze of the J. Walter Tech building, my postdream lassitude was wearing off and I was feeling a little nervous. Carbohydrate time. The dial in the kitchenette produced a fair lasagna, but nothing approaching Paolo Segretti's. I dialed it up anyway and ate it picnic-style on the floor in front of the dataline, while the news babbled at me.

In the seven weeks I'd been at J. Walter Tech, I'd mainly spent my time plugged into Jascha's dreamfeeding system, absorbing technical information about brains and systems and mindplay in general, or hooked in with Pyotr Frankis. There had been a few dips in the pool for training in dealing with consensual reality, and a fair amount of socializing in real time with the other mindplayer candidates. That was J. Walter's official term for us: candidates.

The candidates were a pretty mixed bag, without many overt similarities. J. Walter's program was just as diversified: there was no set time when everyone's training began or ended. You started when you came in and you left when you were finished. The average length of stay was around a year, but that was just a statistic; the only time frame that meant anything at J. Walter was your own.

They didn't expect you to replace your eyes, either, which was something else I liked about the place, although I'd thought that would be a requirement when I'd arrived. My arrival had been rather low-key. Jascha had met me at the front door when I stepped out of the groundcab that had brought me from the tube station in the center of town. J. Walter sat on the fringe of the mid-urban area, housed in an old stone building that looked as if it had been some kind of temple once, before it had been built up and added onto; flanking the wide front steps were a couple of stone lions, almost featureless. The curious minimalism of their faces gave me pause until Jascha explained they'd been reconstructed from the days of acid rain, but the finer details had been lost.

Jascha had explained a lot to me in the beginning. He'd showed me to my living quarters, an efficiency slightly smaller than the one I'd left behind. Along with the usual features, including meal dial and lavabo, it had its own scaled-down system and the dataline that was presently telling me what was going on in the rest of the world.

It was easy to lose touch with that sort of thing at J. Walter. Hell, it was easy to lose touch with night and day, you spent so much time plugged in to one thing or another. It surprised me how quickly I got used to that, being plugged into a system, with or without someone else. The awfully mental life I'd been leading, I supposed. As though I'd been training for something like this for years.

But then, it helped that it was Pyotr Frankis I'd first plugged in with and not Jascha, probably because Pyotr Frankis wasn't real.

I finished the lasagna, tossed the pan in the disposal, and settled down in front of the dataline again. They were running old footage of the Malaysian war split-tank with present-day scenes of the Restoration, ten years after. It might have been anywhere. The Malaysians didn't look too happy. I wondered what they would have made of my father.

Sometimes I thought about calling my parents, but mostly, like now, I thought of not calling them. As far as I knew, they were still franchised. Being franchised doesn't leave a lot of room in your head for anything else, or so it seemed. The easy life, if you could qualify. Surprisingly—or maybe not so surprisingly—plenty of people couldn't. I'd never cared to find out, even just for curiosity's sake, but something told me I was completely ruined for it now.

Closer to home, the dataline told me, mindsuck was on the upswing again. There was an interview with one of those impassive Brain Police officers. The sight of him emotionlessly reeling off some of the latest cases so unnerved me I switched off and put a music spike in the dock, Coor and Lam's *Transcontinental Elopement*. It was nearly ten years old but I never got tired of listening to it, maybe because I'd never listened to the whole thing. But it was 408 hours long and somehow I'd never found time for one of those listening parties where everyone gets together and camps out for the whole two and a half weeks it takes the piece to run. Too busy putting on madcaps or hanging in limbo, I guessed. That was where my life had gone, too.

And here I was hanging around again, except now I was preparing myself for a visit with Pyotr Frankis. What a name—Pyotr Frankis. I wondered who had made it up for him. Pyotr Frankis, Jascha—Slavs all over the place, it would seem. Just like my great-grandmother. I felt for her in my mind about the same way you'd feel for a stray piece of food in your mouth with your tongue, but as usual, I had no sense of her beyond a particularly intense memory. Paolo Segretti felt about as vivid to me, though his aftertaste had faded quite a bit over the weeks.

I looked at the clock over the dataline. There was another hour before I had to present myself to J. Walter's system. No one had said I had to stay in my apartment, so I went down to one of the outside courtyards, using the exterior gallery promenade. The claustrophobia I'd felt when Paolo Segretti had stuck my head into his system seemed to have extended itself to elevators and laterals and other small enclosed spaces. Even the tube ride up to J. Walter had given me some bad moments.

The garden courtyard was beginning to fill up with people taking a break between mindplay appointments. Waving to a few familiar faces, I found the Extremely Identical Twins, Dolby and Dolan, having a late lunch at a small round table under an elm. They were both the same fraction over six feet tall, with the same amount of minor plumpness around their middles. Their straight reddish-blond hair grew at the same rate and fell into the same patterns (and cowlicks). Their taste in clothing ran to the same kinds of loose, frothy shirts over leggings, though they stopped short of dressing exactly alike, and their eyes, too, were different. Dolby had malachite biogems while Dolan had opted for reproductions of his (or their) original hazel pupils. They claimed not to know which had been born before the other; apparently, no one had ever told them.

"Allie," they said almost simultaneously as I joined them. They adjusted their chairs so they seemed to be exactly the same distance from me on either side and offered me the same portion of their identical tomato sandwiches.

"Thanks, but I just ate," I told them. "I'm murdering time before I have to go see Pyotr Frankis."

"Murdering time," said Dolby. "Sounds too serious. How is it, being mentored by a composite?"

"Does it feel different than hooking in with a real person?" Dolan asked. "Clare mentors us. Never both at once, though."

"It's different," I said. "Though I'm not sure I could explain how. Part of it is the way it draws so much on me for a lot of things. Hooking in with a real person, that doesn't happen in quite the same way."

"It sounds like you're inventing your mentor as he mentors you," said Dolan.

"Weird," Dolby added. They paused, looking at each other intently.

"But probably no weirder than anything else," Dolby said, and offered me part of his sandwich again. I took some, figuring I could use the extra fuel, and then had to take some of Dolan's to even them out. No weirder than anything else. And Jascha couldn't understand why I was unable to dream lucidly. How could I? *Everything* was absurd, whether it was dream real or really real, so how was I supposed to be able to tell when I was dreaming?

"We've finally come to a decision," Dolan said, holding off on finishing the last bite of his sandwich so his brother could catch up. "I'm going to be a belljarrer and Dolby's going to be a thrillseeker."

I looked from one to the other, suppressing the urge to laugh. The Twins had been at J. Walter for two months longer than I had and they'd been coming to a decision every week. "I thought Dolby was going to be the belljarrer and you were going to be the thrillseeker."

"We talked it over," Dolby said. "Dolan is really more suited to belljarring. I'm slightly better at finding a thrill in someone's mind than he is."

"Actually," said Dolan, "I'm slightly better at inducing sensory deprivation is what it is. Positively no trauma, none whatsoever. I'd ease you into the belljar so carefully, you'd never miss your senses."

"I'd find you a thrill you'd never forget," Dolby said, not to be outdone. He popped the last bite of his sandwich into his mouth at the same moment as Dolan. "But it would be a safe one, too, not something that should stay buried in your mind. There was this woman I heard about whose big thrill—true case—was walking a dog."

"That doesn't sound terribly thrilling to me," I said.

"*She* got a big charge out of it, though. Of course, it had to be a certain kind of dog and the walk had to be in a certain place and go on for a specific amount of time—I can't remember all the details. But it's pretty exciting work. I mean, it *can* be, looking for bona-fide thrills in people's minds. You know, most people are looking for thrills and they don't really know what they are. And most of it's a lot more than walking a dog."

"I hope so," Dolan said. "For your sake."

They gave each other another one of those looks. "Are you sure you don't want to be a thrillseeker?" Dolby said after a moment.

"We decided," Dolan said. "I'm better at belljarring than you are."

"You could both be thrillseekers," I said.

They stared at me.

"Well, surely you've thought of that, haven't you?"

"Yah, we have," Dolby said uncomfortably.

"But there's a problem. The Kibitzing Factor."

"We do things differently, see—"

"And we'd be jumping in on each other's work even worse than we jump in on each other's sentences," Dolan finished in a rush.

"Oh," I said, mollified. "Well, I suppose it'll work even better with one thrillseeker and one belljarrer. After people are overstimulated from Dolby, they can go to you and take a rest under the belljar."

The Twins nodded together. "That's the idea," said Dolan. "It'll work out just fine."

Unless he decided to become a pathosfinder and Dolby chose to go into neurosis peddling instead. I couldn't picture either of them as pathosfinders—they didn't seem to have the temperament to work with artists, helping them find what was basically the soul in their work. Pathosfinders delved other kinds of professionals as well, usually as part of some kind of therapy, but I couldn't picture that either.

Twin neurosis peddlers was a more likely scenario, I thought. I could just see them giving people some kind of obsessive-compulsive ritual or a minor recreational fetish. I was considering neurosis peddling myself. If I knew anything, I knew neurosis.

And then again, I thought, anything could happen and all three of us might end up as reality affixers. *Oh, sure,* said a small voice in my mind. *But in three different realities.*

The Twins began another discussion of who should be the belljarrer and who should be the thrillseeker. I listened to them until the appointment chime on my collar went off.

P Y O T R
F R A N K I S

The attendant on the system worked as fast as he could to minimize the lapse between the time I stuck my head into the system and the time the connections touched my optic nerves, but I still hit the relaxation exercise with a bang. There was no way to modify the institute's system the way Jascha had changed his for me, rigging up a blindfold-type sling to secure my eyes while I was plugged in. The institute's system was worse than Paolo Segretti's had been; it molded right around your face and fed you air instead of letting you breathe undisturbed. No matter how much I relaxed myself before climbing onto the slab, every nerve in my body turned into an alarm bell as soon as I put my head in the hole.

The system was patient, once I was inside. It just kept washing colors over me, working with my synesthesia to get me down off the ceiling of my skull and into a receptive mode.

Pyotr Frankis always appeared after the colors began to fade rather than feeding himself in as one of them, the way Segretti had. Probably because he wasn't real, I figured. Except, when I was hooked in with him, he felt as real as anyone did.

He looked real, too. His composer(s) had made him a fairly diminutive person, always dressed in dark, loose clothing that seemed to be hiding a bony frame. His straight black shoulder-length hair was starting to get a little white in it, just like anyone real. The silver eyes, however, were just a little too much, at least in my opinion. They would catch light at odd moments and glow at me. I'd thought I might laugh about that effect but somehow I never did, even afterward.

Today, there was a pause between the end of the relaxation exercise and his appearance. I waited, drifting bodiless in some kind of undefined open space, and then I saw them.

Snakes.

Well, that was new. They congealed out of the air—or whatever—moving slowly, floating along with me. I didn't know anything about snakes but something told me they weren't the kind even an expert could have identified. They were all colors, some bright, some pale, some dark, some almost invisible. It wasn't unpleasant, having them there with me, and I was no longer given to snap judgments about symbolism so I wasn't upset by them. They swam through the nothing for a while and then, almost casually, they all grabbed their tails in their mouths and began to spin.

I tried to back off but it was like trying to recede from my own shadow. They stayed with me, spinning faster and faster, becoming rings of colored light, giving off sparks. I felt something vibrating inside me, answering somehow. Sympathetic excitation.

Then they were gone and Pyotr Frankis and I were sitting across a desk from each other.

What was that? I asked, breathless, as it were.

Alerted Snakes Of Consequence.

Pardon?

Pyotr Frankis smiled at me. *It's a joke. Altered States Of Consciousness. Alerted Snakes Of Consequence. Life is funny, Allie. You should remember to laugh. But that's not to say you shouldn't watch out for the Alerted Snakes Of Consequence all the same.*

The environment switched without so much as a blink to a large empty room. Pyotr Frankis and I were sitting on the floor in the center of it, reddish-gold afternoon sunlight pouring over us from the oversized mural windows to my right. Outside I could see a hazy city skyline that looked vaguely Byzantine. The environment tended to switch without warning when I was hooked in with Pyotr Frankis. I wasn't sure whether it was a peculiarity of his program or something of my own, perhaps a sort of mental nervous twitch.

Pyotr Frankis was looking at me dreamily, stroking his own hands one against the other as though he were a magician preparing for his next trick. *Now,* he said, *tell me you can't dream lucidly.*

I can't. I'd try, except I don't know when I'm dreaming so I don't know when to try.

Try now, he said.

Now? But I'm not asleep now.

No, but you're dreaming.

Well, yes and no, I wanted to say but I had a sense of not wanting to argue with him. Instead, I got up and went across the room to one of the windows. The skyline seemed to shimmer like a mirage, the haze more like red dust resting thickly in the air. Minarets and spires gleamed in the sun, swollen to three times its normal size as it floated downward. Far off, I could see the points of a familiar cathedral.

Without thinking about it, I put my hand through the glass. It felt as though I were reaching through something warm and soft. The sharp points of the buildings touched my fingertips. I was a giant; the skyline outside was miniature.

I touched the cathedral, running my hand over the roof, the spires, the buttresses. My fingertip was larger than the front door. I could find no evidence of the patched places I'd seen when I'd visited it before. Some things were visible only from very close up.

My hand closed around the tallest spire. In one stroke, I could have pulled the cathedral up like a root. If I did, would everything come with it, or would I just pull the housing off the foundation, leaving everything inside exposed?

My attention pulled back, turning inward so that the mental flow of time halted. Not this; you don't go exposing your private places just for the sake of having done something. I let go of the cathedral.

Abruptly, I was sitting on the floor again, facing Pyotr Frankis. There were still indentations from where I'd been holding the spires.

No one is prepared for such an extreme action, Pyotr Frankis said. *Not you, certainly not me. Mental activity does not need to be so drastic. If I were real, I would be unable to cope with being a witness to such an act of self-*

exposure. And even so, it might have done something to my configuration.

But suppose I took you there and showed it to you?

That would be different, he said. *A revealing rather than an exposing, which is quite something else. It would be in context, and so appropriate for you to do that.* He laughed a little. *Or would you really like to try ripping off your undergarments before you remove your outer clothes?*

Oh. I heard something slither dryly across the floor behind me but I didn't turn around. *Alerted snakes of consequence?* I asked.

I told you to watch out for them, said Pyotr Frankis, mildly amused. *Say it with the capitals. Alerted Snakes Of Consequence.*

Alerted s-s-s-S-snakes of conse-con— I shrugged. *Sorry. I guess I just can't accept them. I mean, they're a joke. Aren't they?*

He was smiling at me.

All right, then, what are they? Really.

Is really *the word you want to use, Allie?*

I did my best to convey *glare* as a total sensory experience, which amused him.

Think of them as . . . oh, perhaps something you hadn't thought of. How much of the consequence of anything can you foresee? And everything has consequences, Allie, especially in the mind. You have to be— he beamed like a small sun—*alert.*

Okay. I'm alert. What now?

We were sitting on a bench in a courtyard not unlike the one where I'd left the Twins, except this one was an island in the middle of an endless sea of low shrubbery. Pyotr Frankis was on my right, gazing up at the pale blue sky. *I see forever,* he said. No, what he'd actually said was, *I can see this is going to take forever,* but somehow it had gotten compressed. He reached over almost casually with his right hand and pressed the palm to my forehead, which materialized as soon as he made contact. I jumped. There was pressure and a flash memory of the last several days. Tendrils from his fingers unwound, going deeper, touching even earlier events.

Switch. The memory probe was over and now we were ambling along the green bank of a river, Pyotr Frankis still on my right, closer to the water.

I have some things for you to do, he said. *Perhaps they will help. First, you will fast two days out of seven. Two days in a row, forty-eight hours. Only water those days, lots of it. Start today, as soon as we finish. Spend at least an hour every other day in the pool, longer if you can manage. Take walks. Dream vigorously.*

Except for the fasting and the frequency in the pool, I do all of that already, I said.

Now do it in a mode of following my instructions.

All right, I said, *but tell me something—all I've done since I've gotten here is have my dreams fed, paddle around in the pool, and meet with you. When do I take the other forms of mindplay?*

The time will come. This is just the beginning for you, Allie, and everything begins in dreams. He smiled up at me. Being closer to the water, he was shorter than I was. His silver eyes gleamed as he leaned forward and kissed me. Nothing much, just a brush of lips (I'd gotten so used to being without a head that it was somewhat jarring when it sprang into existence for any reason). Then he turned and went toward the river.

He didn't do anything so ostentatious as walk on water. He just walked into the river and disappeared beneath the surface.

Colors fell over me like a soft rain of veils.

G O I N G   F A S T

Two days out of seven. It was hell. I took to marching through the city by myself (walks he wants me to take, I'd think, well, I'm taking them, this is a walk, maybe I'll walk off the edge of the world, lucid walking, we could call it), glaring straight ahead without really seeing anything. Then I'd feel bad because I knew that wasn't in the spirit of what Pyotr Frankis wanted me to do, so after I could eat, I'd go out again and look at real reality as though I were a tourist.

There were still regular appointments to keep with Jascha, fasting or not. My dreams had to be fed even if I went hungry. The fasting dreams were not all about food, but they always contained some element involving consumption, much more so than the dreams I had when I wasn't fasting. Jascha would feed in some element—an image of a piece of sculpture, a stranger entering the room, music playing—and whatever it was, I would find some way to consume it.

But never lucidly. I still behaved as though I were in real reality, even as I was absorbing a futon or a holo-tank. If it continued to frustrate Jascha, he didn't say anything about it.

The pool was a different experience. The hookups were buried in the J. Walter sub-basement, a collection of pods watched over by several attendants who installed people and removed them again like batteries in a power pack. I had to spend half an hour breathing myself into a near trance just to get near one of those pods. The attendants didn't seem to care. They were a curiously bland group, all of a kind; I often wondered how they'd come to do what they were doing, and what they'd been doing previously. But after a bout of swimming around in consensual reality, it was a relief to surface to one of those nondescript beige uniforms who would help me out of the pod without comment and send me off.

The pool fascinated me, as it did just about all the candidates and even the resident mindplayers, who dipped into it almost as often as we did. You couldn't always tell who was who in the pool—people wouldn't necessarily manifest in a form you would recognize from the outside world. Sometimes you couldn't even tell which were the real people and which were pool phantoms, a phenomenon nobody understood completely. The prevailing theory was that they were leftover waking dreams or visualizations that had taken root in the reality, like feedback loops or something. Aside from the general bizarreness of the phantoms' existence, it meant that you couldn't always be sure of exactly how many people were really in the pool at any one time.

After my first few dips in the pool, I stopped trying to figure that out while I was still in, although I had a feeling Jascha wouldn't have approved. Not lucid enough. Well, there were times to be lucid and times just to go with it, I reasoned. Maybe someday I'd strike a balance.

Entering consensual reality was different from meeting someone mind-to-mind in a system. Things were already in progress; you had to visualize a place for yourself in the middle of whatever was going on. Breaching the boundary conditions of the environment (or whatever) was sometimes easy, sometimes not. Occasionally, I found myself watching for several mental minutes before I could get the gist of what was going on and find a place for myself in it.

After that, it was almost easy. Sort of. You had to concentrate to hold up your end of the reality. If your energy flagged, you'd find yourself locked out of the action, watching as though from behind a transparent screen. Eventually, you learned how to keep pedaling, as it were, without devoting the greater part of your attention to it.

In spite of the strong mental image Paolo Segretti had said I had of myself, I was surprised to find I didn't always join the pool in an easily identifiable form. Preexisting conditions might dictate something entirely different than how I usually saw myself and my unconscious (or something) complied. It was quite natural. The day I faded in to find a playground scenario in progress, I joined as another child. Another time, the pool was flying a jet stream so I came in as a flyer, complete with flashy paint job and chrome accents.

Scenarios seldom persisted for very long, however, and there wasn't always a great deal of continuity. The pool system provided a backup environment in case things dissolved, so we wouldn't all be drifting around in our private conceptions of limbo—a pool of the swimming kind, with deep end, diving board, and even a smell of chlorine. But you still had to work to keep your part in it going.

Generally, I took a walk after a session in the pool even if I was exhausted, probably as a reaction against knowing I'd been shut up in a pod barely larger than a body bag. I'd walk halfway across the city sometimes, past the business district, through the residential area, all the way to the lake harbor, and then grab a flyer back.

I began to get into a kind of rhythm that wasn't exactly a routine but more a matter of knowing what I had to do and what I could leave open. It figured, I thought; Pyotr Frankis had to exist the same way, since he wasn't real.

Well, *I* felt real enough. The only times I didn't feel quite real were on fast days, when I wasn't sure I could generate enough presence to hold my place in real reality, let alone in something as trippy as the pool. Nonetheless, I managed, not always lucidly, and I might have gone cycling my way through my life almost indefinitely, except that McFloy showed up. And that changed everything.

THE EYE TRICK

I was eight hours into another bout of fasting and the pool had gone pastoral, rolling hills bounded by lightly wooded areas, mountains in the distance under an overcast sky. The pastoral scenario was a variation on a recurring environment, fairly undemanding in terms of how much it took to make a place for yourself in it. The air seemed charged with collective conscious energy. Must be a full pool today, I thought, settling down in a small stand of trees on the fringe of the forest. Whenever the pool was full, the situation simplified to accommodate all the presences at work in it. I coasted for a while, watching two men directly in front of me set up a sketchy campsite with a barely realized lean-to and some vague equipment. One of the men was very old, the other just out of adolescence. The Twins, I guessed and wondered how they appeared to each other. How I was seeing them wasn't necessarily how they were seeing themselves.

A little ways off from them, someone in a clown suit was juggling an indeterminate number of brightly colored balls. No, not balls—eyes. That had to be Felicity, I decided. Felicity was about to leave J. Walter at any moment for a career as a thrillseeker. She had all those thrillseeker characteristics, extroversion, tendency to act out, energetic style, the dramatic gestures Pyotr Frankis had accused me of, as well as real talent for finding bona-fide thrills locked in the unconscious. But there was one last step for her and it hadn't come yet. She had explained some of it to me not in the pool but one night when insomnia had hit us separately and we'd found ourselves in one of the Common Lounges, the only people awake in the whole world. In real reality, she was an expansive kind of person, always looking as though she were taking up more space than she actually was. Perhaps it was the hair, which seemed to have been colored by a primitive artist and designed by an admirer of Van de Graaff. In the pool, she often manifested as an odd element that somehow always found a niche. A clown juggling eyes in the country wasn't the most unusual thing she'd ever done with herself.

There were a few other people sitting on the grass, some alone, some in small groups of two or three or four, some wildlife running around, stray flowers appearing and disappearing as someone thought about them and then forgot them again. Someone I couldn't identify waved at me, an androgyne wearing an expensive-looking velvet suit. I waved back. Overhead, the trees whispered in the wind and I heard a faint mumble of thunder from far away.

The androgyne melted into existence next to me, leaving the little group s/he'd been sitting with. It's hard to say what happened next. When you're in mind-to-mind contact with just one other person, the exchange is fairly clear-cut. But there was something about the pool that tended to make certain things blur. Kind of. Maybe it was the fact that everyone was acting on everyone else all at the same time, just by being present. Or maybe it was because the contact wasn't as direct in the pool. Individual events could take on a virtual aspect and you'd have to figure out what happened later, after you were out in real reality.

Some kind of contact was made, some exchange took place. Eventually, I looked up and saw a man sitting in one of the trees directly above me. The androgyne was gone.

This is my first time in, the man in the tree said. The words were quite clear, not muddied the way a lot of first-timers' were. I was impressed.

What are you doing up there? I asked, standing up to get a better look at him. If his words were clear, his face wasn't. I seemed to be looking at him underwater.

Getting the lay of the land. Pause. *As it were.*

As it were. And then I was in the tree with him, perched on a branch at right angles to his. I didn't know whether that was my idea or his, or maybe someone else's entirely, like the androgyne. Another branch obscured my view of him, so I broke it off. For a few mental moments, his image rippled in front of me, as though he couldn't decide on something. Then it cleared and I nearly fell out of the tree.

Jerry Wirerammer.

Jerry Wirerammer and none other. The same insubordinate sandy hair, the same cat's-eye biogem eyes, the same mildly goofy expression of *Who, me?* and *Come on, dare yourself* all at once. The tree began to sway.

Did I do something wrong? he asked.

Not Jerry Wirerammer. Definitely not. *Did I do something wrong?* was not a Jerry Wirerammer question.

We were sitting on the ground, some distance behind the campers, whose lean-to had vanished. Somewhere in there I'd told him he looked like someone I'd known once and he'd acknowledged it but he still looked exactly like Jerry Wirerammer.

If Jerry Wirerammer did not exist, it would be necessary to invent him, he said. *The spirit of Jerry Wirerammer moved upon the waters and found it good.*

What? I said.

I was just thinking, he said. *Jerry Wirerammer sounds more like a force of nature than a person.*

You were talking like he was God.

Isn't God a force of nature?

The scenario was evolving as we spoke, or whatever we were doing. Now it was a large indoor room with grass carpeting and odd potted plants in the corners. The person who had been the androgyne was now more female than male; she was traveling around the room a few inches off the floor. I couldn't find the Twins. Maybe they'd become plants for a while.

It's disconcerting. You looking like that, I told him.

I don't know how else to look, he said, almost sadly. *I think I've always looked this way.*

I've never seen you before.

Well, I did tell you it's my first time in the pool.

There was music, something I couldn't quite identify, and we were all outside again on a terrace, attending a formal evening dance under an impossible sky of multi-colored stars.

Does it always change this quickly? he asked.

Not always.

I may have danced, alone or not, but I kept returning to him. We sat at a tiny metal table in the same respective positions we'd occupied in the tree. For a while, the eyes Felicity had been juggling sat in a pile on the table between us and he examined them all carefully, occasionally handing one to me. We talked, but I wasn't always sure what we were saying.

Not Jerry Wirerammer, he said at one point, *but McFloy. Just McFloy, nothing else*.

There's always something amusing, if that's the word, about one-name people. You wonder what they do when they run into two-name people whose first or last name duplicates their one. Three-name people like me rarely run into two other people with names that duplicate two of their own—the equally amusing possibility of Alexandra, Victoria, and Alexandra Victoria all swimming around in the same pool.

He picked up a little of it from me; someone else caught more of it and passed it on to little effect. The music faded away and there was the sensation of a lot of time passing without any time passing at all. Eventually, the environment moved back inside, but the terrace was still visible through a pair of tall French doors.

McFloy looked around the brightly lit room from where we sat together on an indeterminate antique divan. *I liked it better outside*, he said.

And then we were outside again, just him and me, looking back at everyone still inside from the other side of the French doors.

That's pretty good, I told him. *Not many people can manage that on their first time in the pool*.

I'm a prodigy, he said distractedly, reaching into his jacket pocket and pulling out an eye. Not one of those Felicity had been juggling. It had a gold-flake pupil. *You recognize this?*

It looks like Jascha's.

He balanced it on his palm. *He doesn't know I have it. Should I give it back to him?*

That gave me a chill. *Yes. Right away.*

He rubbed the eye between his hands and then paused, smiling at me. A man materialized on my left. He had two eyes, but the right eye was blank. It changed to a gold-flake biogem; McFloy's hands were empty. The man turned to me; he didn't look at all like Jascha and he melted away when I tried to speak to him.

Not terribly ethical, I said, *borrowing a piece of someone without his permission. The eyes Felicity was juggling were of her own imagining, they didn't really belong to anyone.*

That wasn't Jascha. It was a phantom. Some people leave them behind, I've noticed. They can persist for mental days before they finally fade away. McFloy smiled Jerry Wirerammer's loopy smile at me. *Here's something else you should know about.* He reached into his pocket again and held out a gold-flake eye—the same one.

Very prodigious, I said, feeling uncomfortable. Jerry Wirerammer had been in the habit of cloning mental bits from other people, too.

Jascha was still here when I joined the pool. And he still doesn't know. He never will. Unless someone tells him. He closed his hand around the eye. When he opened it again it was gone. *See?* he said, smiling at me. His right eye was now gold-flake, mismatched to the other one. *Everyone's got a blind spot. Never mind, I haven't diminished him. I've just cloned something of his and now we both have it. Allie.* A new eye appeared in his hand, not a biogem. The pupil was brown with green flecks.

I put my hand up to my eyes, but there was nothing to feel because I had no head. My blind spot. I moved to the center of the terrace, wishing the eye back into the head I didn't have. It vanished from his hand.

Don't worry, Allie, I haven't diminished you, either, he said, still grinning at me in the loopy way. *What I'm really interested in is your mind.*

Time to go, I thought, and went.

* * *

The damnedest things affect you in the damnedest ways. I kept seeing those eyes resting in the palm of his hand, first the gold-flake biogem and then my own. Quite a mental trick, and he'd accomplished it effortlessly, or so it seemed. I wondered if anyone at J. Walter knew there was a prodigy loose who was capable of appropriating other people's points of view. Or maybe I was the only one bothered by it. People traded points of view all the time in real reality—figuratively, of course. So maybe it was just the way it translated so literally into the eye trick in the pool that bothered me. Maybe it was just my initial resistance to mindplay resurfacing.

I looked for McFloy in real reality but almost no one seemed to know him, with the exception of Jascha.

"I'm dreamfeeding him, the same way I am you," Jascha told me somewhat shortly when I questioned him. I couldn't stop looking into those gold-flake eyes. Did he have any idea someone had stolen part of his vision? But if it wasn't actually missing from him, had it been stolen at all?

"I was just curious," I said, hoping I sounded harmless enough. "I'd never met anyone named McFloy and he looks exactly like Jerry Wirerammer."

"No, he doesn't. Not out here, anyway. He leads an awfully mental life, too."

I kept looking at Jascha as I stalled with talk about McFloy so I wouldn't have to get up on that too-soft mattress, and gradually I became aware that I was reading his Emotional Index by sight.

Training in reading an Emotional Index by sight or while you're in the system was rather vague. Somehow, you were just supposed to start doing it. It was easier in the system, since things tended to become palpable. Sight-reading in real reality was a lot less certain. So much depended on body language of a particularly subtle sort—movements performed in a certain order, the tilt of the head, certain facial expressions of course, but you couldn't always depend on that, either. It had to be a gestalt kind of thing, where you were perceiving everything at once, situation and mood as well as appearance. When you could make it work, however, it was extremely revealing. Not quite mindreading, Jascha liked to say, but more like being able to read the graffiti on the walls of someone's skull.

The graffiti on the walls of Jascha's skull said he was troubled, by McFloy and by my questions about him. He didn't like McFloy, or he didn't like something about him, which was almost the same thing, and he had to work extremely hard to hold it in.

It was a little embarrassing, as though I'd peeped into his room and caught him talking to himself or something. After a long moment, I realized he was staring back at me just as hard; he knew I'd been reading him.

"Hey," I said, hopping up onto the techno-bed to cover my embarrassment. "Lucid living. You know?" The bed didn't give the way it usually did. I pressed the mattress with both hands. "You put in a bed board!"

"I told you I would," Jascha said, almost sullenly. "Think you can dream lucidly now?"

"No."

I was right about that, too.

Maybe it was because of Jascha's reaction as well as my own curiosity about McFloy, but I started spending more time in the pool. Neither Pyotr Frankis nor Jascha commented on it; the attendants installed me and took me out with their usual neutrality. And McFloy was always there, as though he lived there. If Jascha hadn't told me he was dreamfeeding him, I might have come to believe McFloy was actually one of the stronger pool phantoms, invented by all of us because he didn't exist. It wasn't that he didn't seem real, but then even the pool phantoms seemed real while you were in.

McFloy and I became shadows to each other, always within easy mental reach. The pressure of his presence was unmistakable; I always knew him, no matter how he appeared, and his image would always resolve itself into the form of Jerry Wirerammer. Like a mental landmark for both of us.

Occasionally he did the trick with my eye again, producing it from a fold in his clothes or some other hiding place, once from his mouth, which was rather alarming. I couldn't reciprocate with one of his cat's-eyes; the mental acrobatics of just appropriating his point of view without his help were beyond me. Reading his Emotional Index wasn't easy, either. It seemed to be something he was already familiar with and was able to guard against, showing me only the more predictable feelings without the undertones. Once in a while I caught him out, but not often. Not often enough, as far as I was concerned.

The walks in real reality took on an intermission quality, as though I were using them to rest up for dreamfeeding with Jascha or the occasional conference with Pyotr Frankis or the pool. Maybe mostly the pool.

Maybe? Well, I fooled myself about that for a while. Mindplay never meant you couldn't fool yourself as much as you wanted. I took to the pool as though I were trying to emulate Pyotr Frankis in his form of existence, meeting McFloy in the sky, in realms built out of group fantasies, in places that were so common I wasn't always sure I was really in the pool, except that I would look over and see him in his Jerry Wirerammer suit.

Eventually, I realized he'd had my eye for longer than when he'd first shown it to me on that terrace. I wasn't sure why I hadn't caught on sooner. Maybe because I couldn't live lucidly enough. I wondered if he had a complete collection of eyes. But mostly I wondered how I could find him, out there in real reality.

You don't need to find me out there, he said. *It's enough that you found me in here. What I'm really interested in is your mind.*

We were sitting in another variation of the pastoral scenario where I'd first met him; his words startled me several inches off the grass. I hadn't mentioned I'd been looking for him out there in real reality.

Come down, he said, amused. *I didn't mean to alarm you. The sensation of searching has been pouring out of you for some time.*

That obvious? I reached down and dug my fingers into

the aqua grass, trying to pull myself down again; my buoyancy fought me.

For anyone who wants to see it. The cat's-eyes shimmered. *Everything is obvious for those who want to see it.* His left eye was blank now; he was holding one of the cat's-eyes out to me. *What would you like to see, Allie?*

I was fasting that day, and very hungry. I took the eye from him.

What I'm really interested in is your mind.

That's the sort of thing you should think over, especially when a mindplayer says it to you. Even a mindplayer candidate. The first thing I saw were a series of parquet deformations. He watched them with me as the patterns evolved, drawing on the shapes in the pool reality.

Do you keep this running all the time? I asked. There was no answer. The deformations cleared and we were floating in the system pool. Some kind of mist or fog was rising up from the water, thickening in the humid air. I was disappointed; I'd thought he would show me more than a few of his personal visuals.

We're the last two left, he said. *There's no one else in the pool but us.*

I might not have known it if he hadn't told me, and with anyone else it might not have mattered. I could detect no difference in the feel of the hookup; it wasn't as though we were hooked in only to each other, and yet now we were. The only thing between us was the pool itself.

This was bound to happen, he said, treading water lazily. *With all the time you spend in the pool now. Sooner or later you were bound to end up alone, or just with one other.*

With you, I said.

With me. His admission stirred the water gently. The fabric of my thoughts rippled in sympathy. His left eye was open now, brown with green flecks in the pupil. I was no longer holding the cat's-eye in my hand, but I knew where it was.

Let me look at you, he said.

In the act of letting him, we bypassed the pool medium and it vanished. Now we were hooked directly in with each other, by virtue of the eye trick, an exchange of vision.

Paolo Segretti's carnelian eyes had changed to cat's-eye in the memory, shimmering as I accused him of being about to mindrape me. Pyotr Frankis's cat's-eye pupils caught the light more intensely than silver and shone like small, distant suns. Jascha asked me about a bed board, the cat's-eyes alternating from light to dark with each small movement. As though they'd been there with me all along and I was only seeing them now. Even my great-grandmother's portrait looked down at me with them, casting their light over everything in the cathedral.

Did anyone ever tell you you lead an awfully mental life? someone asked.

He moved through all of it, touching the memories carefully, handling the pieces of my life as though he were looking through a small box of treasures. I could feel his curiosity, his amusement and compassion and, strangely, envy and a kind of longing as he went back and forth among them.

Where did my life go?

You are the One Chosen. (That one seemed to amuse him greatly.)

On the contrary. I didn't think I looked that good. Hey. Lucid living. You know?

Alerted Snakes Of Consequence. Life is funny, Allie. You should remember to laugh.

McFloy's longing seemed to swell in volume like music or water; it flowed in between the memories and I felt myself resonating in sympathy. My resonance drew him in further. Something in him gave, or perhaps it was something in me. The cat's-eye he'd given me seemed to blaze up brightly, illuminating both of us. Surrounded by the elements of my life, he could not do anything but consent to my own request.

Let me look at you, I said. *Let me look—*

Panic flashed briefly, but it was too late for him to be afraid.

Getting the lay of the land. As it were.

I think I've always looked this way.

The powers of visualization greatly exceed the stage of development in this subject; he can already produce a fully-realized mental scenario with a minimum of detail-smudging. This is virtually unheard-of in regenerated subjects at so early a stage. The recommendation is for training, beginning with the subject's discharge from the facility—

I think I've always looked this way.

What I'm really interested in is your mind.

I could have held all of it in my two cupped hands. He was only two years old. Beyond two years was the solid blackness of nonexistence.

Mindsuck.

Everything stopped. McFloy was gone. I found myself alone in the pool, staring at a single cat's-eye biogem floating in the water. I grabbed it up just before it would have sunk.

I tried to get Jascha to talk to me about McFloy but he refused. Under any other circumstances, I would have considered it none of my business, except I still had a sense of McFloy when I thought about things, about Paolo Segretti and Pyotr Frankis, about my great-grandmother, even about the holo display I'd walked through a lifetime ago when Segretti had taken me to his office and introduced me to mindplay.

It was the eye, of course, McFloy's cat's-eye, that I'd saved from the pool.

I locked myself in the efficiency, put out a Do Not Disturb flag and shut off the dataline. I needed time and space to think but I wasn't ready to go under a belljar to do it.

Even if I hadn't had his eye, it wouldn't have been hard to put the bare bones together. Two years before, McFloy had been someone else and someone had sucked him. It happened, mostly to artists of some kind, holographers, composers, dancers, actors, writers, generally just as they were about to achieve their first recognition. Full-blown celebrities were more inaccessible and their minds more traceable to the chop shops where mindsuckers parted them out and sold off the memories and talents to people who craved the overlay of someone else's experience on their own.

It had happened to McFloy. No, not to McFloy but to someone else entirely, who had then been taken mindless but with his brain intact to a hospital quarantine where a new mind had grown into the vacant neurons and axons—and behold the man, McFloy, born full-grown from his own empty forehead. In his own words, a prodigy.

I could get a glimpse of it through his cat's-eye, if I concentrated, brief scenes from his hospitalization, a fleeting memory of a doctor's face. But mostly what I could see through his eye was myself, perched on the branch of a tree, sitting on a terrace under the stars, suspended in the pool, about to accept his eye and give him one of my own. I looked amazingly like myself; I couldn't tell whether that was because he actually saw me that way or because that was how I saw myself even through his sight. But the reason didn't matter as much as finding him and reversing the eye trick. He'd been right when he'd told me he hadn't diminished me.

He'd added to me, and I wasn't sure if I could live with that. It was hard enough living just with myself.

I couldn't find him, in the pool or in real reality.

Mindplay candidates came and went. Felicity made the last step, whatever it was, and went off to seek thrills in the minds of the hard-core jaded. New faces, a rainbow of new eyes, rushed in to fill the place she'd left. The Twins and I remained. The Twins and I and, somewhere, McFloy. J. Walter was a big place; I hadn't met half the people I knew from the pool in real reality. It wasn't hard to find strangers and I found them in droves, sitting in the Common Lounges, loitering in courtyards, passing through the halls, but none of them felt familiar, I could find no sense of McFloy in the plain faces, the polished ones, the dyed ones, nothing of McFloy's essence looking out from any of the biogems that looked at me, cat's-eye or not.

The days slipped through my hands less lucidly than ever.

Jascha fed me a flower. It turned into an eye. Cat's-eye. The dream trailed away into a non-event and Jascha woke me with a curtness that had become routine with him, at least as far as I was concerned.

"Still no lucidity," he said, making himself busy with the connections by cleaning them carefully with a sonic needle. In the wall over the bed, the monitors were dark and silent. He'd recorded the dream to analyze later, I knew; there wouldn't be much to analyze this time.

"Maybe if you weren't mad at me," I said, "I'd make some progress."

He looked up from the connections with genuine surprise on his face. The gilding had worn off his mustache and eyebrows. He appeared younger without it. "Mad at you? I'm not mad at you."

"You're mad at someone. Or something."

"It's not anger," he said, going back to his busywork. The needle vibrated around the nearly invisible tips of the connections. He pulled a drawer out from the wall and carefully stuck the connections into a bowl of solution.

It must have been somewhere in the dreams, I thought, forcing myself not to smile. It must have been in the dreams, the memory of McFloy looking at me through Jascha's perspective with those cat's-eyes. Maybe Jascha felt invaded or used or something. But it hadn't been *him*, not really. His Emotional Index indicated some kind of anger but perhaps he wasn't thinking of it that way.

"I'm putting in a recommendation for a pathosfinder," Jascha said abruptly.

"For what?"

"For you."

I sat down on the bed again. "For *me*? Why?"

"You're stalled. Or stalling. We're just rerunning the same pattern over and over and you're not any closer to dreaming lucidly than you were when you first came here. A pathosfinder might be able to shake something loose."

I laughed a little. "If you want to shake something loose, a thrillseeker would be more appropriate. Maybe what I need is a nice, homegrown thrill."

"You've been thrilled enough. That's the whole point, Allie. You're letting things happen to you but you're not making anything happen. You're in the passive mode."

"Not always," I said, feeling stung. "I hold my own in the pool."

"You've got a lot of help in the pool. Consensual reality nudges you around some, but you still float a lot."

I hadn't been floating that last time with McFloy but I didn't say anything.

"Don't look so unhappy," Jascha said, sitting down next to me. "I'm trying to help you, not hurt you."

I stared at my hands, which were gripping each other in my lap. "I don't think it's a pathosfinder that I need, Jascha."

He was amused. "Well, what, then?"

"Someone else entirely." I got up and left.

"I'm *still* putting in the recommendation," Jascha called after me. I didn't have to look at him to know he was angry, or something, again.

I found the Twins glued to a dataline in one of the Common Lounges, watched a news item about a pair of women called the LadyBugs.

"Who are they?" I asked Dolan.

"Listen," Dolby said while Dolan kept staring at the two identical women on the screen.

". . . another day in court for the former Dolores Messer and the former Iris Feder," said the newscaster's voice. "The panel of judges is still deadlocked over the women's request, the first of its kind. What happens in the end will set a precedent, the repercussions of which are incalculable. Counsel for the women has been silent, unlike the LadyBugs themselves . . ."

The woman on the right leaned forward, grinning away, and spoke into an unseen pickup. "We are simply fighting for our right to be different by being the same. We don't feel there's an issue here at all."

"No, we don't," said the other one. Her grin was looking a little forced. "If we want to be identical, it's our perfect right. The problem is that no one else is identical, not as identical as we want to be."

"It's not as if we're asking the government to pay for it, or—"

I reached for the remote and lowered the sound a little. "Why are they called LadyBugs?" I asked.

"They're as alike as LadyBugs," Dolan said, giving in and looking at me.

"Even more alike than we are. Amazing."

"What's the problem?" I said.

"They want their brainwaves synchronized," Dolby told me. "Jiggered around within the area of the patterns traced by both their brains so they'll match perfectly, apex to trough. Completely congruent."

"Nobody wants to make the adjustment, though," said Dolan. "Permanent alteration of brain tissue as well as the mind. Mind control. Nobody wants any part of it, so the LadyBugs are suing."

"Suing who?"

"The Mindplay Bureau. To make them get someone to do it."

I looked up at the screen. One of the grinning LadyBugs waved at someone. "They're crazy."

"Oh, yah? You think so?" Dolan sat up a little straighter on the couch and squinted at me.

"You don't know," said Dolby. "You're not a twin."

"Neither are they, really. I heard their names, they're not even related."

"Kinship without blood ties. Haven't you ever felt it?"

"And besides," Dolan added, "maybe if they were related, they wouldn't feel the need to be so much alike. Think how compatible they are. And they're not even getting married."

"They're not even *lovers*," said Dolby. "They told the news. They're just very best friends who have found that the person they each want to be is a combination of the two of them."

I was lagging several beats behind them. "'Compatible.' Why do you think they're compatible?"

"Are you kidding? Aren't you compatible with yourself?"

I gave a short laugh. "Depends on who you ask."

"Well, *you* can't imagine. The Joy of Congruence is completely beyond you."

"I hope you won't be offended if I take that as a compliment."

As soon as I said it, the word lit up in my head. Except it was spelled *complement*.

"Are you okay, Allie?" asked Dolan, taking my hand. "What's wrong?"

"Maybe you better sit down," Dolby said and half pushed me onto the couch next to his brother. "You looked like someone told you you were going to die."

Complement. When two elements combine and make each other whole. Kinship without blood ties. Sometimes a thing isn't fully in existence until it is named, and then there's no turning away from it.

I *had* to find him now.

I stayed nearly to the limit of my neurotransmitter in the pool and he never showed up. Exhausted, I went comatose for five hours afterward with an IV patch releasing a tyrosine compound into my neck and came out of it still feeling mildly dead.

For some timeless interval, I floated in half-consciousness, dreams flickering in my brain. Eventually McFloy appeared, looking more like Jerry Wirerammer than ever, and I was overjoyed to see him again.

We were back on that terrace, where he'd first done the eye trick. I could hear the people and the music inside as clearly as I'd heard them when we'd been in the pool. The goofy Jerry Wirerammer smile suddenly turned kind. *Not a single thing that's passed between us has been real and yet you've been hunting me like the hound of heaven.*

It is real and you know it. If it weren't, I wouldn't have something that belongs to you. And you wouldn't have something of mine.

But it happened in a dream. How can a dream be real? The smile faded a little. *You'll just have to keep it. If it's so real to you. I'm hardly real, myself.*

I'll find you. Then you can tell me that in person. Unless you're too unreal.

Ghost lightning danced bluely in his hair. *It's the most real part of me that you have, Allie. Nothing of me could ever be so real.*

The eye was there in my hands. I lifted it up to look at it. *Why are you hiding from me?*

The answer, if that's what it was, was so garbled I couldn't make sense of it. There were hints of fear, a strong feeling of wistfulness, a sense of being inadequate, of being full-grown and only two years old. And something else, something I didn't call love for fear the word would shatter him and scatter the pieces beyond my ability to call them back.

It went on for a long time and then, suddenly, I caught a coherent thread. *—said I was a prodigy and sent me here. They told me it was the best thing. Half my life wasn't real. In the quarantine where this person came into being, this McFloy came into being in a dream where they gave me language and humanity but no history. But here, I learned to do what you call the eye trick, to see with others' vision. It's the only time I'm real. When I see through someone else. When I see through you.*

The eye in my hands was glowing like a coal.

I shouldn't be. I should never have come into being.

I wanted to look at him but the eye wouldn't let me. *It's no different for anyone else, really,* I said. *Who ever asked to be born?*

Pyotr Frankis is more real than I am. You're the sum of everything you've done. What do I have but a little of someone else's vision?

There was nothing but the eye now, and me.

But I gave something to you. No one else, just you. For me, it's too much and not enough, all at once. I don't know how to be real on my own. You take it. Make me real. Somewhere, then, I'll live for real, even if it's just in a dream. Your dream.

Why, McFloy?

A little amusement, followed by a memory of a memory. *You are the One Chosen.* The memory faded. *I love your life, Allie. I love you.*

In the pupil of the eye, I could make out the form of a snake in a perfect circle, mouth gripping its tail.

Where are you? I asked. Did I really expect an answer? This was *my* dream. Wasn't it?

The phone's chiming startled me awake, shattering the dream. I rolled over on the futon, putting my back to the screen. Taking a phone call was about the last thing I wanted to do.

On the fifth chime, the recorder kicked on.

"I really expected you to be there," Jascha said, sounding miffed. I rolled over again and looked at the screen. Jascha was looking straight ahead, like someone having a mug-holo shot, an expression I still knew pretty well. His own screen was showing him a Not-In reading. "I called to tell you I've made an appointment with a pathosfinder for you. Her name's Benedict, she's quite good. You're to see her this evening, after supper. I'm putting a page out for you so you can't pretend not to know about it." He paused, looking troubled, seemed about to say something else, and then disconnected.

I wanted to laugh out loud. I didn't need a pathosfinder to help me learn how to dream lucidly any more. The clock over the dataline told me it was an hour until supper. Maybe that would be enough time.

Where are you? The beach was miles long, stretching far ahead of me. The tide was coming in under the afternoon sun and it seemed as though I could feel every grain of sand under my bare feet. The seashore scene was relatively rare in the pool, at least when I was there. It felt especially strange today, built up from minds new to me. I wondered how many people were in the pool today.

After a while, I became aware that someone or something seemed to be pacing me, but when I looked around I couldn't see anything, only a little movement in

my peripheral vision. I let it be and kept moving,
holding McFloy's eye.

If I hadn't been hungry, I told myself, it never would
have happened. Damn Pyotr Frankis and his bright
ideas about fasting for enlightenment. If fasting really
had anything to do with enlightenment then millions of
people throughout the ages had died of the secret of life.
And the secret of life was, in its entirety, that starvation
hurt like a bastard.

Several people wading at the edge of the waterline
beckoned to me. I paused, scanning them carefully, even
though I knew it was unlikely that McFloy would be
among them. Overhead, seagulls called out to each other
with almost human voices.

There was another movement in my peripheral vision.
I turned and saw that a large umbrella had materialized
on the sand to my left. I trudged up to it and sat down in
the shelter of its shade. I was tired, I realized. Tired
enough to sleep.

I lay back on the sand, resting McFloy's eye on my
chest. There was a moment of dizziness and disorientation; it seemed as though I could feel every little bit of
movement in the universe, the rise and fall of the waves,
the earth turning and turning as it swept around the sun,
the whole solar system traveling on the fringe of the
galaxy as it revolved in endless night.

A thousand faces snapped into focus on the inner bowl
of the umbrella, a good many of them my own. The rest
were McFloy's.

Everyone has a blind spot, said McFloy's faces.

I was asleep and dreaming in the pool. Nobody did
that very often in the pool but it happened once in a
while. From everyone else's perspective, I would seem
to have vanished. That included McFloy. I was more like
a pool phantom now.

My dream self sat up. The beach scene appeared in a
kind of negative to me, an orange sky burning over violet
sand. I raised my hands but there was nothing to see.
Dreaming, I was invisible even to myself. I looked back
at where I'd been lying and there I was, asleep with
McFloy's eye resting on my chest. Beneath my closed

lids, I could see my eyes moving back and forth as I dreamed lucidly. I turned away and paused, staring at the handle of the umbrella. It was a snake. A Snake. Just a joke, but that didn't mean I shouldn't watch out for them.

The beach seemed to brighten, the light very hard, almost blinding. I concentrated into the orange glare on the water and eventually I saw him, standing near the water's edge a little to the left of my focal point, still decked out in all his Jerry Wirerammer glory.

Carefully, not wanting to wake myself up, I moved my perspective a little closer to him. The tide rushed up around his feet and slid away again, taking a little of him with it, as though he were made of sand.

No, I thought. Don't. Please don't.

You don't know, said the McFloy faces in the umbrella. *For you, staying real is effortless. You'll always be real. You've had a lifetime to get used to it.*

The sea was becoming rougher now. The waves came in higher, hitting him in the back, and McFloy was smaller when they washed away.

I knew as soon as I came here I wouldn't be able to stay, said the McFloy faces. At the waterline, McFloy himself said nothing, but I thought I saw a change in him, as though he sensed I was nearby.

There are other places to go, I said silently. A gull was calling, except it sounded like an alarm bell for some reason. The sea looked as if it were boiling; far out, larger waves were building, rushing toward the shore.

I don't mean J. Walter, McFloy's faces said. *I mean here. This reality.*

If we could have met, I thought, you could have seen how real you were to me.

I'll always be real to you, Allie. More waves crashed over him, melting his shoulders, eroding his body. *Remember that I never really took anything away from you. Remember what I gave you. Let it be your third eye, if you want. If there could be such a thing.*

That damned gull kept screeching. I struggled to wake myself up. From the corners of my eyes, I could see people gathering on the beach. The air quivered with their agitation.

A hard, high wave rose up and I thought I could see a thousand phantoms in its glassy wall. McFloy turned and looked directly at my sleeping self. He smiled; *Allie*, he said silently. Then the wave pounded down in an explosion of fiery orange froth.

The people on the shore scattered, several of them popping out of existence as they ran. The gull screamed and screamed and screamed.

The attendant was tapping my face lightly with her fingertips. "You in there? Say something."

"I'm—what. What's going on?" I could still hear the seagull, except it was unmistakably an alarm bell now.

"Who are you?" demanded the attendant. "Do you know who you are?"

"Sure. I'm—" I looked down. My hands were still cuddled up to my chest, cupped as though I were holding something, but of course there was nothing there. "I'm Allie."

"Good. You can go." The attendant gave me a little shove toward the door and went to the pod next to the one I'd occupied, yanking open the cover. All around me, the attendants were pulling people out of the pods as soon as the indicators on the covers showed their eyes had been reinserted by the pool system. I found my way over to a chair near the door and sat down, trying to clear my head. Being yanked up through two altered states was a lot like taking a hard one to the skull. My eyes felt as dry as cotton balls.

I don't know how long Jascha was standing over me before it finally registered on me that he was there.

"I was afraid I'd find you here. You're supposed to be with the pathosfinder," he said.

I pushed myself up from the chair. The room was empty now except for the attendants gathered around one last closed pod in the center. The indicators on the cover were dark, inactive, except for the ones measuring blood pressure and respiration. Low-average readings; the person inside was still alive.

I went over to them. "Aren't you going to open it?" I asked the one who had pulled me out.

Behind me, Jascha said, "Allie, I don't think—"

"It's okay," I said. "I knew him."

The attendants looked at each other. All of a kind. I don't think I'd have recognized any one of them if we'd met again in the next two hours.

The readings on the cover of the pod began to fail. Another indicator light went on to show that emergency life support was standing by. If I didn't see him before that happened, I'd never get another chance.

I pushed past several of the attendants and knelt to unlock the cover. Someone made a move to stop me and then thought better of it for some reason. Later, I thought Jascha had probably told them to let me go ahead.

I didn't take a long time. Just long enough to know that he didn't look the least bit like Jerry Wirerammer.

"Flat-line," said one of the attendants. "All readings."

It took me several moments to realize he wasn't talking about me.

Jascha helped me up. "Call Stanwyn, the belljarrer. Right away."

"I don't want to go under the belljar," I said, but no one seemed to hear me.

UNDER THE BELLJAR

HOW TO FIND
YOUR PATHOS

The LadyBugs had been grinning out of the screen for several minutes before I registered on them. I tuned out the audio. It had been two days since I'd come out of the belljar and I just wasn't in the mood to hear about their struggle.

The door chimed. I gave it some thought before I got up and answered it. It was Jascha. I let him in anyway.

"You've missed two appointments. Should I phone the Brain Police and tell them you've reconsidered?"

I wandered back to the sofa and curled up on it. "I've overdone the mindplay lately. I have to sit things out for a while." I reached for the remote, intending to shut off the screen.

"No, leave it on. I'm dying to see what happens with those two. I think they're loony, myself, but it's going to be a landmark case." Pause. "You did as much as you could."

"I know," I said, a little impatiently. "So did you."

Jascha settled himself on the couch a respectful distance from me. "You were in shock. You had to go under the belljar. Shut down the organism, let it rest. You can't still be mad at me for that."

I didn't say anything. All I could think of was how much it reminded me of McFloy's time in the darkness while he was regenerating. In the five hours I had spent under the belljar cut off from all sensory input, his eye had shown it to me. Not a lot, because he couldn't remember it consciously; just little flashes that resonated with my own absence of light and sound and feeling. Resonating. McFloy and I had done a lot of that in a small space of time and I hadn't always realized it.

"Look," Jascha said after a bit. "It happens sometimes with mindsuck cases. Not often, but it will happen. It's too much for some people to be forced to full maturity in the space of a year."

"Two years."

"All right, two years, if you count the year he spent in quarantine along with the year as an outpatient. They were impressed enough with the strength of his mental life to send him here, thinking we'd make some kind of mindplayer out of him."

I shrugged. "He might have made it."

"He didn't have a chance. I knew it as soon as he taught himself to do the eye trick. A person who has to mooch bits out of other people because he can't find enough in himself can't make it."

"The eye trick. Yah. I know all about the eye trick. That one got by me. Just because I was hungry. I had to consume something, and there he was with something I could consume. His eye."

Jascha moved a little closer to me. "There's all kinds of hunger. When you love somebody—"

I groaned loudly. "*Please*. Spare me. When you say stuff like that out loud, it always sounds trivial."

"You were the only one he gave an eye to. Everyone else he just took from. I don't think that's so trivial."

"No, it isn't." I paused. "Sometimes giving can be like taking, Jascha. Especially when someone gives you part of himself." All he'd been interested in was my mind. Whenever I closed my eyes, I could call up the image of that third eye as clearly as life, the cat's-eye pupil shimmering. Except now I always saw it with the Snake making a circle inside it.

He said he hadn't diminished me, I remembered. And he hadn't. Except by his death.

"Pyotr Frankis wants to see you again," Jascha said after a bit. "That was what I came here to tell you."

"You could have phoned."

"I also came to escort you personally to his hookup."

I sighed. "Can't it wait? I told you, I've overdone the mindplay, I need time just to breathe in and out in real reality. Feel real air on my face, hear real sounds, see real things. I feel like I've been in dreamland for a hundred years. Maybe *I'm* getting less real now than I used to be."

"He's going to pathos-find you."

"Pyotr Frankis? He's not a pathosfinder."

"He's whatever his configuration says he is."

I supposed that was true enough, but—Pyotr Frankis? "What about your pathosfinder friend?" I said. "The one I didn't keep the appointment with."

"Pyotr Frankis and I agreed that it wouldn't work to bring a third party in on things at this point. Before McFloy's drowning, it might have—"

"Drowning?" I stared at him. "Is that what you're calling it?"

"What else would you call it?"

I thought about it. "Dissolution. Disintegration."

"It's the same thing, really. They had to, uh, they had to drain the pool."

"What?"

"They had to shut it down and run the program bit by bit." Jascha looked at me. "Searching for his remains."

"Did they find any?"

"Some. The rest is so embedded in the program now it doesn't make any difference whether there's anything of him there or not."

I stared at the LadyBugs on the dataline screen without really seeing them. "Then, it's like . . . McFloy *is* the pool."

"No," Jascha said firmly. "He disintegrated."

"If you shatter a hologram," I said, "you can pick up any one of the pieces and regenerate the whole picture. And the mind is a hologram."

"Not without life, it isn't. The pool is not alive. And neither is McFloy, anymore." Jascha glanced at the clock. "Pyotr Frankis is waiting for you."

I got up. Jascha leaned over to shut the dataline off. "No, just leave it on. If a dataline is running and there's no one there to watch it, has anything really happened?"

Jascha frowned at me. "What kind of silliness is that? Do I have to send you back to mindplay kindergarten?"

"There is no mindplay kindergarten."

"Congratulations," Jascha said dryly.

* * *

We were walking on the bank of that river again, Pyotr Frankis and I. The scene felt a little sketchier than usual. I wasn't exactly putting my heart into it.

Always the dramatic gesture from you, Pyotr Frankis said. *Even the dramatic non-gesture.*

I'm tired of mindplay. It's nothing but trouble.

You might as well say you're tired of thinking. Or that you're tired of life.

Uh-huh.

But you're not. He stopped and gave me a little shake. *Pull yourself together now. That's all you have to do.*

That's all? What kind of a pathosfinding is this, where you just tell me to pull myself together?

His amusement rustled the trees around us, made the river gurgle. *I could give you a lot of double-talk, but yes, that's really all. Come now; give yourself to your concentration. You can visualize better than this.*

A tree that had been a vague blur on the other side of the river came into focus. I recognized it as the tree McFloy and I had been sitting in when we met, and I looked away, half-afraid I'd see him on that same branch, getting the lay of the land again.

Ah, Pyotr Frankis said, studying the tree. Abruptly, we were standing under it. I made a move away from it but he kept me there firmly and yet somehow without real force.

You see now how things can be and not be simultaneously in the mind, he said. *I hold you here without holding you. Now, this is how you pull yourself together.*

What happened next wasn't clear. For some timeless interval, I seemed lost in a jumble of half-formed images—Paolo Segretti, the Brain Police, Jascha, my unlucid dreams, Jerry Wirerammer, my old efficiency. The pieces of my life. You don't keep the pieces of your life in any particular order, they're all over the place.

When the storm cleared, I was standing in front of the cathedral.

It had been a long time since I'd seen it close up. It looked the same on the outside, except it seemed heavier, more solid, as though the whole structure had been reinforced.

Things hadn't changed much inside, either. Some of it had been rearranged but my great-grandmother's portrait was still in the same place and the pose hadn't altered.

I found the eye right away, of course; it was on the table near the crystal vase and the phone and the small holo of Jerry Wirerammer. I held it up to the light. In the cat's-eye pupil, the Snake was clearly visible, still gripping its tail with its mouth. As I watched, it revolved very slowly. Marking the passage of some private time, I thought; maybe sometimes the Snake revolved more quickly. Perhaps there were times when it actually spun.

Ouroboros, said my great-grandmother's portrait. *Alerted Snake without end.*

It was just a joke, I said, putting McFloy's eye back on the table. *Altered states. Alerted Snakes.*

All right, then, altered state without end.

I gave a short laugh. *I suppose you're right. And everyone's got to go somewhere, don't they. Only—when I go, where will that leave you?*

We'll be wherever you are, of course, my great-grandmother said matter-of-factly. *Altered state without end.*

She means it, said a familiar voice. I turned; Paolo Segretti was sitting on an antique divan, plump enough to be real.

Where have you been? I asked.

Here. Where I've always been. You just never got around to me before.

I went over and sat down next to him, surprised at how comfortable the stiff-looking divan actually was. *I didn't think I'd gotten around to you now,* I said.

You triggered me, Segretti said amiably. *I don't just run around in here on my own.*

You told me once that there was only room for me in my mind. That part of me would have to be excised for someone else to fit.

That's true.

Then, how can part of someone else be here in my mind?

If it's here, then it must be part of you. Just as I am. Are you going to use it? he asked.

Use what?

That part of you. The eye was in his hands. Then it vanished and reappeared in his own head, replacing his left carnelian biogem. *I see,* he said thoughtfully. His features blurred, taking on some of McFloy's characteristics.

Something in me leaped to do something about that. Abruptly the eye was gone and Segretti was completely Segretti again.

Suppressing the eye isn't going to solve anything, he said and his voice sounded a little like Pyotr Frankis's.

You bet it's not. I need a dry-cleaning, not a pathos-finding.

It won't' work. Look. Segretti held up a mirror. McFloy's eye looked out at me from my left socket. *You can't dry-clean out part of yourself.*

It's not me. It's him, it's McFloy.

Oh, it's you, all right, whether you want to claim it or not. For better or worse. If you'll pardon the expression.

I lowered the mirror and glared at him.

You want to dry-clean something out just because it hurts? It was Pyotr Frankis sitting next to me now. *Sorry. Can't accommodate you.*

You refuse to understand. But that's all right. I reached up and took hold of my left eye, pushing my fingers into the socket.

Stop! Look at what you're doing! Pyotr Frankis held the mirror up again. My left eye was my own once more, brown with green flecks. I looked over at the table. McFloy's eye was back where it had been. *Do you see? If you try to cast it out, you'll end up crippling yourself.*

I sat back on the divan, feeling suddenly drained. On the table, the eye gleamed at me in the soft light of the cathedral. *All right,* I said after some immeasurable mental time. *Then, I'll live with it. But in my own way.*

Pyotr Frankis laughed. *Of course in your own way—who else's way could it be?*

His, I said. I got up from the divan. *Can we go now?* Pyotr Frankis nodded. *I'll wait outside for you.* He was gone and Segretti was in his place. *And I'll be waiting in here for you*, Segretti said. *Altered state without end.*

And in McFloy's eye, Alerted Snake without end. I headed for the door, pausing at the table. Jerry Wirerammer's holo looked up at me and grinned hugely. That Jerry. What a kidder. Next to the holo, McFloy's eye trembled. I pointed at it.

STAY, I said firmly.

So where else would it go? said my great-grandmother's portrait.

I looked up at her. *You know what I mean*, I said, and got out of there in a hurry.

Pyotr Frankis and I met in the room with the large windows and the alien skyline outside. *It's like being a ghost without being dead*, I said. *Which I guess would make the system a haunted house*. I paused. *Or me. Can a haunt be haunted?*

I cannot answer that, Pyotr Frankis said, *on the grounds that the theorem of incompleteness makes it impossible.*

What?

That there is nothing on this level of existence that can fully explain this level of existence.

What? I said again.

If a haunt is haunted, it's on a different level of reality. Not this one.

But which level is this? I asked.

Whatever level you're on, of course.

I remembered the sign in front of the cathedral: YOU ARE HERE. (WHERE DID YOU THINK YOU WERE?)

I think I've had a satori, I said. *Is there a light bulb on over my head?*

In here, you don't have a head. You must also be careful not to mistake a satori for a sartori, which is the realization that you haven't got a thing to wear. The silver eyes twinkled, sort of.

More jokes.

Life is funny, Allie. Try to remember that, or tragedy

will overtake you and wash you away. In a different fashion, perhaps, but just as thoroughly.

I looked out the window. The cathedral spires were visible just as they had been the other time. I no longer had the urge to go over to the window and toy with the idea of pulling the cathedral up like a flower. Or a weed. Even at that distance, it seemed as though I could feel McFloy's eye where it rested on the table.

Tell me, I said, *what the difference is between reality affixing and pathosfinding.*

Pyotr Frankis was amused. *In reality affixing, you come to me and say, Am I here? And I help you see what you need to see so you can answer that question. In pathosfinding, you come to me and say, I'm here, but am I any good at it?*

There was a rustle of snakes—Snakes—somewhere out of my field of perception. I laughed.

That's reducing it to rather simple terms, he said. *But my configuration tends to do that.*

I'll accept it. But then I have to tell you, I don't think it was successful.

Pyotr Frankis' silver eyes gleamed. *Why not?*

I showed him the scene of myself in the cathedral, ordering McFloy's eye to stay there.

Where else would it go? he said.

You know what I did. Locking it up. I don't think you meant for me to do that.

You do what you need to do, Allie. A Snake materialized between us, coiling lazily. *As for pathosfinding, why do you think the results have to be immediate?*

The Snake looked at me expressionlessly. Of course; what kind of expression could a Snake have?

The mind is a dynamic thing. It will go on and on, changing, reshaping itself, Pyotr Frankis said. *Someday you may go to your cathedral and find it's become a shoebox. And everything that was in it . . .* He paused, looking at me solemnly.

And everything that was in it will be pretty jammed together, I finished for him.

His laughter filled the room. *All right, have it your way, Allie.*

I will, I said. *My way and no one else's.*
But that's what I've been telling you.
I let it go at that.

In spite of my having locked the eye in the cathedral—
or maybe because of that—he began to appear in my
dreams. Not the ones I had by appointment with Jascha
but in the ones I had in my off-hours, the dreams I was
allowed to keep for myself. It was as though he knew the
difference. He would emerge from strange countrysides,
appear in mirrors, walk through open doors. He was just
a dream phantom, little more than a memory. Always,
one of his eyes was blank.

I should have been afraid, but somehow I never was,
not in the dreams. He was just there, taking it all in. If
he got in my way, I simply moved him aside and went on
with the dream. He might have been watching a play or
a holo program. Near the end of the dream he sometimes offered a comment, but not always. Eventually, I
started taking his presence for granted even while I
worked around him, never allowing him to change
anything or participate. My way and no one else's.

The change in my dreaming processes extended to the
ones I had with Jascha. "You're dreaming lucidly all the
time now," he told me after one of our longer appointments. "You're not letting the dreams run away with
you. I told you you'd be able to do it someday."

I was lying on the techno-bed staring out the window.
Below was an empty stone courtyard. No one sat on the
sterile benches in the late afternoon sunlight. In the
middle of summer, the place looked cold. "If I have to
dream my life away, I might as well be in the pilot's seat.
Or at least the navigator's," I said without actually
realizing I was speaking aloud.

"You're catching on," said Jascha approvingly. He
tucked away the connections and shut down the system.
"You want to go somewhere?"

I looked at him in surprise. He was gilded again, his
skin newly polished. The gold flakes in his eyes struck
sparks. "Don't you have another appointment to feed
someone else's dream?"

"I'm taking the rest of the afternoon off. You don't think people mindplay without a break, do you?"

Why not? *I* did.

There was an empty flyer waiting at the stop a block down from the stone courtyard. Jascha hired it and shooed me in. "Where are we going?" I asked, plopping down on the worn overstuffed cushions in the back.

"Somewhere. Everybody's got to go somewhere." He leaned forward and spoke to the control deck. "Overfly the city."

The flyer lifted immediately, rising at a steep angle. We strapped ourselves in.

"I'm not normally letting anyone make a decision for me these days," I said.

"Understood." Jascha turned on the dataline screen in the ceiling. I groaned at the sight of the LadyBugs and he shushed me. "No, listen. It's the ruling, they said it would come today."

". . . precedent-setting ruling that the LadyBugs have, indeed, made a psychotic request and thus are petitioning for a license for psychosis, which is their right under the law. The approval has already come in from the local registrar, and tomorrow the LadyBugs will report to a psychosis clinic for their brain-wave synchronization. The National Institute of Mental Activities is drawing up specifications that will describe this new form of psychosis and name it formally."

"I always said they were crazy." I reached over and turned down the sound.

Jascha nodded, smiling at me. I leaned back against the cushions and watched the toy skyline glide by below us.

"Why so deadpan?" he asked me after a bit.

"I was just thinking. If I'd been able to afford the LadyBugs' lawyers, none of us would be here right now."

"Yes, but where *would* you be?"

"Of course, if I'd been able to afford the LadyBugs' lawyers, I probably wouldn't have been *there*, either."

"Where?"

"Hanging around an efficiency with an overdrawn kitchen, waiting for someone like Jerry Wirerammer to show up—" I stopped. It was the first time I'd thought of the real Jerry Wirerammer in some time. "I wonder what ever happened to him."

Jascha's expression was unreadable. "If you wait a few minutes, you'll probably find out."

"What's that supposed to mean?"

"Just wait." Jascha was looking up at the screen again. The story on the LadyBugs wound down and faded to a commercial. Jascha turned the sound up. It was for the Power People franchise but I stifled the urge to groan again.

The overdone camerawork showed hordes of dreary, dull people marching along, suddenly, a golden arrow materialized and touched the shoulder of a middle aged man. He stopped and looked heavenward with an expression of childlike wonder.

"Have you ever wished you were more than just another warm body in a world of warm bodies?"

The scene switched to a party, where our hero was standing in a corner with a drink in his hand, nodding his head thoughtfully. Someone passed him a platter of artificial-looking hors d'oeuvres and he sent it on without looking at it. The sound of a roomful of people giggling madly came from off-camera.

"Have you ever wished you had more personality? The kind that could enchant, amuse, *involve?*"

Switch to our man alone in a room. He hesitated, then went to the phone and punched the buttons with enthusiasm. Switch to a view of the phone monitor. A ridiculously beautiful woman appeared: "Power People—we have the person you want in your life!"

"You can be enfranchised!" crowed the narration. "It's simple, it's fun, and it's not as expensive as you'd think! Due to the breakneck pace of scientific and technological research, personality rental is the most reasonable it has ever been—and with our seasonal specials, you can pay even less!" Quick succession of shots of our man going to Power People for consultation, then sticking his head into a system, after which he was wheeled into reconstructive surgery ("On the premises!" the narrator said assuringly). I thought of the LadyBugs, but it wasn't quite the same thing. Getting franchised involved an overlay on the core person, the mental equivalent of a mask, if a bit more complicated. The physical surgery wasn't absolutely necessary but most people seemed to prefer going the whole route. Rampant brandname-ism. They wanted everyone to know which designer personality they had.

"Over a million outlets worldwide, waiting to serve *you!*" Pause; final shot of our man, now unrecognizable as a ridiculously handsome type, being entertaining at a party with a woman under each arm.

"And just *look* at this week's *specials!*"

We looked. Portrait of a striking older woman staring off into space. "Anya Mukherji, a real person who modeled her life on Indira Gandhi's!" Change to a slightly younger woman with sequins glued to her bald turquoise head. "Yvette La Due—the life of any gathering, anywhere, any time!" The portrait winked. Change again, another face. "Jerry Wirerammer—if there isn't one in every crowd, there ought to be!"

I didn't gasp or yell or even move. He must have sold himself for salvage to pay the fines, I thought, and somehow Power People had found something in him that real people wanted. I thought of McFloy finessing his image out of me without my even knowing it. But then, McFloy had only been two years old, his own life hadn't been enough.

So when had that ailment ever been confined to recovering mindsuck victims?

"Now you know," said Jascha, and he shut off the screen as a story on the breakup of the Coor and Lam composing team was fading in. "Do you want to talk about it?"

If Jerry Wirerammer did not exist it would be necessary to invent him. "No." It didn't make that much difference. Jerry himself was probably wandering around somewhere tickled to the point of spasm that people were paying good money—or bad money—to feel like they were him. And they all lived happily ever after. As each other.

"Look, I know you must be feeling a lot of things about it right now—"

"I'll just keep my feelings to myself for the time being, if that's all right with you." And everyone had to go somewhere, McFloy, Jerry Wirerammer, even me. Except that by licensing himself for franchise, Jerry had gotten to go and stay at the same time. Just like— I clamped down on the thought and shut it off.

"Deadpan Allie," Jascha said.

"What? That sounds like a bad neighborhood."

Jascha laughed a little. "Just a thought."

D E A D P A N
A L L I E

I wasn't sure who I surprised more, Jascha or myself, when I took the pathosfinding option. Pyotr Frankis wasn't surprised at all, but then, surprise probably wasn't in his configuration. The Twins would have been surprised if they'd had time; they were packing to leave the day I told them. Oddly enough, they were unleashing themselves as twin neurosis peddlers on an unsuspecting world.

"It's the only way," Dolby said as he rearranged the contents of one of Dolan's suitcases. "Otherwise, we'd never be sure if we were in the right roles."

"What about the Kibitzing Factor?" I asked, sitting on Dolby's bed and handing some of Dolby's things to Dolan, who was, of course, repacking one of Dolby's suitcases.

"Kibitzing is neurotic," Dolan said cheerfully, holding a tube of depilatory in one hand and a bottle of cologne in the other. "We'll be able to roll with it, work it right in with no problem. This looks like my stuff."

"Of course it does. All my stuff looks like your stuff."

"Not all of it," Dolan said a little darkly.

"Well, *that* stuff looks like your stuff."

"Then, where's *my* stuff?"

"With your other stuff." Dolby held up two identical items.

Dolan frowned. "That looks like *your* stuff."

"Yes, I know," Dolby said patiently. "I just explained that to you."

"No, wait now. There's a dent in the middle of this tube, see? I saw a dent like that in your tube."

Dolby looked at the tube he was holding and pressed it with his thumb. "There. Now they're both dented and it doesn't make any difference."

"But I want my tube—"

It was too much. At any moment I expected to find

Alerted Snakes crawling out of the walls. I jumped up and grabbed Dolan in a clumsy hug. "I'll say good-bye now. I've got a full schedule this afternoon." That was a lie but they were driving me crazy. Just as well I hadn't gone into neurosis peddling after all; I just didn't have the temperament for neurotics, or anyone who wanted to be that way.

Dolby rushed over for an identically clumsy hug and I felt sadder than I'd wanted to allow myself. J. Walter was full of new candidates I barely knew now and the last stretch of my training would be rather lonely. Once again, I'd set myself up to go it alone. I'd probably end up packing to leave by myself and wondering where this part of my life went.

"We'll let you know where we are," Dolby said.

"And maybe you'll drop by for a little fetish or something," Dolan added. "Have I got a fetish for you."

"I've got one, too." Dolby said, glancing at him.

"Great, I'll get a two-fer if I'm ever in the neighborhood." I headed for the door before a small war could break out.

"Allie," one of them called after me (I couldn't tell who without looking).

"What," I said, pausing with the door open.

"Pathosfinding?" Dolan said. "That'll be good for you."

"It'll be good for somebody," I said.

Dolby grinned. "So will you."

Jascha was waiting in the hall for me at my efficiency.

"You haven't come to cross-examine me about my decision to be a pathosfinder, have you?" I said, pressing three fingers to the print-lock panel.

He shook his gilded head. "Pyotr Frankis gave his approval so I have nothing to say about it."

I opened the door and stopped. My futon had been exchanged for a much wider one.

"Your doing?" I asked, looking over at him.

He shrugged. "I always felt bad that you were never able to get comfortable on my bed." He wandered over to the couch and sat down. His Emotional Index could have been a flashing LCD display but apparently he didn't mind. I closed the door and kept my distance.

"It wasn't so bad after you put in the bed board," I told him.

"But it wasn't the same."

I went over to the futon and sat down on it. "You did your best."

"Deadpan Allie."

"What."

"Nothing. Just Deadpan Allie. I used to be able to read you with my eyes closed. Or out. Now I have to be mind-to-mind with you, feeding your dreams. And sometimes even then I'm not always sure. Not right away, anyhow."

"Pathosfinders can't go spraying their own feelings all over their clients' minds."

Jascha nodded. "Benedict told me you were a quick study. But I'm not a client."

"You're my dreamfeeder."

He smiled. "Yah. When you put it that way, it sounds as good as it is. Being your dreamfeeder. At least I did that, even if I wasn't really the one who got you to dream lucidly. But I'd like to think that I helped in some way." He fell silent for a moment. "There's a lot I would say now but I don't want to make anything sound trivial. And I'm not deadpan. But I've been about as professional as I can be with you and I've reached the limit. So I guess what it comes down to is, if you can't be comfortable on my bed, maybe I can be comfortable on yours."

There's all kinds of hunger, he'd said. There were all kinds of fasts, too. Pyotr Frankis' had been over for weeks. It was time to end this one, too.

Very ethically, Jascha ceased to be my dreamfeeder. I wasn't taking much in the way of dreamfeeding by then, anyway. Mostly I worked with Benedict, first in a monitoring mode and later on the receiving end. Her approach was different from Pyotr Frankis', which still seemed like more of a reality affixing to me than anything else. But I was getting somewhere, and everyone had to go somewhere. Some things happened and some other things didn't, and at one point I found I'd gone to a place where I married Jascha.

Pyotr Frankis had been right: life was funny. It was also reasonably good and so was the relationship. And after the divorce, I got a job.

ALTERING
STATES OF
CONSCIOUSNESS

THE PATHOSFINDER
GETS A JOB

"Kid," said the big little man on the couch, "it's a good thing you're a pathosfinder and not a neurosis peddler. Neurosis peddlers are a buck a gross in this town." He rolled over onto his back and watched the dancers on the ceiling. A year before, I might have rolled over to watch them, too, drawn by the faint, classical music flowing under our conversation, but Jascha had tipped me off to that tactic. Let prospective employers divide your attention like that and they can get you to agree to all sorts of things without your realizing it, the more unscrupulous ones using posthypnotic suggestions keyed in with symbols. Or they can use subliminals to convince you that you don't want the job, if *they* don't want *you*. It saves them the trouble of arguing with you. So I held my position, reclining on my left side with my hands composed in front of me, resisting the urge to pick at the lamé upholstery. Only someone as successful as Nelson Nelson would have lamé couches. I was dying to look at the ceiling; whatever those dancers were doing up there, he was enjoying immensely. But I kept watching him watching the holo until he acknowledged my self-control and rolled back over onto his side to face me.

"All right," he said, smoothing out a wrinkle on his loose tunic. Loose tunics were all the rage these days; even I was wearing one. "All right." He touched a button on the low desk between us and the music faded. "Bolshoi, about seventy years ago, just before they went weightless. They're all twelve feet tall now. You like ballet?"

"A lot." I was glad I hadn't sneaked an eye at the holo. I would have been lost in the performance until he wheeled me out a side exit, couch and all.

"Me, too. You're good. Takes more than a holo-tank to frag your concentration, isn't it so? Sure. But you'd be surprised how many get caught in that little trap." He lit a cigarette. "Want one? Imported. Straight tobacco, I wouldn't try to drug you. I hate drugs." He tossed me the pack and I plucked it out of the air.

"Thanks," I said, lighting up by the glowhole in the couch frame.

"You impressed? That I can throw around imported tobacco?"

"More satisfied, actually."

Nelson Nelson laughed. "You'll do. All right, you can work for me. That's a privilege, kid, I don't employ many people. I've got a client waiting-list that could stretch to the moon and I like it that way. We'll start your training as soon as you move in."

"I'm already trained," I said, feeling like I had nothing to lose. If he let me get this far, he wasn't about to throw me out now. "J. Walter made me the best pathosfinder in town."

"I know that. Here's something else I know: the best institutes in the country don't train people in how to work. All my staff I train myself. I'm gonna strip you down and build you back up again. When I'm through with you, you'll be the best pathosfinder in the country. If you're not, you can sue me and I'll settle with you for any amount. What's your full, legal name again?"

"Alexandra Victoria Haas."

"Okay, Allie, just a few things before I show you around. You don't like what you hear, get up and walk. Fair?" He nodded for me. "Fair. You're gonna have to lose those eyes." He paused, waiting for my reaction. "That scare you?"

"No, I—"

"Okay. I didn't know. You don't see a lot of people wearing the eyes they were born with any more. I thought maybe you were queer for organics or something. A lot of agencies let you keep them until they wear out, but I say, why wait? You're gonna be hooked up to the system more often than anyone in any other profession. Living eyes weren't made to be popped in and out that often. Pretty soon you've got a couple of rotten eggs endangering your optic nerve. The eyes I'm gonna give you reattach to the muscles easier, not to mention the optic nerve, which I already mentioned." NN took another pack of cigarettes from the desk, waving away my offer of the pack he'd tossed me. "Keep 'em. Happy birthday." He lit up again and blew smoke toward a far corner of the room. "They come in here from the best institutes in the country thinking they can get away with a little fudging. But you can't fudge in this business. The last time I had the best pathosfinder in town on that couch, he was a chubby little guy who wanted to hook up to the system through the ears. Said it was just as good. I said, "How you gonna hear me tell you what a lousy job you're doing with your ears plugged up like that?' He took a stroll. He's not the best pathosfinder in the country, that's for sure. Then there was the guy with a *socket* in the back of his head. I said, What are you, a federal employee or just a freelance zombie? *He* said he could hook directly into the vision center of his brain, bypassing the optic nerve altogether. I showed him out. I don't have that kind of equipment." NN leaned forward and squinted at me. "*You* don't have any sockets in *your* head, do you?"

"No, I—"

"Just checking. There may be a better method than the optical system, but as far as I'm concerned, it hasn't been invented yet. Hooking up through the ears is complicated, time-consuming. Ever seen the inside of an ear? What a *mess!* Going in through the ear is like hacking your way through a jungle when there's a perfectly good freeway with no traffic on it you could use instead. And connecting right into the visual center of the brain is more direct, sure, but the brain doesn't like that. It likes to get its pictures through the optic nerve, the way it *always* gets its pictures. Sockets in the head! Goddammit, why do people think they have to break into the skull like burglars when they've got two perfectly good entrances right here?" He pointed two fingers at his own eyes and I thought for a moment he might accidentally poke himself.

"NN, I'm all for the optical system," I said quickly, before he could draw another breath. "J. Walter's system could accommodate organics or replacements. But I came here knowing your policy."

"Then, there's no problem." NN's smile was blissful. "It's so nice when there's no problem. I just hate it if I want to send somebody out on a job and it's no-go because the eyes are rotten eggs and the optic nerve's infected and I have to spend even more than I lost on the job getting the mess fixed."

"Not to mention the person in question having to sit around blind for months," I added.

"That's right, Allie. You take care of your part, I take care of mine, and everyone gets rich. But you won't have to worry about the eyes I'm gonna give you as long as you treat them right. I got a contract with the best eye house in the hemisphere. The retinas are guaranteed— you couldn't detach them with a twenty-mule team. The company kicks in for replacements if they spoil and the tissue is replaced every five years. They're the finest eyes in the world. If you don't think so, you can sue me and I'll support you for life."

We laughed together, both of us knowing he could probably wiggle out of that one even though he was recording.

"Your new eyes can be just like your old ones or you can have your choice of the weird stuff or any biogem you like—bloodstone, onyx, fire opal, cat's-eye—"

"I'll take cat's-eye," I said before I even realized it.

"Ah? Good for you. I like it. It'll be striking. Like a trademark. Good for business. You'll get a following." His foxy old face was all lit up. "I can see it now— Deadpan Allie, sees in the dark." He winked at me, popped his own eyeballs into his palms, and then clapped them back into the sockets without breaking the connections. "See? They're that easy. What do you think?"

"I think it could give new meaning to the sentence, 'My eyes dropped to my soup.'"

NN guffawed so heartily his couch shuddered. "Not bad, Deadpan. I can see already you're going to do well with us. You want to look at the setup?"

We took his private lateral to the west wing, where the

system was housed. I hesitated before getting into the lateral; it was only seven feet square. NN noticed and said nothing. He knew how I felt about small enclosed spaces from my profile and was probably waiting to see if I'd throw up on a moving conveyance or save it for later, after I got home. Some employers keep testing you right up to the day they ask you to leave.

It took about a minute to reach the west wing. NN kept me distracted with chatter. Just about the time I got the urge to punch holes in the walls, the lateral stopped at a darkened room, dimming its own lights. Blinking into the darkness, I could just make out the supine form of what seemed to be a headless man on a table. From the neck up, he was engulfed in the system, which took up most of the room. A pair of bloodstone eyes were waiting in a clear bowl of solution.

"That's Philbert," NN told me. "I'm switching him from pathosfinding to dreamfeeding. He was a good pathosfinder but we both thought it was time for a change. There are hookups for twenty more in here, not that I keep twenty more around to use them."

Stepping into the room, I looked around. I couldn't see much detail but I could tell it was the biggest mindplay single system I'd ever encountered. It rose from floor to ceiling, the latter invisible in the gloom so I couldn't tell if it ended twenty feet up or two hundred. I got the impression that if I yelled, it would echo. Areas of it jutted out like promontories on a cliff born in the mind of a cubist sculptor. Nothing showed, no wires, no dials, no lights, just a black facade, part of it eating a man's head. The man's body twitched a little. NN beckoned me back into the lateral.

"There's another lateral moving in behind this one. Someone else wants in," he said, pointing to a flashing blue light next to the doorway.

"Only one entrance?" I asked as we rotated and started back to his office again.

"A couple of emergency exits but besides those, yeah, just one. Keeps it private. You know, sometimes you come out of there and you don't want anyone to see you for a while."

My couch was gone when we returned to his office. He sat down on his and turned on the holo again. "That's all, kid. For now. Any questions?"

"Not yet."

"Still want to work for me?"

"Sure."

He leaned back on one elbow and cocked his head. "You really are deadpan, kid."

I wasn't sure if I was amused. "How'd you hit on that nickname?"

"It's in your profile. Go back and cash in your apartment or wherever you're living—say, you haven't become a Two, have you?"

"No, I'm single. Uh, not married."

"Good. I don't lust after taking on half a couple at this level of development. But I don't discriminate. One of my people is a Four. Anyway, you move in here tonight. I want you living at the agency while I train you and for the first year after. Then you can live wherever you please as long as you can get here when I need you. Suit?"

I nodded. "Just one other thing. Why is it—"

"—that I bother with educated people if I insist on training them over from scratch? Everyone wants to know that. If you weren't already trained, I wouldn't know you were trainable. I let the institutes weed out the failures and the missionaries for me. See you tomorrow."

I left him to the Bolshoi and slipped a tube back to my apartment.

Jascha's face looked a little older in the phone screen. Maybe it was because he wasn't using gilt these days. "I'm not surprised Nelson Nelson took you, Allie," he said. "And don't kid yourself, he probably knows all about you. There are all kinds of ways they can get around the privacy seal in your records. The smart ones can, anyway, and he's about the smartest one there is."

"'Kid.' That's what he calls me. 'Kid.' It's weird. Like meeting someone from a past time."

"Yah, well, he's *old*. How old I'm not sure but he's

probably giving your great-grandmother a run at the record."

There was a long silence while we just looked at each other at an exorbitant per-minute charge. "Listen, I think I'm going to be incommunicado for a while. While he strips me down and builds me back up again. Unquote. Jesus, all I could think was, 'Not *again*.'"

"That's the way he works. You'll be okay, though. He'll see to it." Another long pause. "I'm, uh, well, I'll leave callback so you'll know where to reach me."

"Do you *want* me to call you?"

"Who else would you call—Pyotr Frankis?"

I gave a short, uneasy laugh.

"Ah, Christ, Allie, everybody's got to have someone to trust. I could have done worse than to be yours."

And I had done worse than to be his. But all I said was, "Thanks, Jascha." I couldn't even bring myself to tell him about the cat's-eye biogems.

The screen blanked as Jascha disconnected. I sat there, feeling pretty disconnected myself. Another part of my life over with. Or maybe vice versa.

I began to understand a little of how McFloy had felt. I had a past but everything in it seemed to be receding from me faster than the speed of light. The way I'd been cut off from my old life (such as it was), the days of the drugs and Jerry and madcaps and then J. Walter and Pyotr Frankis and McFloy and Jascha, I might as well have been a mindsuck starting over myself.

I was still sitting in front of the screen pondering how it was I kept ending up alone contemplating my life when the phone beeped, startling the hell out of me. It beeped twice again before I jumped for the answer pad, thinking it might be Jascha calling back to say he wanted to see me the instant I was out of training. And I'd do it, I thought in the split second before the screen lit up. And if he wanted to give it a try again, I'd do that, too, what the hell, I didn't have to drift through my own outer life without any ties—

"Heya, Allie."

The features looked a little more world-weary than I remembered them but they hadn't changed much. I closed my eyes briefly, seeing that face in my mind's eye, or in some mind's eye. Identical, except I could discern the differences in spirit that moved behind each one.

"Jerry, what are you doing calling me?" I said. "I thought the conditions of your sentence specified no contact with—"

He giggled. Same old Jerry Wirerammer giggle. "Hey, is that any way to greet an old war buddy? After all we've been through together. Didn't you get even a little nostalgic seeing me around?"

I squinted at the screen, feeling uneasy. "Is this the *real* Jerry Wirerammer, or a Power Person?"

He giggled again. "Oh, it's really me, all right, Allie. They wouldn't let me clone off my memories. Not legally, anyway. Whaddaya say, can I come see you?"

"I'm not supposed to see you, Jerry. What are you doing calling me after all this time anyway?"

"Because we're old friends, like I said." He looked hurt. "And it wasn't any too easy to find you, either, even for an old hack like me. I had to access your great-grandmother's records."

"I ought to report you," I said darkly.

"Come *on*. Give an old friend a few minutes before you go off to be a big hot-wire mindplayer."

I stared at the face on the screen. Identical to McFloy and yet it didn't look a thing like him. In some ways, at least. Of all the images in my head, why had McFloy pulled out that one? Maybe because of the weakness he'd sensed I'd always had for Jerry. Or maybe because I felt responsible for Jerry's getting caught. He hadn't had to take me to the dry-cleaner's that day a million years ago. He could have left me insane and gotten away.

"Allie?" Jerry said hopefully.

I sighed. "Where are you?"

"No problem, I'll come up."

"*No.* I'll meet you somewhere. Just tell me where you are."

He thought for a moment. "There's the fetishizer's on the east side where I've been doing a little work. I'll meet you there. Say you're there for me and go into the back room—"

"I'll meet you out in front, on the sidewalk," I said.

"Why? I thought you were worried about being seen with me."

"I'll pass you off as a Power Person or something if it comes to that, but I'm not walking into some fetishizer's back room alone. Give me the address."

He punched it in and a tiny line of print ran across the bottom of the screen. "Half an hour okay with you? Or is something wrong with that, too?"

"Half an hour's fine. Just be there because I'm not going to wait."

That giggle. "I've done a lot of things, Allie, but I've never been late to do them."

I disconnected and found myself rushing for the door. I forced myself to slow down. Why the hell was I hurrying to consort with a known mind criminal, especially when it would violate the conditions of my own sentence—or rather, reprieve. Jerry had been the one who'd been sentenced.

Running out to see McFloy's face. But even as I thought it, I knew that wasn't it. Well, that wasn't *all* of it. Not even most of it.

It's just a way of putting a real end to the days of drugs and madcaps, I thought as I pulled my credit chip out of the stash bag at the head of the futon (old habits die hard). Just a way to tell Jerry good byo once and for all.

And I really believed it, too.

"Actually," Jerry said with that goofy smile, "I'm in kind of a tar baby."

"Why am I not surprised?" I asked the low, gray ceiling in the fetishizer's back room. We faced each other over a workbench where a small mindplay system was lying half-assembled, spilling its guts onto the grainy surface. I still didn't know much about hardware but I could see that a lot of the connections were definitely Jerry-rigged. "Something to do with the 'work' you've been doing here?" I gestured at the system. "Illegally."

Jerry spread his hands. "Hey, even a convicted mind criminal retains the right to turn a screwdriver if he wants to. Nobody has to know what on. I've got to eat, don't I?"

"What's the matter, are the residuals from Power People running a little slow?"

"You know I can't collect on that. All proceeds go to the state. The No-Profit law—no criminal shall see material reward from the commission of a crime blah, blah, blah, and blah. They could make a big-budget holo about my life and I wouldn't even see a free ticket to the premiere." He shrugged. "Crime's not supposed to pay. I get by, the state and Power People are getting fat. Real fat, from what I hear. Maybe there ought to be a law that no one should be able to profit from someone else's mind crime."

"What did they do to you?" I asked.

He gave a carefully casual shrug with one bony shoulder. "Oh, nothing much really. Some enforced belljarring with amnesia, a few thousand hours' community service, some fines. They let me hook up with Power People to pay those. My contract's up with them next year but they'll probably sign me on again. The Jerry Wirerammer property'll outlive me, I think. Which is kind of the problem."

The fetishizer poked her head through the black curtains in the doorway. "Are you getting anywhere near finished with that system?"

Jerry held up a screwdriver. "Still working. My consultant here tells me half the parts are obsolete."

"You said she knew how to update them." The fetishizer glared at me. I didn't glare back. She was a husky woman, laced into an old leather oversuit with nothing underneath. The pupils of her eyes were black spiders, and at either temple, her long black hair had been molded into two horns that looked sharp enough to pierce flesh. Giving people fetishes was a hell of a way to make a living and you wouldn't have thought there'd have been enough of such a specialized trade to keep fetishizers in business, but there was. You could get the same thing from a neurosis peddler but a fetishizer was far cheaper, if somewhat cruder in approach. Or so I'd been told.

The door buzzer went off in the other room, signaling a new customer and saving me from having to say anything to her. Jerry had hustled me in past her with some double-talk about my being a hardware expert. She'd taken an instant loathing to me and told him I'd better be worth the extra fee. Which Jerry had apparently pocketed, figuring it would be all right with me.

"What's going to happen to you when she finds out you're no further along on this pile of junk after I leave?" I asked in a low voice.

"Maybe she'll kill me," Jerry said cheerfully. "And maybe I should let her, which would solve all my problems. Of course, she's treading lightly herself with the law these days, so maybe she'll just beat me up a little, which won't solve anything and probably get me caught."

"Caught for what?"

Jerry winced. "Bootlegging."

I almost didn't need to ask. "Bootlegging what?"

"Myself."

I had to try not to laugh. "Oh, chris*sakes*—"

"Hey, I've got to *eat*," Jerry said plaintively. "I wasn't seeing anything from Power People, I could hardly get any work, for a while I had to sleep in a parking space, not even a flop but a *parking space*, and once I got towed off when the meter ran out—and I didn't even have a *vehicle*. *You* try living that way sometime. Then when somebody offers you a deal that'll make you a little more than sub-subsistence, you'll jump for it without a second thought, too."

I stared at the disassembled system so I wouldn't have to look at Jerry. "That's great. Who are they, the same people you used to fence stolen memories to?"

There was a long pause. "How'd you know about that?"

"Did you think I wouldn't have been told?"

"Well, what do you care? I never got any of yours."

"I never gave you a chance at them. Lucky for me."

"I wouldn't have done that to *you*, Allie. We're old war buddies."

"*What* war?"

"The war of life."

I wiped my hands over my face. "I don't think I can handle philosophy from you, Jerry, so just tell me what it is you think I can do for you and let me get out of here before your girlfriend decides to beat me up a little along with you."

Giggle. "You got any money?"

"Not much. Not enough to buy you out of either contract."

"It wouldn't be for that."

"Jesus, Jerry, *why?* Bootleggers usually clone their goods off one of the enfranchised people. Why couldn't you just let them work from one of your copies—"

"Well, they were. But then they found me, and everyone know you get better results from the original template."

"Is that what you are to yourself now—an original template?"

Jerry shrugged. "You think differently when something like Power People gets through with you."

"And whose fault is that?" I slipped my credit chip out of my shirt pocket. "Never mind. I've got a little money on this. Not much. I won't be needing anything after today, you can have it. But maybe you should just turn yourself in. Or leave town."

"Forget it. I'm travel-restricted. They'd just catch me, and I'm not going under the belljar with amnesia again."

I couldn't blame him for that. I was about to say something else when the fetishizer reappeared in the doorway, looking meaner than ever.

"Well?" she said.

Jerry jumped up. "We've got to go out for a part." He ran around the bench, grabbed my arm, and pulled me toward the back door.

"*What* part?" the fetishizer asked, staring at me with those spider eyes.

"A part you don't have," I said and slipped out the door before she could say anything else. Jerry was right on my heels.

We hurried up the narrow alley to the street. "What's

she going to say when you go back without a part?" I said as Jerry pulled me past a trip parlor.

"I don't know. Don't worry about her now." Jerry kept pulling me along the street, looking at the storefronts until he stopped abruptly in front of a memory-wipe place. "You got that chip?"

"You can't use it until I sign it over to you."

"Don't sign it over to me, sign it over to them." He jerked his at the memory-wiper's.

"What? Why?"

Jerry looked at me as though I were mildly retarded. "I've got to get rid of the memory of bootlegging myself before Power People calls me in for template renewal tomorrow, of course. Otherwise they'll find out what I did."

I blinked at him. "Jerry, if you can't remember what you did, how are you going to avoid the bootleggers?"

"Oh, they'll put me on callback here and resell me the memory. I've done it before. And who says I want to avoid the bootleggers? They're the only thing between me and starvation."

I shook my head. "I thought you wanted me to *help* you."

"This *is* helping me."

"I don't think so."

"Come on." Jerry herded me into the memory-wiper's.

The woman behind the counter looked like a raccoon, down to the black band painted over her eyes and the little black nose and whiskers grafted onto her face. She was actually kind of cute, if animals were your weakness. Right then, I wished they were mine instead of Jerry.

"Hey-*yo*, Rammer-Jammer!" she said, showing her sharp little teeth in a grin. "Thought you were about due for another visit." The bright animal eyes took me in eagerly. "Bringing me new trade, too."

"Not me," I said, "I'm just the wallet here."

She spread her hands, showing off her raccoon claws, which weren't so cute. "So that's pretty handy, having a wallet that follows you around. The usual, Rammer?"

Jerry nodded. "She'll pay you, Bandit. Including the callback and resell."

"That's all right by me, it's your memory. But don't you think there's some things better left forgotten?"

Jerry disappeared through a doorway at the back of the shop without answering. The raccoon-woman beckoned to me with one claw as she turned to a console at her right. "Cash or chip?" she asked me.

I put the chip on the counter and somehow she managed to pick it up without the claws getting in the way. She saw me staring.

"Just like fingernails," she said, "only more useful in case of an emergency."

I nodded. "I'm signing everything on the chip over to you for Jerry's account. Can you keep my name out of it?"

"No problem, milady." She pushed a small pad of numbered squares at me. "Enter your unlock code and I'll do the rest." She worked on the console for a minute, checking a screen I couldn't see on the other side of the counter. "Personally, I wouldn't use a 'bearer' chip—too easy for people like your friend the Rammer-Jammer to hackity-hack the unlock code."

"I never cared to pay the feds for a personal account ID."

"Can't fault you for that." She made what I supposed was a raccoon noise as she looked at the screen. "There's a little left over even after the callback and resell. Sure there isn't something *you'd* like to forget about? Like the Rammer-Jammer maybe?"

I shook my head. "Too many associations. It would wipe out half my life, maybe more. I've never really understood how some people can just come into a place like this and forget whole blocks of things so easily."

The raccoon-woman clacked her claws together. "Well, for some of us, it's just this episode and that episode, one thing after another, and not too much relates to anything else. It's one way to live. Not the worst way. Nothing haunts you."

"Yah. I'll wait outside for, uh, Rammer-Jammer."

"Right. Come back any time," she called to my back.

I found an empty parking place a few feet up from the wiper's, fed the meter a token, and sat down on the curb. Jerry came out twenty minutes later looking relaxed, refreshed, and ready to goof up anything. He glanced at me, did a double-take, and came running over.

"Allie! What the hell! I never thought I'd see *you* again!"

I opened my mouth to say something and then realized he'd had to wipe the memory of calling me along with his bootlegging. "Just passing by, Jerry. Some coincidence, huh?"

"Yah, synchronicity in all her glory. Heya, I'd invite you for a drink or a pop but, you know, I don't think we better take a chance on getting seen together." He looked up and down the street. "I don't care about me, but they'd go hard on you."

"Yah." I looked at the meter; there was another five minutes on it. "Listen, I've got to sprint. You want a parking place for five minutes?"

"Yah, sure!" He sat down and stretched his legs out. "You're a real friend, Allie."

"I sure am. Seeya, Jerry." I walked off as fast as I could without running and without looking back. One thing after another and not too much relates to anything else.

And I'd thought *I* was disconnected.

THE PATHOSFINDER
DOES A JOB

I canceled my lease, sold off the big stuff to General Stores, and took one suitcase back to the agency. I found my new quarters easily enough, even though there seemed to be no one to show me around. The big building was a windowless maze inside, but the laterals and passageways were color-coded.

My name was already up on the apartment door—as Deadpan Allie, not Alexandra V. Haas—and the door was set to my handprint. It opened to a three-room apartment superior to anything I'd had in the last several years. I had cooking privileges in the elaborate kitchenette or I could dial up meals. There was an area set up for entertaining, complete with stocked bar; NN apparently believed in socializing. He probably liked having his staff talking shop and picking each other's brains. I wouldn't have called the bedroom luxurious but it wasn't a monk's cell either (if there were any monks left). The bed was big enough for five and firm enough for me and I wondered how Jascha had managed to include that in a recommendation.

There was a conch shell sitting in the middle of the bed. I tossed my suitcase into the autovalet and sat down. There was a note in the shell reading simply, *Welcome*. It wasn't a cultured shell but the real thing, unpainted and unvarnished. NN sure was ostentatious. I put it carefully on the nightstand and dialed up a mushroom-and-algae casserole for supper. I found an orientation program cued up and ready to run on my dataline so I lingered over my food, reading about the history of the Nelson Nelson Agency and NN's personal feelings about mindplay.

What he had to say didn't differ much from J. Walter's line, except for a small paragraph on the last page. NN felt that mindplay was a necessary tool for the evolving, expanding mind, and that the next evolutionary step would take place in the brain, generated voluntarily by humans themselves. That was nothing new. There were plenty of people in the if-god-had-not-meant-for-humans-to-mindplay-he-wouldn't-have-put-ergot-fungus-on-bread camp, and a lot of them had been at J. Walter.

Eventually, I found myself nodding out at the screen. I undressed, sent the empty casserole down the chute, adjusted the room temperature, set the bed for six hours, and slept hard.

The next day, and every day after for six months, were all hours full. I had my eyes out early that first morning and spent the following three days waiting for my optic nerves to heal while I got acquainted with Rich Lind-bloom. She had the apartment next to mine. NN had assigned her to be my seeing-eye person. She was a big one, almost seven feet. After I got my eyes, I saw that she was also navy-blue-skinned and orange-haired. Not a permanent dye-job, she told me. She liked to switch around. NN employed her as a thrillseeker. I thought she was a walking thrill all by herself.

Most everyone else besides Rich and Philbert, who was still switching tracks—Fandango, the neurosis ped-dler; Deacon and Sara, the belljarrers; and the other pathosfinder, Four L. N. (a single parent with three cubs, something you don't see much)—were in and out as business required, mostly out. NN made himself scarce as well once the training began. He slipped in a few times while I was sleeping to check my brain wave personally. I guess he liked what he saw because he never bothered to wake me.

I spent a lot of time letting the system eat my head. There was no way to modify it in a fashion that NN would allow, but at least it didn't grab your face. I had to take all the mindplaying over again, too, administered by the appropriate employee, who approached things as though I were an actual paying client. NN wanted me to be on the receiving end of the agency's preferred techniques. Fandango came up with one of those cleanliness obses-sions for me with a side tendency to become sexually aroused by the color orange. The bit with the orange was pretty interesting, if kind of kinky. I wondered where she'd learned it.

Rich dug down into my mind, found a thrill, and arranged it for me. I was kind of nervous about that but she showed good judgment about what could be brought up out of my subconscious and what should have stayed buried. It was a very satisfactory thrill, though I suspected she was getting back at Fandango for making me go into rut every time she brushed her hair.

Philbert finished switching tracks, so I let him practice his dreamfeeding on me. He was pretty good—he had to be or Nelson Nelson wouldn't have kept him around—but he was no Jascha. I managed to keep him from picking up any of that feeling from me, though. They didn't call me Deadpan Allie for nothing.

Belljarring I couldn't look forward to; it still felt too much like being buried alive. Or something. Deacon was sensitive to my dislike of being cut off and worked to give me an impression of people-just-in-the-next-room without stimulating any senses. It lasted half a day and it was just fine, when it was over.

Four L.N. and I spent some time hooked in together so I could get the feel of how he worked. Interestingly enough, he'd been at J. Walter several years before I had and there were overtones of the institute technique, especially in the relaxation exercises. But through the years in private practice, his methods had evolved into something that was actually quite different. What I noticed mostly was how skittish two pathosfinders were when they were hooked in mind-to-mind. The first couple of sessions were like The Great Stone Face Meets The Other Great Stone Face. When we were finally able to let out some with each other, I saw he had developed a persona that was strictly activated within the system, his own mental mask. It made me wonder if he hadn't had a franchise personality at some time in the past, but of course he didn't tell me.

And once in a while, when there was a free moment, I paused in front of the mirror in my apartment and looked at myself with those eyes. Of all the biogems I'd had to choose from, what had possessed me—

Bad way to put it. Try again. Why *those?* That's all. Just *why*.

Because I liked them. Honestly, truly. And what I liked best about them was that they didn't look a thing like McFloy's eyes in my head. If anything, they seemed to be more me than McFloy. I hung onto that thought.

Training concluded, NN gave me a week to breathe in and out in any fashion I chose, so I went off with Rich to a sky-island owned by the agency. It was about the same as any of the other flying resorts circling the world, except it wasn't crammed to the weight limit with tourists and businesspeople on working vacations. Entertainment was the finest in music, dancing, even some theater, works in progress or recently finished, things that wouldn't see popular release for months. Rich told me it was all provided by the agency's clients who chose to pay partially for services by playing the island. We spent a lot of time free-fall sailing and exercising mindlessly and I decided I could get used to being a member of the Jetstream Set.

It was all so wonderful I was suspicious of what would be waiting for me when I bounced down out of the clouds again. Probably a killer assignment, Rich theorized. NN's vacations weren't usually so lavish. We were both right.

Jascha's phone asked who was calling. I punched in my code and instead of an answer blank, it tossed up a videotaped message. "I've left J. Walter and gone back into private practice," Jascha said. He was using gilt again and also a little face paint, just a tasteful floral spot design. The resolution on the answer tape wasn't good enough to let me see exactly what kind of flower it was. "This is my office number, but if you need to, you can pry my home code out of the answering machine. I've put you in as one of the very few who can access it. Just tell it your name." He paused and I almost shut the screen off, thinking the tape was over.

"I've remarried, Allie. I guess I should have told you that in person but I wanted you to know before you called. You *can* still call me. If you want to. I want you to. I just don't know how you'll feel about it. So it's up to you. I'll always take your calls. I've just got this screening process because I'm not with an agency." He glanced at something, or maybe someone, beyond the screen. "I don't know if you *will* call now. In case I don't hear from you for a while, I bet you're a hell of a pathos-finder . . . Deadpan." The screen faded to white with an asterisk cue. I punched in an end-it and plugged into my system access for a round of calming influences. Just a few mental hours of mental fingerpainting. I mean, what had I expected, after all?

One minute to the week my time off was over, I found myself reclining on the couch in NN's office, listening to him tell me about Marty Oren, the actor who had started to make sensations two years back just before he'd retired to an anti-mindplay enclave with his new wife.

"But now he's back on the outside, wife and all," NN told me. "He tried old-style theater while he was in and apparently found it extremely unsatisfying. How you gonna keep 'em down on the farm, I guess. He was vague about it on his preliminary application. Truth to tell, I think the adulation of a few hundred people was too little for him. Anyway, his old company kept letting him know regularly they were ready for him any time he wanted to come back. So he's back. He and Sudella Keller are in Restawhile, Kansas."

"Restawhile? *Kansas?*"

NN shrugged. "It's kind of a year-round resort-cum-village, very quiet. Ideal for making a transition back into the mainstream."

"Transition? How do they live in those enclaves—in mudhuts?"

"Not exactly. It's a difference in sensibilities. Without a transition period, the culture shock could make him psychotic. Kind of like if you took an eighteenth-century hermit and dropped him smack into the middle of

Commerce Canyon out there." He jerked his chin at the window.

"Marty Oren isn't an eighteenth-century hermit. After all, he grew up—"

"Only recently. He's just twenty-two years old, a comparative baby."

"Compared to who?"

"You. He went through his second puberty in that enclave. And don't look at me like that, a lot of experts call the years between eighteen and twenty-four second puberty."

Involuntarily, I felt my face with my hand.

"Relax, Deadpan. It's just because I know you so well. Didn't know I knew you so well, did you? Well, I do. You don't have to agree with me about second puberty, you just have to do your job. Besides Oren's well-being, there's also his wife to consider."

"What's she going to do—make the transition with him?"

"Hell, no. She's just as anti-mindplay as she ever was. She's your stumbling block." NN smiled pleasantly. "All those jobs have stumbling blocks, did I ever mention that? So it's going to be hard for you to work with him while she's there. The only thing you've got going for you is her respect for his personal choices, but she's bound to inhibit him in some way.

"*Also*, Oren's always had this bitter streak he's had to keep in check, which I think is why they've always worked him with pathosfinders rather than dreamfeeders, like some actors. After being out of things for two years, he needs a pathosfinder more than ever. That's why the company asked the agency to handle him instead of turning him over to their resident pathosfinder. Next month, they want to put him into rehearsal for *Two Moon Night*, the play about the guy who died alone on Mars."

"I'm familiar with it. Isn't that kind of industrial-strength material to start him off with? I mean, a man in that part has to go through all kinds of things—raptures, hallucinations—he's got to run the emotional gamut.

Experienced actors have taken year-long recuperations after doing *Two Moon Night* because they were too wrung-out to work afterwards and Oren's been out of touch for, what, two years?"

"If he's not ready for it, you'll tell them."

I was really looking forward to something like that. NN's smile was broader and more benign than ever. "If he's as sheltered as you say, I don't think he'll be able to deal with it. We could just phone the company now."

"Your compassion is showing, Deadpan."

I sat up and folded my arms. "Empathy's a bitch."

"What isn't?"

"So I get him into shape for the play. Or I try to get him into shape. Then what?"

NN looked blank.

"What about his wife? He can't very well move into a city with her."

"They haven't let me in on their plans." NN sounded just a bit sour. "I imagine she'll be staying in Restawhile when he's working. It's far enough out in the country that she can avoid most problems if she's careful. Anyway, they want to stay together. Don't ask *me* why. Neither one of them is about to give so much as an angstrom in their viewpoints. He's going to mindplay, she's dead against it. It's going to screw his emotions around."

"It could be a good source to draw on."

"I doubt it, but use your own judgment. They're both a couple of very defensive people right now."

"I'm not sure if I'm going to be able to make any progress, then. The ideal thing might be to work with both of them, but if she won't—well, it's their time."

"And their marriage. Don't bust it up."

Maybe I should have told him my new hobby was not busting up marriages. "I won't. But they can't blame me if after he—"

"They most certainly *will* blame you, they're the sort of people who tend to lay blame for their own messes. So watch where you step. He probably wouldn't sue us but she most definitely would. And I don't want that, not at all."

"Is she well-connected?"

NN flipped on the ceiling holo and the familiar Bolshoi music filled the room. "Sort of. She's my daughter."

Oh.

I went underground tubeway to Wichita and rented a flier to take me and my equipment east to Restawhile. I spent the time on the tube getting acquainted with Marty Oren's old notices and re-reading *Two Moon Night*. It was a powerful piece of work, heavy on emotion and full of tenuous science, with the potential to be a tearjerker instead of an honest study of a dying man.

When I got a look at the flier in Wichita, I nearly turned around and went home. It was an airplane converted to computer autopilot and seemed to have been put together with masking tape and spit. It did fly, albeit roughly; the rolling Kansas landscape, pretty as it was, gave it a lot of trouble. By the time I got to Restawhile, a hamlet nestled around a lake, it was late afternoon. I circled the lake several times before I realized the autopilot was locked in an electronic argument with itself as to whether the water could be landed on. I ended up landing the thing myself and took a few turns on pontoons before I found the dock I wanted. I might not have found it at all, except Sudella Keller was standing on it, watching.

She looked large in her loud, flowery-print muumuu, but when I climbed out of the cockpit and onto the dock, I could see she was nearly swimming in diaphanous material. Her wide, elegant face was made up subtly but effectively and it bore absolutely no resemblance to NN's foxy pink features. Her eyes tilted up at the outer corners without actually being Oriental. Her nose turned up, too. Great body engineering. Apparently bodyplay was all right if mindplay wasn't. Interesting. I chided myself for being catty, but it didn't make things any less interesting.

We just stood taking each other in for a few seconds. "You must be Sudella Keller," I said, making an extra effort to be cordial.

"You must be Daddy's thug," she said, also quite cordial.

Ah, I thought, court is in session, the judge is on the bench, and I'm already in contempt.

"I could have told by your face who you are," she said. "Deadpan Allie. What's so important about being deadpan?"

"A professional mindplayer has to remain neutral at all times. We aren't judges of human behavior. Clients have to remain unaware of our approval or displeasure, so they won't attempt to gain either."

"Well, I see you've swallowed Daddy's menu first course to dessert."

I almost asked her why she was so bitched at Daddy, but it wasn't my business. Instead, I asked if it would be all right to bring in my equipment.

"I'll show you your room. Then you can decide whether you want to or not. It isn't much bigger than the inside of your flier and you didn't mention how long you'd be staying."

"I'm not sure. But I don't have much with me."

"Good thing."

She led me down the pier to the house. It was an old-fashioned cottage with a bare minimum of conveniences, none of which were in the broom closet they called a guest room. It had a water bed taking up most of what space there was. I stood in the doorway staring at it and trying not to think about my mattress back at the agency. "Nice woodwork," I said lamely.

"It'll be pretty cramped."

"Doesn't worry me," I lied. "Where's Two Oren?"

"Gone fishing. Know anything about fishing?"

"Not freshwater. Just mid-Atlantic shark-fishing." I winced inwardly. If I couldn't be more deadpan than to one-up fish stories, I was going to make a bigger mess than the one I was supposed to straighten out. But somehow it seemed to have been the right thing to say; she almost smiled at me. Perhaps she was surprised that I didn't spend all my waking hours letting Daddy's system eat my head.

I had already decided to sleep on the roof and was wheeling the last components of my portable system over the extendable ramp from the flier to the dock when

Marty Oren came home, rowing himself in a rowboat. I stopped to watch, wondering what part of the lake he'd come from that I hadn't spotted him from the air. He looked tired, disgusted, sunburned, and very attractive. His hair had grown down below his shoulders and was plaited in two gold braids. The gold was strictly his own, probably maintained from childhood by something in his diet. As he got closer, I saw that his face was more angular than it appeared on holo. Lots of cheekbones. Your basic leading man.

When he reached the dock, I leaned down to give him a hand up and was surprised to see that he had cat's-eyes. They looked better in his head than they did in mine.

"Deadpan Allie." He smiled warmly. Inside, I felt a chord being twanged, which is what's supposed to happen when a leading thespian smiles like that in your direction. I didn't make anything of it but I was sure plenty of people had tried to in the past.

"Nelson Nelson gave you a big buildup," he said and something changed in his face. He had shut himself off from me at his own mention of his father-in-law. It was as sudden and effective as a slap. "We'll have some food and then get started. If you haven't eaten." He looked back out over the water, which was turning gold as the sun began to edge toward dusk. "Nice day."

"Lovely."

I wheeled my equipment ahead as we walked down the dock to the house together. Sudella was waiting like a statue at the door.

The meal was roast duck, which Marty cooked in an old microwave, a real, functioning antique, taking all of twenty minutes, including the algae. We sat around the table passing each other orange sauce (which stirred a few decidedly unusual memories) and not saying much. I felt like I was in a holo period piece, complete with anachronisms. Marty and Sudella loosened up a little but it was more resignation than relaxation. I tried reading Marty's Emotional Index by sight but I couldn't get much feeling for his state of mind. Sudella's was only too clear.

Afterward, they cleared the table, leaving me the coffee. I pretended not to watch them as they put the reusable dishes in the washer. For a few moments, their guards went way down. Obviously they loved each other a great deal while being in conflict with each other's desires—pretty normal. But the love part seemed strangely intensified, like sunlight reflected on water, as though one of them were wearing an amplifier. It bothered me. If I could have delved Sudella—but by law I couldn't even ask her. I'd just have to work their puzzle with half the pieces.

They dawdled by the dishwasher as long as they could but finally Marty came over and sat down across from me.

"Do you want to start?"

"Only if you think you can."

He glanced at Sudella, still over by the dishwasher. "I want to get this over with as soon as possible."

"This isn't something you can rush, remember. There's no way I can tell how long it's going to take until we're in." Peripherally, I saw Sudella cross her arms and stand up a bit straighter, ready for a siege.

"I hadn't thought there'd be much to do. It always went pretty smoothly before."

"You've been out of touch."

"Well, I've always worked with pathosfinders, so I'm used to it. Or I was."

Sudella suddenly turned and strode out the front door, leaving it open behind her. Marty started to get up.

"Sit where you are. Sudella is showing us a great deal of courtesy. I think we should respect her by accepting it."

"But she left because—"

"A lot of the right things get done for the wrong reasons. If I gave you a soft purple sponge, what would you do?"

"Hold it in my hands and squeeze it." He twisted in his chair.

"If I gave you a green hat with a brim all the way around, what would you do?"

"I'd see if it was my size."

He went on for close to half an hour, longer than usual, but I thought he would enjoy playing *What Would You Do?* Most people did. They forgot it was less a game than a relaxation exercise geared to provide a pathosfinder with some hints about what kinds of things were wandering around in their heads. He got involved in it, and by the time I asked the last question his answers were spontaneous and his mind was (mostly) off Sudella.

I gave him one of NN's expensive cigarettes to keep him busy but idle while I wheeled out my apparatus and put it together. It was like playing with a giant set of cub's blocks, three big pieces and five smaller ones. When I finished making the connections, I had a portable version of NN's cubist cliff, looking off-balance but actually quite stable. It wouldn't eat our heads; instead, the connections were external, so as to keep the system as compact as possible.

I pulled out the drawer with the four connections and the thermos tank of solution for our eyes. "Ready?"

"Do you know there are no longer any actors alive today who still have their own eyes?" he asked suddenly.

"Does that bother you?"

"It seems strange. Drawing on life and looking at it through artificial eyes."

I remembered my own eyes with some fondness, but it was rather nice not to have to put up with having my astigmatism worked on every few years. Pushing the tank over, I showed him how it was compartmented so we wouldn't be groping for our optics later. He made three tries at getting his eyes out before I did it for him: his eyes were deepset and he was out of practice. After I hooked him into a relaxation exercise, I made a quick check of his connections. The tissue and insulation would be good for another year at most; then they would have to be replaced or he'd go blind. I wondered how he'd planned to do that from an enclave, or if he even knew what condition his eyes were in.

After a minute of deep breathing, I hooked myself in, making my presence felt gradually, so he wouldn't feel like I was bursting in on him. He was in the middle of a chromatic, making colors. Surprisingly, he didn't seem to have any enthusiasm for it. I made a few with him—navy blue to jade blue to scream blue to milk blue, and he yielded the whole thing to me with juvenile boredom. Maybe I'd relaxed him too much and he was getting antsy. I put the colors aside and indicated we could start.

Nothing happened.

I prodded again and then again before I got any results. We were in a bare, sterile room, no windows, no doors, nothing, just smooth white walls. The Infamous White Room; most people are stunned to find out how common an image it is. Marty was sitting in one corner with his legs stretched out in front of him, hands resting on his thighs. I seemed to be invisible.

Marty?

The figure in the corner slumped and became a marionette. I was suddenly awash in waves of *reassure me, reassure me.*

Not my job, I told him as neutrally as possible. *Let's do some work.*

The marionette persisted a little longer, as though he thought he might get me to believe he really did need reassurance, that he wasn't just a pawn by sheer stubbornness. Then everything faded, leaving us in limbo, aware of each other's presence but alone. Lots of people felt that way, though few were so textbook in expressing it.

You have to help me, I said. *I can't carry us both.* Not strictly true, but the idea was to keep him thinking for himself rather than following my lead.

No response. I checked his vitals; he was still conscious. He just didn't seem to care.

Well, that was a hell of a note—my first job and the client was more deadpan than I was. It was more than a hell of a note, though; it was all wrong, and in the worst way. So. I could fumble around for a while and get nowhere or I could give him a direct mental jab.

Disregarding NN's warning, I showed him a visualization of Sudella watching us from across the room and then suddenly walking out. He clamped down on his reaction quickly, but not quickly enough to hide a sense of responsibility or obligation for something that Sudella may have done for him that was, to his way of thinking, somewhere between a service and an outright favor. Then the rest came out of him involuntarily and I saw that if I were willing to pick up doing this service/favor where Sudella had left off, I could gain his responsibility/obligation in her place.

They don't call me Deadpan Allie for nothing. I let it pass and took his Emotional Index, looking at all the little domino feelings that led up to the reaction. I had to take it several times just to be sure. It kept coming up *like* hunger but definitely *not* hunger—like someone who wanted food just because it was there.

Over his protest, I went for a walk through his life. He tried to keep me distracted with the recent past, his sense of triumph and accomplishment after each performance. It disturbed him that I noted only his orgasms during applause. I went back further to the time before he became an actor, for a look at his family.

He'd been a Three, an only child between two parents, a tripod, which some diehard experts were still claiming as the most stable of family configurations. I found it unusual that it was *so* nuclear. Pressure on each corner of the triangle had remained constant until sometime after he reached puberty, when his corner had begun to spike up and down before ascending rapidly out of plane. So much for the stability of the tripod.

His first mindplay experience had been a full two years after he'd come of age, at eighteen. His first acting audition had paired him with the company's pathosfinder. I went back and checked carefully to make sure I hadn't missed any suppressed thrillseeking or illegal madcaps but there was nothing.

The company's pathosfinder had been an incompetent. No, not really—just overworked. It figured. The emphasis had been on turning out performers in a hurry. Rather than working with Marty Oren's inexperienced mind, the pathosfinder had done a rush job, teaching him by example rather than helping him find his own answers. After being the focus of a tripod, Marty had

simply accepted the attention and mimicked the appropriate responses.

He'd gone on to his next play with conditional notices;
apparently someone had noticed there was something
lacking in him. Then he'd suddenly switched companies
but the next pathosfinder was no better. The troupe was
on a tight schedule and they got exactly what they
wanted from him. By the time he'd joined his present
company, his mimicry of real emotions had been perfect-
ed. All he had to do was reflect the pathosfinder's
expectations back to the source.

I sat on my anger and told him he should have gone for
help. A feeling of *I didn't need help, I was doing fine on
my own* came out of him.

We can put this right, I said.

Put what *right?*

He became an observer while I searched around for
things he cared about. A two-dimensional image of
Sudella slipped by me before I could catch it, turned
sideways, and disappeared. I went after it through a long
hall lined with locked doors. He made no attempt to stop
me as I jerked them open; I received the distinct
impression that somehow it no longer mattered.

Sudella's image, still two-dimensional, stood in a room
of mirrors with a fixed smile on its face. Mirrors; he'd
done enough with mirrors. It was time for someone to do
something else. I ignored the toy Sudella and looked
deliberately into his mirrors to be sure he could see what
I was doing. If everything he cared about was two-
dimensional, he could deal with me alone.

I plucked my eyes out of my head.

It was a purely figurative act but the feeling of reality
in it hit him hard and he couldn't maintain the mirrors.
Vision heightened rather than destroyed, I went back to
the locked places I had forced open.

The hallway was shadowy, empty, abandoned, a place
no one had ever come to. I went along it slowly, pausing
at each of the doors to look into the rooms beyond.

They were all empty. There was nothing to see in any
of them and no sign of anything ever having been there.
Occasionally there was a strong smell of something

spoiled but it was just a smell. Once I heard something large and wet shift its weight, but it was only a noise.

I let him close the doors after me, locking each one tightly, not against me but because there was no point to leaving them open. It was just a place in his mind. His body was an instrument rather than a live thing, his face a device, his eyes windows where no curtains had ever hung. He didn't hate. He just couldn't care.

In his own way, he was possibly one of the best actors of all time. Only there was no audience for his best performance.

And there was no such classification as emotional criminal. Which, I reminded myself, was a good thing for all of us.

Emotional cripple, then. But I wasn't a doctor. I couldn't even diagnose him, officially. I was only there to help him with what he had. If it wasn't there, I had no job to do. I started to withdraw.

Wait, he said.

I waited a long time. Then a landscape began to form around us, all from him though I could feel him trying to draw on me. I clamped down and he didn't like that much, but I wasn't about to let him tap me. On his own, all he could manage was bare earth under a colorless, sunless sky, none of it feeling terribly real.

Help?

I didn't say anything. He strained a little and I felt the ground against my feet, like cardboard.

Better? He was looking around for me now and I jumped into his blind spot. *Allie?*

There's nothing more to do, I told him.

Nightmare purple flickered like heat lightning; fear. He was capable of a few emotions. *Are you going to turn me in?*

As what? To whom? It's not against the law to—to be the way you are.

Can't you tell me what to do? He was still looking around for me, confused. But he had a big blind spot; there was room enough in it for me, Sudella, and most of the country. *I need a pattern to follow, that's all, for me it's just as good . . .* Suddenly we were in a huge

empty theater. He was onstage; I was looking up at him
from the audience. He smiled down at me triumphantly.
No blind spot here; he knew exactly where to find
everything and everyone in his theater. I had to withdraw quickly or I was going to give him what he wanted
after all.

I jumped up and hurried along the row of seats toward
the aisle. He laughed a little and suddenly the aisle had
receded to a vanishing point; the row of seats was
endless. I paused, trying to form a clear picture of the
aisle as it had been, without letting him see it, too.

See? he said. *This feels good, doesn't it? It feels real,
doesn't it?*

Didn't you think someone would find out someday? I
asked him, covering the image of the aisle. I almost had
it. *Another actor, a better pathosfinder, or even Sudella?*

Sudella's two-dimensional form appeared in the row
behind the one I was in. She was smiling and applauding.

*Sudella loves the reflection of her love. And youth is
forgiven many things, including its callowness. I am as
good a mirror out there as I am in here. The world is my
oyster. I am the pearl.*

There was a time to argue the case that youth won't
persist forever, or even as long as it thinks it will, and a
time to cut and run. I lunged for the aisle, which
materialized just as I hit it. Before Marty could react, I
tossed him into another innocuous relaxation exercise
and broke the contact between us. The image of the
theater persisted, fading slowly as I ran, and ran, and
ran.

Eventually, I reached a small, safe, private place in
the system, where I could take a few free mental breaths
before I had to go back into real reality, or whatever that
was out there where Sudella and Marty went through
their shadow play of a relationship.

Even real reality is full of unreal things, said a voice.
It sounded a little like Pyotr Frankis's and a little like
Jascha's, with the intonations of Paolo Segretti. I didn't
look around; at the moment, I didn't have enough will to

visualize anything more than mental fog. *Some will choose an empty exchange over a real one. Because they refuse to see that it is empty.*

Abruptly, I was facing a cat's-eye with a Snake around the outer rim of the pupil, holding its tail in its mouth.

The emptiness is real.

I had no reply. The eye faded away as I let myself be drawn out of the system.

When I disconnected and put my eyes back in, I saw that Sudella had come in out of the dark and was standing behind Marty. She was very pointedly not looking at the eyes. They *are* a bit grisly when they're out if you're not hardened to that sort of thing. I reached into the drawer and ran down a line of switches. Each of Marty's limbs gave a small jump, separately and then all together. Sudella made a gasping noise.

"What are you doing to him?"

Nothing, compared to what he tried to do to me. "Making sure his motor controls haven't suffered. Routine." I unhooked him, popped his eyes back in, and turned him around to Sudella before he could say anything. He stared up at her open face, which was filled with longing and compassion and love for him. Sudella in the empty theater, applauding for all she was worth.

"You must be exhausted," I said. "Why don't you lie down?"

"I think I will." He turned back to me and I saw a trickle of blood leaking from the corner of his left eye. Sudella wiped it away with her fingertip.

"He's hurt."

"He's all right, he just ruptured a capillary. It happens sometimes, when you're out of practice." I nodded at Marty. He gave me that smile again, but this time all I could see were lips and perfect teeth. For an empty package, he sure had a beautiful wrapper. Then he went into the bedroom and shut the door.

"Now what?" Sudella lifted her chin belligerently.

"Now I leave." I started dismantling my apparatus under her startled gaze; she hadn't been expecting that.

"Marty will explain everything. He's decided to return to the enclave with you. He's—" I paused. "He's who he is."

"I know." She took a tiny step closer to me. "He never needed your stupid mindplay. It's indecent to go running around in a person's mind like that. You find things out you shouldn't know."

I stopped what I was doing and leaned on my equipment. "Why not? Why shouldn't we know?" I asked gently.

She looked at me and for a moment it felt like we were hooked in together. Of course. Rudimentary telepathy. Not developed enough to be useful, just enough to hurt.

"Some of us can live with our illusions." She looked down at her arms, which were folded tightly against her chest. "For some of us, it's good enough if you can't get the real thing."

"If that's what you want to settle for."

"If the alternative's nothing at all, what choice have you got?" She was close to tears now. "Maybe we can't know ourselves as well without mindplay but it's the human condition to struggle for it. It's the human condition to try alone."

I didn't comment on Marty Oren's condition. I didn't have to. It might have been different if she'd mind-played—and then again, probably not. He wouldn't have given her an eye. He didn't have one to give.

Nelson Nelson didn't have much to say about my report, but then I'd left out what I knew about Sudella being telepathic. It didn't make any difference; the only one it really mattered to was going back to the enclave with Marty Oren.

He made a business of getting the receipt chips for my expenses in order, scrutinizing each one on the screen in his desk before punching them into final entry. I made a business of lying on the couch not looking curious.

"So tell me, Deadpan," he said after a bit, "how it was that you caught his problem when it eluded people who had been practicing for years?"

I was ready for that one. "I had no expectations. I

didn't stereotype him and I was thorough. You said I'd be the best pathosfinder in the country—I did a superior job."

"Only it was too superior, eh?" NN waved away anything I might have said. "Forget it. You did what was best for everyone. The theatrical world won't come to an end without him."

"What about those pathosfinders who aggravated his problems?"

"He's got only *one* problem. I congratulate you for not dismissing it as a superficial manifestation of an overblown ego but recognizing it as the fabric of his reality. Woo, what a speech, eh, Deadpan?" He rubbed his wrinkled pink chin with one finger. "Say, you'd make a good reality affixer."

"No, thanks."

"Good, because I don't need one. Yet." He rolled onto his back and put his hands behind his head. "I've turned their names in for recertification testing. The Mindplay Bureau may get around to calling them in sometime. Bureaucracy stinks."

I shifted position uncomfortably. "Look, if they aren't found and stopped, we might as well go back to lysergic acid and watching the ceilings roll by. Without holotanks."

"Incompetence and mediocrity are everywhere. But what do you think you're here for?"

"Pardon?"

"It's the nature of any discipline to stagnate for a while, for the superficial to be received as something of depth and meaning. Mindplay doesn't mean that people won't go right on believing what they want to believe. Even— *especially*—in the name of *love*, of all things. But sooner or later some smartass comes along and points out the emperor is naked."

"And nobody loves a smartass," I said.

NN gave me a sharp look. "How right you are, Deadpan. Now get out of here and leave me alone with the Bolshoi."

I got. I didn't like the sound of *What do you think*

you're here for? Just what did *he* think I was here for? Some pathosfinder—my first job was a success because the patient died, as it were. As it were. One session with me could end a career. What the hell *was* I here for anyway?

I didn't get an answer for a long time.

JERRY WIRERAMMER REDUX

"**H**eya. Remember me?"

I shook my head at the phone screen. "The correct question, Jerry, is, do you remember *me*?"

"I never forgot you, Allie, I just didn't remember everything. But I do now. So you're a big hot-wire mindplayer these days."

"And real busy. So tell me you're not calling to get another memory wipe."

He giggled. Same old Jerry Wirerammer giggle. "No, nothing like that. I gotta remember everything I can, can't forget a thing."

"Well, it's nice you remembered me, but I've just come off a job and I'm tired—"

"Yah, saw it in the dataline. That holographer, Bonspere. Did you know you got coverage on that one?"

"Strictly gossip-column, society-screen stuff, Mr. Up-Town tells on your favorite celebrities. I didn't think you'd care to follow that kind of news, Jerry."

He gave me his goofy grin, but it looked a little strained. "Oh, yah, all information is valuable. Whaddaya say we get together and talk over old times? And new times."

"No."

"Allie, please?" No grin, no giggle.

"I'm too tired for you right now, Jerry."

"Then how about tomorrow? Or the day after," he added quickly, before I could say no again. "Or any time you say. *Please?* I wouldn't ask if it weren't real important."

Real important. The words echoed in my tired brain. The damned thing about it was, I *wanted* to see him and I couldn't kid myself about why. It was like a last connection to McFloy, even if I didn't give McFloy another thought as soon as I was with Jerry. That face. As long as it existed, it would haunt me.

But then, it would exist as long as I did, wouldn't it?

I brushed the thought away. "You can't come here, Jerry."

"Yah, I think the Nelson Nelson building's beyond even my considerable talent for hackity-hack. But that's okay, you can come here." He punched the address in and disconnected before I could put him off till the next day.

I was impressed by the west-side address, impressed by the maxecurity luxury of the building, even impressed by the size of the elevator/lateral that took me up to the extra-private penthouse apartment levels stacked atop the rest of the structure, very impressed at being delivered directly into the living room. But I was most impressed at being greeted by three Jerry Wirerammers.

They stood side by side by side, grinning at me goofily and looking pleased with themselves. I turned to get back into the elevator/lateral.

"No, Allie, it's okay!" The Jerry Wirerammer on the left end darted forward and grabbed my arm. "Here I am. This is me."

I studied his face carefully. It seemed to be the original. I walked over to the other two for a closer look and right away I could see the differences. They were small, perhaps even unnoticeable to someone who didn't know Jerry as well as I did, but now that I saw them, I knew I'd never get them confused. The middle one didn't have the grin quite right—it was almost a sneer with cynical undertones—while the other one had tense eyebrows. Almost before I realized it, I'd taken their Emotional Indices. The one with the tense eyebrows was scared, probably of me but of something else as well; the middle one didn't believe in something, probably Jerry as well as me, and might have been ready to do something dangerous about it.

Jerry stepped up and put his arm around my shoulders. "This is her, this is Allie. The pathosfinder who did your friend Bonspere. I told you I knew her. Allie, this is—"

"Shut up," said the scared Jerry. "She doesn't have to

know anything other than we're you." And then, absurdly, he giggled.

"Oh, she knows more than that," said the other Jerry. "Maybe not everything but she can tell us apart. Can't you, Allie?"

I shrugged, forcing myself not to dive for the elevator/lateral as the doors whispered shut behind me. "It's harder to fool a mindplayer, I guess."

"Ah," said Jerry, "she *can* tell us apart but I bet she can't tell which is the bootleg."

The other two stiffened. I pulled away from Jerry and headed for the elevator doors. "Great to see you, Jerry, gotta sprint."

He caught me in half a hug, half a restraining hold. "Heya, *heya*, Allie, there's no hurry!"

"Let me go, Jerry. I haven't seen a thing and I don't want to see any more."

He pushed my face into his shoulder. "Leave us alone a while, how about?" he said to the other two over my head. "We got some things to talk over. You know how it is when you haven't seen someone for a long time." Giggle.

There were two answering giggles. Twenty minutes max before that would have driven me killing mad. I could hear the dry brush of their feet on the thick white carpet; then, silence.

"Are they gone?" I said into Jerry's shoulder.

"Yah."

"Then, let go of me."

He released me and stepped back with his arms up. "Heya, you're free."

I glanced at the elevator doors. "And you're not. Am I right?"

Jerry looked sheepish. "Sometimes life is just one tar baby after another." He tilted his head and squinted at me. "Is there something wrong with your face?"

"My *face?*"

"Yah. Did you get the nerves cut or something? You haven't changed expression since you came in here."

"Just a habit."

"Then, you really *are* Deadpan Allie."

"You knew that."

"Yah. I just didn't know it so much. You want a drink? Birch beer or something?" He went across the room to a fancy bar near a mural-sized window that looked out over the skyline. It was just starting to get dark; Commerce Canyon was a murky spot against the coming evening. I followed after him slowly, taking in the expensive freestanding holos, the harsh lines of the nouveau furniture, and the indirect wall-well lighting growing brighter as the daylight faded.

"Hell of a place, isn't it?" he said, setting a tall glass of birch beer on the bar. "Lots better than fetishizer back rooms."

"Different," I said, sliding onto a tulipesque stool in front of the bar. "Not necessarily better. What do you need me to do for you now, Jerry?"

"Like I said, talk over old times."

"Our old times consist mainly of your bringing me drugs and madcaps."

"Yah, those were the days. I thought we could talk about them."

"*Jerry*. I think I just said about all there is to say about them. You want me to describe them in detail? How my old efficiency looked, what I was wearing, what you were wearing, how many times you used the lavabo?"

He grinned a little too brightly. "Sure. Why not?"

"*Why?*"

"Because if I don't come up with some more memories for those two guys, they're probably going to kill me." He grabbed my hand as I started to get off the stool. "Okay, not *kill* me. I mean, not *dead* kill. Probably. But they'll be mad enough to kill. And then I don't know what they'll do but maybe afterwards they won't kill me even if I beg them to."

"Who are they? No, don't tell me. I don't want to know. Just explain to me why they seem so enamored of being you."

Jerry grinned goofily at a point somewhere over my head. "I don't know if it's that they want to be me so much as it is they don't want to be them. If you see what

I mean. Maybe you could understand that better if you knew just how much I wish I weren't me right now."

"Yah, I think I can understand that pretty well."

Jerry pushed the birch beer at me. "'Drink up, Shriners.' Anyway, these two guys, they're just a wealthy married couple, bored, they've spent so much with Power People, they should probably be half-owners. So one of them rented the Jerry Wirerammer property and liked it so much he talked his husband into it, and *I* said he could buy direct from me and I'd give him a break on the price."

"You're bootlegging yourself on your own now? What about the bootleggers you were working with?"

"Jerry Wirerammer's still moving well for them, they've got no complaints."

I touched my face casually; ever the professional, I still hadn't changed expression. "Don't you see the problem with that? Or are you that much dumber than I ever thought?"

Jerry shrugged theatrically. "Heya, it's not something I'd make a habit of. I just wanted to give these guys a break. Mostly, I let Power People and, uh, the other company do the selling for me."

"How did you meet these two?"

He looked pained. "You know, that's the one thing I can't remember. I guess it's not important."

"Only to them. So they aren't happy with the product?"

"Sure they are." Jerry's grin faded a bit. "They just wish there were more of it. They keep after me for more memories. I've given them everything, including stuff I didn't even know I had. But I'm going dry. I need help. And here you are." He pushed the glass a little closer. "'Drink up, Shriners.'"

I shook my head.

"Come on, Allie, all you have to do is talk over old times with me. Prime the old memory pump."

"Jerry, you were a long time ago. It's like someone else's life to me now."

"No problem. They've got equipment here."

I blinked.

"You know, enhancers. It'll be like reliving everything."

"You're not getting access to my mind. That was the one thing you never talked me into and you're not going to talk me into it now."

He looked down at the glass of birch beer. "Yah, that was the funny thing about you. You'd do just about anything except mindplay. That was before you became a big hot-wire mindplayer, though. They have to pay for you now, right? Suppose I offered to pay?"

"Call the agency in the morning. Nelson Nelson'll put you on the waiting list. If you want to hire a pathos-finder."

Jerry leaned his elbows on the bar and rested his chin on his hands. "I'm not asking for anything you haven't got, Allie."

"You don't get in. That's my final word."

"Well, I had a feeling this was how it would go, but I was hoping." He nodded at the glass. "'Drink up, Shriners.'"

"How come you keep saying that? What are 'Shriners'?"

"I don't know. It's something I picked up from my two, uh, fans. They say it all the time. 'Drink up, Shriners.' Sounds kind of cute."

"Actually, it sounds like maybe you've picked up more from them than they have from you. They aren't really very much like you, Jerry."

"They're resting their imprints right now. They were me all day. You should have seen them then."

I was glad I hadn't. "Listen, I think I can help you after all."

He perked up, complete with goofy grin.

"No, not that way. Suppose I get you out of here."

Jerry waved a hand at the expensive room, including the mural window. "Get out of here? What for? So I can go back to sleeping in parking spaces and rewiring fetishizers?"

"Does all of this really mean that much to you? It's just *stuff*, Jerry. It's just expensive *stuff*. You're risking your—your *self* for a goddam nouveau *couch!*"

"What else is there for me? I'm a convicted mind criminal. I'm a mind *felon*. I'm out of the game you're playing in, they didn't offer me a rehab deal."

"Not that time. But maybe they did once?"

He mirrored my expressionlessness back at me, with an edge. "I don't remember."

I nodded. "Yah. I guess you also forgot that things you can't remember still happened anyway."

"I'll tell you what I *do* remember—taking someone to a dry-cleaner's when I could have pissed off and gotten away."

"*I* remember who gave me the madcap."

"And *I* remember there wasn't any gun to your head to take it, either."

We stared at each other. "Old times," I said after a few moments. "Those were the days."

Jerry burst out laughing. Not giggling but laughing. "Yah, they sure as hell were. I remember how you'd do just about anything to light a fire in your brain. Sometimes I used to wonder what you were after." The laughter subsided. "What *were* you after?"

I blew out a breath. "You're asking me *now?* I'm not sure. Lights. Colors. Patterns. A glimpse of Something."

"Like that mandala on your ceiling."

A vivid picture of the old mandala sprang into my mind. "Yah. I used to wander around in that for hours, just . . ." My voice died in my throat.

"Go on," Jerry said helpfully. "You used to wander around in your mandala for hours, just what?"

I reached over and tipped the glass of birch beer toward Jerry. He jumped back with a small yell.

"What did you do *that* for?" he said, grabbing an expensive towel and mopping at the mess.

"Just to let you know I'm onto you."

"Not a terribly deadpan thing to do," he said, dumping the saturated towel in a small sink behind him and grabbing another one.

"I was deadpan all day. You should have seen me then."

"Glad I didn't," Jerry muttered. I felt a brief prickle of

gooseflesh. "But that's okay if you want to stop now. You've given me enough to work with."

"I have?"

"Sure." Giggle. "Your offer to get me out of here still open?"

"Why?" I said suspiciously.

"Because I need to get out right now."

"All right. I'll get you out."

Big grin. "Hey, Wirerammers!" he called.

A door near one of the freestanding holos slid back and the ersatz Jerrys appeared in the doorway side by side. Neither of them was grinning.

"She says we have to go to her place," Jerry said, gesturing at me somewhat sheepishly. "You know how it is when you haven't seen someone for a while."

"Does she have equipment?" the scared one asked.

"'Does she have equipment.' She's Deadpan Allie, she's got all the equipment in the world."

I hopped off the stool and headed for the elevator doors. "Come on, Jerry, gotta sprint."

"Wait a minute," said the angry one as Jerry hurried after me. I jabbed the call panel next to the doors and kept my back to them.

"The faster we get out of here, the faster I get back with the goods," Jerry said. "Don't worry, it'll be great."

The elevator arrived and I was so relieved that I didn't notice until we'd dropped fifty floors that it wasn't the same one I'd come up in, but a much smaller one.

"Sorry," Jerry said casually, as my breathing became audible, "but you were in a hurry. Otherwise I'd have called the big one. When did you become a claustrophobe?"

"I don't remember," I said with some difficulty. Mercifully, Jerry didn't giggle.

We hit bottom and I spilled out into the lobby. Jerry sauntered after me, watching me with great interest. "Your face really does work after all," he said as he punched an exit code into the front door.

"You can feel privileged that you got to see it," I said, taking deep gulps of the night air.

"I never wanted to see you in trouble. That's why I took you to the dry-cleaner's in the first place."

An airbus went by overhead, the underside lit up with a new advertising campaign for Power People. Jerry's face was not among those on display. He glared up at it for a moment.

"Come on," he said and led me down the steps to the front gate, where he had to punch in another exit code.

"Where do you want to go now?" I said. "You can't stay with me and I don't think a visit to a memory-wiper is a good idea."

"Oh, I'm going back there," he said. "Just like I told them. Did you really think I wouldn't?"

"*Jerry*—"

"But first I've got to get to a memory lane." He punched another code into a stone stanchion on the left side of the gate. "I'm calling the car," he explained. "I'll drop you off at the agency on my way."

"Why are you going to a memory lane?"

"They can take the stuff we talked about and plug it into a more elaborate scenario. Those two'll never know the difference. It'll be easy to fool them since I've never gone mind-to-mind with you."

A private flyer swooped down and landed almost silently in front of us, the door opening automatically, like a mechanical bird wing offering shelter. I hesitated; Jerry gave me a gentle push inside.

I settled into the green velvet cushions while Jerry gave the flyer the agency's address. "That little bit we talked about isn't going to be enough," I said.

"Yah, it will. When they get through with it at the memory lane, it will. Never been to one, have you? Stupid question, yah. In two hours, you and I will have a history rich enough to make a holo and two sequels over." The flyer lifted smoothly. I didn't bother strapping myself in.

"Why didn't you do that before?"

He grinned at me, but not goofily. "I have. With other things. I've been saving you for last. I wasn't going to get to you unless they got greedy." He shrugged. "So they got greedy."

"If you've been saving me for last, you should have had plenty of material."

Now he looked confused. "Yah, you'd think so, wouldn't you? But, I don't know. I got down to you and then I needed you to be there. Damnedest thing." He giggled but it didn't come out quite right.

Organ fatigue. I stared out the window at the city lights passing below us. All the little intrigues and counterintrigues Jerry had been indulging in to keep himself one step ahead of everyone he was double-crossing. The mental strain was beginning to translate into something physical—too much memory-wiping, too many strolls down memory lane to get falsified memories. Probably stripping the myelin sheathing off his axons like cheap paint. He was losing himself. How long before he woke up one day with Swiss cheese behind his eyes?

I forced myself to look at him again. He was lying back on the cushions with the trademarked Jerry Wirerammer grin on his face, staring at nothing.

"Jerry."

"What," he said brightly.

"Has it occurred to you that you can't keep this up?"

"Who's going to stop me?" He paused. "You going to turn me in?"

I shook my head. "I should. It would save you. Maybe I will."

"No, you won't. Because I asked you not to. I know what I'm doing." He sat up a little. "I choose to do it. If they caught me and put me under the belljar with amnesia now, I'd come out a baked potato, I know that. You've been under the belljar, haven't you? Imagine it with amnesia, nothing to draw on to help you through the sensory deprivation. It's cruel and unusual, and they keep doing it because none of *them* knows what it's like. The crazy thing is, you don't remember what it's like yourself afterwards. But your subconscious gives you a little glimpse now and then. You walk around with the creeps for the rest of your life."

"They couldn't Strip-Search you. It was disallowed."

"I'm supposed to feel grateful? They whipped me but thank god they didn't use the really big whip?"

"There's a bright side to everything, Jerry."

"You're such a smartass."

"And nobody loves a smartass."

"Except another smartass." He slumped down on the cushions and closed his eyes. "I know what I'm doing. And you can't stop me unless you want to get in trouble yourself and I don't think you do. You want to stick with being a big hot-wire mindplayer, Allie. And I'll stick to what I've got. I'm living in the outer world and I'm locked out of the one you live in. You're living in yours and you've turned your back on the outer world. That's how it is."

The flyer made a gentle landing on the agency roof. The door swung upward to let me out.

"I won't call you again, Allie." I stepped over him out onto the roof. "Unless I really need to," he added as the door closed again.

F A N D A N G O

"But if you'd gone into neurosis peddling, what would you do to relax?" said Fandango. She'd taken to hanging around my place in her various neurotic drag. This week she was dead white all over with a coating of lanugo. Early Petulant Child, she called it; it looked more like the Invasion of the Giant Baby to me.

"Huh?"

"Neurotics should never go into neurosis peddling. It only encourages them."

"*I'm* neurotic?"

"Sure you're neurotic. All you pathosfinders are neurotic. You have to be. You're always looking for what things *mean*. It's part of your job, of course, but it's still neurotic."

"And what about you? You're not neurotic?"

She shrugged. "Oh, sure. But it's different for me. I'm into it as an art form, like all neurosis peddlers. Can you honestly say you have an appreciation for neurosis as another form of art?"

"No."

"Well, there you have it. You're stuck with pathosfinding unless you quit and you can't quit. You're under contract until you make back what NN invested in training you, plus a twenty-percent profit. That fancy vacation you took with Lindbloom is included in that figure, you know."

I hadn't known. Or rather, I hadn't read my contract carefully enough, but it didn't matter that much to me. After all, I had nowhere better to go.

Fandango popped up off the floor where she'd been knotted up like a sheepshank or something and dialed herself another birch beer. "Anything for you?"

I held up my glass to show her I was only half done with mine.

"You're the first one I know of that the old fox hired in right out of an institute. Everyone else here had a few

years in private practice. Were you some kind of prodigy
at J. Walter?"

"No," I said, laughing a little. "Not me."

"*Ah.*" Fandango ambled over, clinking her ice cubes.
"Then *he* was the prodigy."

"'He'? 'He' who?"

Fandango blinked. Moonstone eyes; they didn't really
become her. "Whoever it was that left such an indelible
mark on your life. Or *she*, excuse me."

Indelible mark; that was one way to put it. "Sorry, I
hadn't realized we'd gone from a discussion of my hiring
to, uh, something else entirely. You were right the first
time. He. Yah, he was. A prodigy, I mean."

"I know what you mean, I'm following this conversation. After all, I started it." She lit on the couch next to
me. "So tell me, was *he* the reason you went into
mindplaying?"

I laughed again, shaking my head. "No, not *him.*"

Fandango's smile got broader. "Outrageous, Deadpan.
Another one. Quite the vixen, were you?"

"Oh, no, not *me.*"

Now she looked puzzled. "Well, then, who?"

"Who what?"

"Who was the vixen?"

I broke up completely. "It wasn't anything like that,
Fandango," I said when I stopped laughing.

She drew back a little, frowning at me. "What's the
matter with you?"

"I don't know what you mean."

"You need a life, Deadpan. Hey, listen to that, that's
the second time I've called you Deadpan. *That's* what I
mean. What kind of a life have you got just pulling down
the big ones for Nelson goddam Nelson?"

"Hey, give me a little time. I'm new in town."

"Not that new. You've been here, what, a year?" I
nodded. "A year and what have you done? I'll tell you
what you've done. You've done Nelson goddam Nelson's
son-in-law, you've done that punchy holographer, and
you've done the Dancing Barbanos." I grinned at her
reference to the half-dozen members of the revival
dance company. I'd helped their sincerity but not the

fact that there wasn't much interest in reviving things like square dancing and demishawn.

"I also did that performance artist," I said. "The one who'd spent a month in creative trance." And then there'd been Jerry, but I'd been refusing to think about that.

"Oh, yah. I remember your performance artist. A few more like that and nobody would need neurosis peddlers. All right, you've got quite the list of accomplishments. What have you got for yourself?"

I tried my best Deadpan face on her. "That's a rather personal question, don't you think?"

Suddenly all the neurosis-peddler facade was gone from her face and we were just person-to-person on the couch. "You know what a mindplayer is without a personal life?" She tossed back her drink and held up the glass with just the ice cubes in it. "This."

"Well, I lead a very mental life," I told her.

"Yah. Your personal life's all in your head, right?"

"Something like that."

"You go and visit your phantoms regularly in whatever kind of little home you have for them in your mind? Tell them everything that happens to you, maybe feast your inner eyes on that old lover preserved for all time just the way he was?"

Some deadpan. I was staring at her with my mouth hanging open.

"Allie, for chrissakes, *I'm a neurosis peddler!* I know every mental kink and twist and trick there is, *what do you think I peddle, pancakes?*"

In spite of everything, I couldn't help laughing a little. "I never thought of that."

Fandango bounced on the couch cushions impatiently. "Goddammit—"

"Okay, *okay,*" I said, "I was listening to you, really, I was. I understand what you're trying to tell me. I'm just, I—" I spread my hands. "It's not that easy."

"You want me to give you an exhibitionistic streak for a while? Great way to meet people."

Oh, my god, I thought. "We'll talk about it after the next assignment."

"What—you got another one already?"

"'Already'? It's been close to a month since the last one. NN left a message in my dataline last night. I've got to see him"—I glanced over at the clock above the screen—"in about an hour."

"You didn't tell me that," Fandango said accusingly.

"You didn't ask."

"What were you going to do, throw me out when the time came?"

I shrugged. "That's what you do to me. Except you're usually over here these days so you just flounce out when the time comes."

"Flounce?"

"Or slither, or toddle, or whatever."

Fandango got up to dial her third birch beer. "You go ahead. Take your assignment, do your usual brilliant job with it. And after that, you see living people."

"I'm going to see living people on the assignment." I smiled into her petulant glare, just being obtuse. Also being wrong.

N E A R L Y   D E P A R T E D.

"Three things," I said, and held up a matching set of three fingers.

Nelson Nelson looked tolerantly amused. "Run 'em."

"One—" I curled my index finger. "I don't do empaths. Two—" I bent my ring finger. "I don't get physical. Three—" I pointed the remaining finger at the old fox on the other side of the desk. "I don't rob graves."

The couch creaked as NN rolled over onto his back and folded one arm behind his head. "Is that all that's bothering you? Kitta Wren hasn't been buried."

"I don't do dead people. If God had meant me to pathosfind dead people, she wouldn't have invented the Brain Police."

A broad smile oozed over NN's saggy features as he reached for a cigarette. He was smoking those lavender things again. They smelled like young girls. "What's the matter, Allie? Are you scared of a dead person's brain?"

"I'm scareder of some live ones I know. Fear isn't the issue. I just have certain beliefs, and this job you're asking me to take goes against every one of them."

"Such as?"

Sighing, I shifted position on my own couch and scratched my forearm. That vulgar gold lamé upholstery giving me a rash. You can dispute taste but you can't stop it. "Such as, death is the end. Of art, I mean. The end means there is no more. Dead people should be allowed to rest in peace instead of having their brains plundered and looted for any last bit of—of treasure, like Egyptian tombs."

NN looked at me with mild admiration. "Eloquent. Really eloquent, Deadpan," he said after a moment. "You're probably the most eloquent mindplayer this agency has ever employed. Someday you might talk yourself out of a job. But not today." He winked at me. "Actually, I respect your feelings. Those are good feelings. Especially for someone who trades on the name Deadpan Allie."

"Being deadpan doesn't mean I don't have feelings. I just don't show them."

"You're showing them now. And I personally don't share them. I feel there's a lot of validity in, say, going in and getting the last measures of unfinished music from a master composer who dropped dead at the harpsitron, or mining the brain of a gifted writer for the story that remained unwritten in life. Postmortem art is highly regarded and a large number of artists, including Kitta Wren, sign postmortem permissions. It's a sort of life after death. The only one we know about for sure."

I scratched my rash some more and didn't say anything.

"Kitta Wren *wanted* a postmortem. It's not grave robbing. If she hadn't signed the permission, that would be different."

"Kitta Wren was a five-star lunatic. I read her specs while I was waiting for you. She had a psychomimic's license and when she wasn't writing her poetry, she was going boing-boing-boing."

"Ah, but she was brilliant," NN said dreamily. I blinked at him, astounded. I'd had no idea he liked poetry, or anything else besides the Bolshoi. "When it came to her work, she was totally in control. Somehow, I always thought that control would bring her down. In a thousand years, I never would have thought anyone would kill her."

I wanted to tear my hair and rend my garment. "NN," I said as calmly as I could, "I *hate* murder. I am *not* the Brain Police. If they want to find out who did her, let them send in one of their own to wander around in her mind."

"Oh, they will," Nelson Nelson said cheerfully. "Right after the postmortem." A cloud of lavender smoke dissipated over my head as NN flipped his cigarette into the suckhole in the center of the desk. "The Brain Police can't do anything until that's taken care of. Otherwise whatever poetry is left in there could be fragmented and irretrievably lost."

The rash had crept up past my elbow. I kept scratching. "You know, there are mindplayers who postmortem for a living."

"I'll pardon the expression. Wren's manager hired you. Come along, now, it'll take you somewhere you've never traveled."

"I've never been to the heart of a white dwarf star and I don't see why I should go."

NN exhaled with a noise that was almost a growl. "Do you *want* to work for me?"

"I'm thinking."

He gave me that oozy smile again. "Deadpan, this is important. And you might learn something." He raised up on one elbow. "Just try it. If you can't do it once you're in, fine. But *try*."

I sat up, scrubbing my arm through my sleeve. "All right. But just don't make a habit of signing me up for postmortems."

The agency's system would have removed my eyes for me but I'd come to prefer doing that little chore myself for some reason. After I lowered them into the bowl of solution, I lay down on the slab and felt it slide me headfirst into the system. Even blind, I could sense the vastness of it around me as it swallowed me down to my neck. You could have spent the rest of your life wandering around in it but all I wanted at the moment was a little basic reality affixing and reassurance. If I was going to run barefoot through a dead lunatic's mind, I needed all the reinforcement I could get. After letting the system eat my head for an hour, I almost felt ready.

I hadn't been gassing Nelson Nelson as to how I felt about postmortems just to cover a corpse phobia. To me, you ought to be able to take something with you—or at least make sure it goes the same time you do—and if it's your art, so be it. Hell, there were plenty of living artists around with a lot to offer. Stripping a dead person's mind for the last odds and ends seemed close to unspeakable.

I supposed the appeal was partly what Nelson Nelson said—life after death. But there seemed to be more than a little thanatophilia at work. Art after death made me think of sirens on rocks, and I wasn't the only one who heard them. Occasionally there'd be an item in the dataline about some obscure holographer or composer— holographers and composers seemed to be particularly susceptible, or maybe there were just more of them— found dead with a note instructing that an immediate postmortem be performed because the person had been convinced that the unreachable masterpiece so unattainable in life could be liberated only by the Big Bang of death.

So there'd be the requested postmortem and the mindplayer who hooked into the brain, which was all wired up and floating in stay-juice like a toy boat lost at sea, would come out not with a magnificent phoenix born of the poor deader's ashes but with a few little squibs and scraps from half-completed thoughts that had turned in on themselves, swallowing their own tails for lack of substance, vortices that had gone nowhere and now never would. Some people aren't happy just with being alive. They have to be dead, too.

At least Kitta Wren hadn't been one of those. The information Nelson Nelson had dumped into my dataline was freckled with little details but was rather sketchy taken all together. I punched her picture up on my screen and sided it with her bio.

She'd been a very ordinary woman, squarish in the face with a high forehead and medium-brown untreated hair. Her only physical affectation had been her eyes. Since the advent of biogems, many people had at least a semiprecious stare. I hadn't seen very many people with my own preference for the shifting brown of cat's-eye and it takes a certain coloring to carry off diamonds, but Kitta Wren had something I'd never seen before.

Her eyes seemed to be shattered blue glass, as though someone had deliberately smashed the gems before putting them in. Her pupils were spiderwebbed with white cracks. I enlarged them for detail and then paused. Wrong again. Her eyes weren't spiderwebbed with cracks—they were spiderwebbed with spiderwebs, thickened as though coated with dew or frost. Come into my lunatic parlor. I wondered how much they had to do with her psychoses.

She'd gotten her first psychomimic's license at nineteen and spent the five years after that almost continuously crazy with a few months off here and there for extended periods of writing. Later, she had begun limiting her psychotic times to summers while she worked on a cycle of poetry. The result, a long series called *Crazy Summer*, had given Wren her first major recognition. From there she'd gone to being crazy only at night, then only during the day, and once she'd spent six months orbiting the moon in high mania.

That was the other thing that was bothering me, of course: the whole psychosis thing. All those madcaps I'd taken leading me step by step to contact with this madwoman who also happened to be dead but still crazy. Did I believe in the Cosmic Practical Joke? And how much funnier was it going to get?

When Kitta Wren had died, which had been—I punched for the date—just the day before, she'd been a week into a general schizophrenia no one seemed to know anything about. Cause of death—I blanched— disembowelment. There was a photograph of her office where she'd gotten it. She'd been strong all the way to the end, walking clear across the room before collapsing. Dead just under an hour when her manager had found her. Not too bad. Five hours was about the limit for an untreated brain. After that, it's not worth trying to hook in with. No suspects and no murder weapon; the Brain Police were holding off their investigation of her brain until after the postmortem. Standard procedure, as their technique tended to wipe a mind clean.

Under Miscellaneous, I found a small picture of Wren's manager, a gold-skinned androgyne named Phylp with fan-shaped eyebrows. The request for a pathosfinder was entered as well. It seemed Phylp wanted someone who wouldn't treat her like just another deader. Sounded to me as though Phylp was hoping Wren hadn't left behind as little as s/he suspected.

.WE ARE GATHERED HERE..

A morgue is a morgue is a morgue. They can paint the walls with aggressively cheerful primary colors and splashy bold graphics, but it's still a holding place for the dead until they can be parted out to organ banks. Not that I would have cared normally but my viewpoint was skewed. The relentless pleasance of the room I sat in seemed only grotesque.

The other two people in the room with me didn't seem to feel that way. One had introduced himself as Matt Sabian, postmortem supervisor. The other was unmistakably Phylp. S/he overshadowed Sabian despite the latter's silver hair, garnet eyes, and polished skin. Phylp was the flashiest androgyne I'd ever seen—most of them preferred no higher an appearance profile than anyone else, but Phylp handled major talent. It was probably advantageous to have such a memorable manager. If anyone could remember the talent after seeing the manager, the talent had to be pretty major. Show biz.

"I understand this is your first dead client," Sabian was saying. The absurdity of the statement made me want to laugh but they don't call me Deadpan Allie and lie.

"Up until now, I've worked only with living minds, yes." I sneaked a glance at Phylp, who was more arranged in a chair than seated.

"You shouldn't have any trouble," Sabian said. His voice had an odd hint of disappointment. "Your own mind will have to provide a good deal of visualization, except for her memories and the like, so I hope you're not given to overly bizarre symbolism. And you have to realize that you'll be *in* the mind, not just in contact with it, as you would be with a living mind. A dead mind can't respond to anything outside of itself. You'll find that everything in a living mind is present in a dead one. Except life, of course. We leave this world as we come into it—without thoughts, personality, memories, talent. When life fades, it leaves these things behind, just like any other material item. Which is why there'll be room for you inside of it."

I didn't like the sound of that but I couldn't decide exactly why.

"You'll have to actively stimulate the mind to obtain anything, as it can't offer it voluntarily," he went on, seemingly pleased to be lecturing. "It takes life to do that. It'll be very much like hooking into a computer program of Kitta Wren's identity."

"But it's not really that simple, is it?"

Sabian was about to answer but Phylp spoke up for the first time. "That's why I wanted a pathosfinder for her."

"Pardon?"

"Someone who would understand that it's not just a matter of searching out data. I want whatever it is that comes out to sound alive. Because she was alive when she created it."

Sabian pointedly did not look at Phylp, who returned the favor. It clicked for me then. Sabian, postmortem supervisor. If Phylp hadn't insisted on hiring a pathos-finder, Sabian would have been on this job. A nice sweet plum of a job, too, doing a postmortem on someone of Kitta Wren's stature. I did a sight reading of his Emotional Index but I couldn't tell who he was angrier at, me or Phylp.

"How well did you know Kitta Wren?" I asked Phylp.

"Not at all. I managed her, but she was a stranger to me."

That was a lot of help. "What about family?"

"Only two brothers. One is at the South Pole. The other is under the Indian Ocean in a religious trance."

"Do you know anything about her early life?"

"Only that her parents gave the children to the state and vanished." S/he spread her/his hands gracefully. "That's all anyone knows. In the five years I've handled her, she never showed the slightest inclination of opening up to me or anyone else. It was a major disclosure if she told me she liked her contracts."

"That extreme sort of self-isolation isn't exactly normal behavior for a poet, is it?"

Phylp frowned at me. "Nothing about her behavior

was *normal*. She was crazy. All the time she was crazy, and when she wasn't, she wanted to be. God knows what she got out of it."

Her poetry, apparently. I turned my attention back to Sabian. "What about the psychotic dead mind? Is the psychosis still operating?"

"Very much, though in a strictly mechanical way." He thought for a moment. "But it probably doesn't know it's dead."

I hesitated "Which do you mean—the psychosis or the mind?"

"Both, I would think."

"How does a mind not know it's dead?"

Sabian lifted his head slightly. "How does yours know it's alive? It's the same question, really." Not the way I saw it, but I let him go on. "Minds contain information, but it takes the presence of life for them to know anything. What does a computer program *know?*" The polished face stretched in a tight, triumphant smile, as though he'd given me a glimpse of Big Truth.

"And where is the brain now?" I asked after a moment.

"Here." Sabian got up and went to a panel in the nearest wall. He punched a few buttons and a section just below opened up. There it was; what had waited behind Kitta Wren's spiderwebs in life now hung in a tall, clear canister of stay-juice, trailing wires like the streamers on a Portuguese man-of-war. The wires went down through the bottom of the canister to the maintenance box, which kept a minimum number of neurons firing. Two more wires leading from the visual center were coiled on top of the canister.

"We're still within the optimum time to go in. One more day and the neurons will begin to cease firing efficiently, and after that, deterioration will be rapid. I hope you'll be able to get everything on the first try."

Looking at the thing in the canister, I hoped so, too.

They left me alone so I could set up my portable system. There was a lot to be said for the ritual of preparation as a form of relaxation therapy; I never needed it more than I did just then. I took my time, working silently and trying not to look at Kitta Wren's mortal remains while I let my thoughts wander.

Eventually I found myself thinking of Jerry Wirerammer and the madcap. A logical association; this was the first time I'd been near a psychosis since my arrest. But it was quite a different thing to deal with psychosis than it was to be psychotic yourself. Given the choice, I would rather have been crazy, but it didn't seem to hold the same attraction for me as it once had. You grew up, Deadpan, I told myself; you grew up and found out reality is crazy enough on its own. Any reality.

Pulling out the drawer with the connections and thermal tank for my eyes, I paused. A living client I would have hooked into a relaxation exercise such as making colors, building landscapes, or running mazes, but what could I do with a dead one? Aside from the fact that it couldn't initiate any action—could it get any more relaxed? I laughed to myself. A little mental humor. Sabian had said I would have to stimulate it. I settled on some abstract moving visuals, made the connections, and then dragged over a chair.

Despite my apprehension, it didn't take any longer than usual to calm myself into a smooth, alert state of receptivity. I had positioned the thermal tank of the maintenance box next to the canister, where I could reach it easily. When I was absolutely sure of its location, I thumbed my eyes out and let them down into the solution. It never ceased to amaze me how well I could function blind; training had given me superior short-term eidetic memory.

The connections crept under my eyelids and found their way to my optic nerves. After a few moments, body awareness faded and I was through the system, into Kitta Wren's mind.

Normally I would have made my presence felt gradually so as not to startle my client by bursting in like an invader. But this client couldn't know that trauma; besides, I was going directly into the visual center instead of using the less abrupt route through the optic nerve. After the slight disorientation of passing through the barriers of personality and identity, I found myself in the thick of random pictures and arbitrary memories. So this was being inside a mind. It wasn't so different from being inside the system, or anywhere else. Everybody's got to go somewhere. Around me, the mind seemed to tense as it felt the addition of something new and unpredictable. Then it ground on as before, leaving me as just another thought.

The abstract-visuals program was still running and I was awash in lazy spiral rainbows and harlequin rivers. I set it for gradual fade-out, and as it went, more of the brain's own pictures appeared, some of them mundane objects remembered for no reason, some of them vignettes from Kitta Wren's life. I let them swirl around while I decided on the best way to go about the postmortem. Hitch a ride on a memory? Follow a random thought? Get hold of some false starts or blind alleys and reconstruct them?

I'd immersed myself in one of her false starts (an image of a walk in the rain in the middle of the night) when the mind tried to think me. There was almost no warning. I was busy receiving multiple over- and undertones accompanied by the memory of the false start's creation and the frustration Kitta Wren had felt before finally giving up on finding anything to do about it. Taste of rain dissolving on lips and tongue and the first line: *Do I drink the rain or does the rain drink me . . . drink? Think?* I was searching it for possible salvage when the mind clamped down on me and the old, unfinished poem together.

It thought the poem piece by piece, starting with the memory. It remembered the night and then the season (why not the season and then the night, I wondered), and then moisture, pausing to associate it with varieties of wetness. I was overwhelmed by the smell of the ocean, followed by a brief image of a coffin covered with barnacles lying on the sea bottom. The taste of rain returned more strongly, eradicating the picture of the coffin (*my brother, that's all*) but not quite managing to suppress a fleeting thought of snow. *Drink the rain*

. . . the rain drinks me . . . drinking the rain I am drunk and am drunk by drunken rain . . . The mind niggled and gnawed out each variation from the original line (what was this big fascination with rain, anyway?). When it was through, I was next.

There is no way to describe being thought, or being about to be thought. If you imagine yourself in, say, a play, it's still not the same, at all. If you imagine yourself recorded on holo, yourself being the recorded image—no, who can imagine that. I still can't, and I was there. I couldn't imagine what it would be like to be thought, either, except I didn't think it would be a very good thing.

Hurriedly, I made a mask of my face and then took it off. The mind reached for me in its purely mechanical probing and I threw my face into its processes. Traveling at the speed of thought, my face was everywhere as the mind tried to find the correct association for it. I saw it materialize on the smooth, blank surface of a writing slate before I slipped through a half-remembered dream—images of cold stone carvings on a cathedral wall and a quick impression of writing about a mad cathedral, which gave me a chill. But it wasn't my cathedral. I made sure of that before I let myself settle down on Kitta Wren's back burner.

There isn't a mind in the world that doesn't have a back burner and it was usually a lot more difficult to get a client to open it up. Sometimes the incomplete puzzlements and notions stewing there were capable of growing into full-fledged ideas; other times, they changed into false starts or shrank away into unexistence. Kitta Wren's back burner was so full of images that some were teetering half-dissolved on the edge of forgotten, as though she had deliberately pushed every idea that occurred to her to the back burner and waited to see which ones wouldn't disintegrate. Not the most productive way to work. I propelled myself through them to see what I might be able to glean, which, I thought, would probably yield more results than looking at false starts and blind alleys. I was learning.

It was like looking at a holo-collage of a beginning holo

student. Kitta Wren's inner voice faded in and out where
she had found words to go with the pictures. In quick
turn I was looking up from the bottom of a deep, narrow
hole at a circle of innocent blue sky, staring across the
surface of a bed at eye-level, watching two people, their
faces in shadow, touch hands while their low, womanly
voices murmured to each other (each was Wren herself).
I was caught in a storm in the desert with rare rain
beating straight down (there was that rain again),
observing a street scene populated only by machines,
my cheek pressed against the pavement, tasting an
empty cup and pretending there was something in it.
That one caught my interest; I reviewed it to see where
she'd gotten it.

Something from nothing, that intelligent-sounding
inner voice said. *Something from nothing.* I saw a
chrysanthemum in the bottom of the cup; it metamor-
phosed from live to painted-on. The center of the flower
was an eye. *Something from nothing. I fill me with
something from nothing.*

I began to get the feeling I wasn't alone. Which was
absurd—even *she* wasn't there any more. I turned my
attention from the cup and waited. Possibly what I'd felt
was the mind reaching for me again. Lowering my
energy level as much as possible, I moved in among the
jumble of unfinished ideas and waited. Rain punched
dents in the sand; the sideways view of the street
shimmered in the soggy desert sky like a mirage.

The mind spasmed. I had given it a new combination
of thoughts by the way I had juxtaposed her old
fragments. It fixed on me and the madness hit.

That was what I had felt approaching, her psychosis,
and it struck like a concentrated, highly localized storm.
I thought my perception of it had been colored by my
exposure to her preoccupation with rain but it remained
stormlike even after the mind separated me from its own
concepts, and I realized the nature of what Kitta Wren
had done to herself.

Had she been alive, I would have been witnessing a
localized psychotic episode, a variety of seizure meant to

produce not a physical convulsion but an altered state of consciousness. Except there was no consciousness.

The seizure tore into her ideas and images and they scattered in all directions, falling flat because there was no one to pick them up and use them. The rest of the mind practically came to a standstill while the storm raged on. She'd been hoping for a literal brainstorm, a creative madness that would tear through her mind, stirring her thoughts into new and better patterns, giving her the stimulation she had refused to seek in the larger world outside herself. The mind seemed to shimmer and its perception of me grew vague. I slipped away down to an area of learned reflexes and automatic behavior to wait things out. As soon as the seizure had passed, I would go back, collect her ideas, memorize them, and get out. Phylp had been wrong. I would have to treat this strictly as a data-retrieval operation, I couldn't deal with the mind as though it were living—

Reaching for a cigarette with only a dim awareness of the act I/she felt the first pain. I/she looked down at the slate on the desk and the stylus in my/her hand. It gleamed like a knife. (Memory run; it was a go; humans keep memory packrat style, who would have thought this one would be in Habits and Mannerisms?) But it couldn't cut away the blankness of the slate to reveal the words that were stuck in my/her mind.

Then I was past the memory pocket and the mind had me again. Tropism—I should have known. Minds were meant to live and be conscious. There had been no consciousness, but now there was mind. If consciousness was there, then the mind must be alive.

Alive. It pulled at me and I passed through the psychosis like a kite in a high wind. The madness clutched at me, searching for a way in, almost as if it were a separate, living intelligence as alien as I was. I tasted anger and spat it out; it came back at me as a sea of strange faces registering disappointment, confusion, hate. Kitta Wren's view of the world, vinegar laced with poison. The mind dragged me onward and I went, trailing the madness and the memory and the madness of the memory through the fireworks display of her life.

Something from nothing. I looked to see who she was speaking to but there was no one. Just a personal affirmation. *Give me nothing; I take nothing. Offer me nothing; thank you. His eye may be on the sparrow but the Wren looks out for herself.* She had worked hard for her unhappiness and her mind showed her efforts to me as though they were trophies and prizes. A coffin under the Indian Ocean, something she'd never seen, an image invented and embellished for her own meditation of bitterness. A silhouette in a blizzard at the bottom of the world. Empty pedestals labeled *Mother* and *Father* and an arena of thick, sweaty faces demanding a show, their greedy voices orchestrated by a golden-skinned androgyne. *Give them what they want; something from nothing. Give me nothing. You take something.*

In her office, she faced the invisible, hungry multitude. The mind tried to push me back into the memory but I clamped down on my energy level again, pulling the image of the desert over me.

I watched through the hard beat of the rain as the seizure leaked into her visual center, causing the slate on the desk to swell to enormous size. She backed away from it, hallucinating patterns on the slate. The patterns became faces. *Give them what they want.*

The pain doubled her over. She straightened up slowly, both hands on her belly. There was a dark stain on the stretchy material of the secondskins, just below her navel. *Something from nothing. Give them what they want.* Her fingers gripped the cloth. Psychotics frequently displayed extraordinary physical strength. And some had a touch of telekinesis, undiscovered, unusable until a moment of crisis. Any crisis; it didn't matter if it took the form of a hallucination brought on by an anxiety attack.

Her hands fell away. The woman who could not open up finally did, and thirty years of misery poured out. She didn't even moan.

The memory went black, along with everything else. Then the mind stirred itself and probed through the desert storm, finding me easily. Kitta Wren might have been dead but her mind wanted life. Any life. Mine would do.

Listen, she said. The memory was so worn now only her words remained. *All they want is the show. Give them what they want, but never ask anything of them. Something from nothing. The Wren looks out for herself.*

I pulled back, preparing to withdraw. The mind flexed and the feel of it was plaintive now. Without warning, I was face to face with the image of Kitta Wren as she had been, spiderwebs glistening in her eyes. They still looked like shattered gems at first glance and they always would.

Unbidden, the memory came to me. Not one of her memories but one of mine. And with it came the thought that there could be a variation on the eye trick.

I concentrated on that thought, sending it toward the image in steady waves. After some timeless mental interval, new lines appeared in the webs, running like fissures. The mind fought, trying to maintain the solidity, but this was right. The cracks crept slowly over her face. I had to strain to keep them going, but they went, dividing her forehead into a myriad of little territories, fragmenting her cheeks, sundering her mouth. The image shuddered, almost held, and then just came apart, every piece sailing away from every other piece. When they were all gone, so was she, and I withdrew without difficulty.

The first thing I saw after I put my eyes back in was the brain in the canister. The stay-juice looked milky now, a sign of imminent decay. Without really thinking about it, I leaned forward and shut the maintenance box off.

Nelson Nelson held up an official-looking chip-card. "This is a lawsuit."

I nodded. He put the card down on his desk and picked up another one.

"And *this* is a lawsuit."

I had my own card and I held it up. "And *this* is a countersuit. In case anyone actually has the nerve to go to court."

NN looked tired. "Everything's already being settled out of court. The agency took your side, of course. No one can say I don't back my people, isn't it so?"

It was sure as hell so. But I could tell by the way that puckered old mouth was twitching that he'd probably thought about filing against me, too, for taking it upon myself to shut off the maintenance box. If the morgue laboratory had not come out and said that the composition of the stay-juice had indicated degeneration beyond the point where the mind could be reentered, I would most likely have been signing my next thirty years of salary over to Nelson Nelson.

"Why'd you do it, Deadpan? What got into you?"

"She was dead. And nothing at all got into me." Not lately, I hoped.

"Sabian says the brain couldn't have deteriorated so quickly between the time you went in and the time you came out."

I didn't attempt an answer right away. The brain had been a lot deader when I came out than it had been when I'd gone in. I didn't know if that was really because of what I'd done to Kitta Wren, and I didn't want to know. "Maybe the solution was defective. Or hadn't been changed often enough." That was the argument in my countersuit, anyway, that Sabian had allowed me to hook into an unstabilized brain which caused me to act in an irresponsible manner by shutting my client off instead of calling for him so he could decide what to do. Sabian was just bitched because it meant he couldn't enter the mind after I was through to do his own little postmortem, to see if there was anything I'd missed that he could sell Phylp. He wasn't gassing me. Nobody filed a lawsuit over a protocol violation.

NN shrugged. "Phylp's charge is more serious."

"Seriouser and seriouser. It'll never hold up. S/he got all the postmortem fragments I could find. I had them all memorized, I did my job. It's not my fault s/he thinks none of them were worth the effort. And I can't be sued for wrongful death of someone who was already dead."

"It's a little more complicated than that, Allie."

"That's what it amounts to. Phylp's charging that before I broke contact—"

"*Prematurely* broke contact."

"—I dissolved her Self and killed her a second time, compounding that by turning off the box."

"That's the way it looks in the transcript of your report."

"That's the way it was."

I thought Nelson Nelson was going to choke. I sat up, rubbing the small of my back with both hands.

"Just between you and me, NN, yes. That's exactly what I did."

He reached down and fiddled with something on the side of the desk facing him. Of course; he'd been recording. He was always recording. This one would have to be doctored.

"You know how a dead body will twitch when you send a current through it? A dead mind'll do the same. It takes more than current, but it's a fair comparison. They had the neurons firing so well, it didn't know it was supposed to be dead and it tried to use me to come back."

"Could it have?"

"I don't know. It didn't work. I killed it."

"But what do you think?"

I sighed. "Possibly I might have ended up incorporating elements of her personality and some of her thoughts and memories. Then you'd have had to have me dry-cleaned to get rid of her."

NN raised his invisible eyebrows. "Now, there's an interesting situation."

More interesting than he knew. "Not for me. I wouldn't want any of that woman in me."

"I mean in terms of the legal definition of existence. If such a thing had happened and the agency did have you dry-cleaned, would we, in fact, be killing her all over again?"

I glared at him. "No. She was *already dead*."

"But if she returned to life in you—well, never mind, Allie. It's just an intellectual exercise. At this point." He waved the subject away. "All this aside, tell me. Did you learn something?"

From a bitter woman who had literally torn herself apart? "I learned she shouldn't have been buying psychoses. She was already fogged in."

"No, now really, Allie. Wasn't there anything in there at all—some insight, or a vision beyond—ah, any final knowledge of any kind?"

I lit a cigarette by way of stalling. Tell him about altered state without end, everybody's got to go somewhere even if they might not be real after they make the trip? Oh, sure, he'd love it. Except what had happened to Kitta Wren? If there was an answer to that—or an Answer—it wouldn't have been in a dead mind because you couldn't ask the right questions in there.

So ask a living mind. Unbidden, the thought came to me with a mental image of an eye with a shimmering gold-brown pupil rimmed with a very Alert Snake, a completely realized eye, marvelously detailed and absolutely unshatterable. Even if I could have shattered it, I knew where the pieces would have gone.

I shoved the thought aside. Instead, I lay down on the couch again and blew smoke at the ceiling. "Life's a bitch. Then you die."

I could almost hear his mouth drop. There was a long, thick moment of silence and then he began to laugh. "That's a good one, Deadpan," he said finally, wiping his eyes. "You know, sometimes, I can't tell when you're kidding."

I just nodded, still deadpan, as though he had caught me out. What the hell. He probably wouldn't have believed me. And then again, maybe it would have been worse if he did.

PART THREE

ALERTED
SNAKES OF
CONSEQUENCE

OLD HOME WEEK

You will go down into darkness before you die.
  You will go down into darkness before you die.
  You will go down into darkness before you die.
  You will—

"Light!" I yelled, sitting up and flinging the cover away from myself. Every light in the place went on and that awful, hateful voice stopped, as it were, dead. As it were.

I sat there looking around at the apartment, making sure I was anchored in real reality. Bed, check; Picasso sheets, check; system access in the wall, check for sure; body, heartbeat, sweat, check, check, check. Definitely back in the real world and not down in darkness of any kind.

It was her, of course. Nelson Nelson would have corrected me and said, *It was she* but the hell with it. *Her.* It was *her.* The growl of that word fit Killa Wren better than grammar.

Shoulda put yourself in for dry-cleaning, Deadpan, I thought. The lawsuits had all been settled, I was halfway through the minimum mandatory rest period before I could take on another job; there was no reason why I couldn't have. Except I'd really thought she was gone.

Well, the agency's system had a superior dry-cleaning program and there was no time like the present. I got up and shimmied into a caftan.

To my relief, no one else had felt called to mindplay in the middle of the night. I stepped off the lateral into the semidark of the enormous system room. Behind me, the lateral hummed slightly as it moved away. The darkness should have made me nervous but I guess I was too relieved to be out of the little box to be troubled by anything else. I hopped up onto the slab, started to remove my own eyes, and then paused. What the hell; for once, I'd let the system do it. Besides, I hadn't prepared a bowl of solution and I was feeling too jumpy to do anything so responsible.

The system had a light, humanish touch. My eyes came out smoothly, the connections going to my optic nerves almost at the same time. I could feel the initiation program running through my vital signs and responding with a near-hypnotic relaxation exercise, colors in motion, to focus my attention. Colors in motion was a bit more involved than color building. You had to add particular kinds of motion to each one—spinning, flapping, swinging, pulsing, flowing—all the kinds of motion you've ever seen. Sometimes you see patterns of different things in the colors, rotating wheels, pendulums, bird's wings. It's actually a great way to focus your attention and calm down without having to work too hard at it right away.

Meanwhile, the system was reading my immediate needs. It had the dry-cleaning program all cued up and ready to go as soon as my mind drifted away from the colors. With me, that usually happened as a result of an accumulation of associations—one idle thought would lead to another and eventually I'd find myself poised for a mental leap. It wasn't really necessary to make a deliberate entry into a dry-cleaning program—it'll just kick in when you're ready to open up for it—but I've always preferred jumping to being pushed, as it were. As it were.

After a short mental moment of limbo, I found myself standing in what seemed to be either an office or a store, staring across a counter at a man who looked like the result of a liaison between my great-grandmother and Nelson Nelson. Except he had cat's-eyes.

Is something wrong? he asked.

Was something wrong. I just looked at him.

Yes, something's wrong, I know, he went on. *I meant, besides that.*

Your appearance is . . . sort of disturbing.

I just incorporate elements that seem to be appropriate. Do you think they're inappropriate?

No, I said, *I just hadn't expected them. It. Oh, hell, you know what's wrong. I don't really have to tell you anything.*

Not if you don't want to. However, experience has

*shown the human need to express one's self outweighs
any benefit of expeditious thought-reading.*

A mental laugh feels pretty much the same as a real-reality laugh. *Nelson Nelson wrote you, didn't he?*

Not the whole program; just the flourishes.

Flourishes. As it were. Well. *There was this dead
woman, a poet. I did a postmortem on her mind,
scavenging for lost fragments of art.*

A terminal had materialized on the counter in front of
him. He was working the keyboard and nodding at me.

*Her mind was attracted to my life. Her mind and her
insanity—she was insane when she died. I disintegrated
her mind but I think some of it splashed on me. I heard
her voice in my sleep. No visuals, just the voice. She
said, You will go down into darkness before you die.*

He looked down at the screen for a moment and then
up at me again. *And you are—?*

Allie, I said, feeling bewildered. *Alexandra. Deadpan
Allie. I'm a pathosfinder.*

Got it. He did something else to the keyboard and
smiled at me. *Yes, I did know that. I just wanted to make
sure you did.*

I'm not that far gone. You can tell that, can't you?

Uh-huh. Just wanted to make sure you could.

Another one of NN's redundant flourishes; I let it go.
Okay, when do we start?

He shoved the terminal aside and reached for my
hand. I felt the most realistic sensation of skin against
skin and then I was gone.

CLEAN, NO STARCH

Afterward, the dry-cleaner put me into a sleep mode and let me dream it off, which I found superior to the programs that would just let you drift. I dreamed about Pyotr Frankis and Snakes. We were walking through a desert-type area together and I was surprised to see how diminutive I'd dreamed him. He was telling me something about multiple levels of consciousness but it was as though his words were bouncing off me; I forgot what he said as soon as I heard it. There were movements in the sand around us, a wiggling that sometimes appeared as a snake, sometimes just bare sand showing indentations from an invisible snake.

Excuse me, Pyotr Frankis, I said at one point, *I'm trying to concentrate on what you're saying but the snakes are back.*

Ah, he said, and at last I heard his voice quite distinctly. *I told you to watch out for them. Say it. With the capitals, Alexandra.*

Alerted . . . s-snakes of . . . c-c-c-c—Konsequence. That still wasn't it, was it?

Keep practicing, you'll get it. Pyotr Frankis' smile was sunny. *Even so, you've made so much progress. You're altering states of consciousness now.*

Yah, but—somehow, it just hasn't been what I expected.

What had you expected?

It was easier to show him than to put it into words. I stopped and looked past him to my right. Jascha was standing there, smiling thoughtfully.

Pyotr Frankis nodded. *I see. Come, we have to keep going.* He took my arm and urged me forward. *You expected to be like Jascha? But you're not a dreamfeeder.*

No, but— I jerked a thumb to my left. Marty Oren and Sudella Keller were sitting at a campfire cooking something in a beat-up old pan. They looked up and glared at me as though I were an intruder. Pyotr Frankis and I kept going. *That was a mess. And then there was—*

A coffin appeared a little further on from Marty and Sudella; there was an empty canister on top of it. *And you know what an even bigger mess that was.*

Pathosfinding can be messy work. No matter how 'deadpan' you are. Pyotr Frankis pulled me along a little more quickly. We trudged through the sand, the snakes flickering on either side of us, sometimes visible but mostly not.

Well? I said after a mental minute or so.

Well, what? Pyotr Frankis was going faster now, almost yanking me along behind him.

That's all you're going to say—'Pathosfinding is messy work'?

Isn't that true?

Yes, but . . .

But you want to be like Jascha. Clean hands, clear conscience, rest at the end of the day. Jascha reappeared ahead of us and to the right, this time with his techno-bed. *What makes you think it was ever like that for him? Don't you know anything about dreamfeeding?* Pyotr Frankis slowed for a moment, looking over his shoulder at me. *Ah, it's Jascha you don't know about.*

Hey, I was married to him. But as soon as I said it, I knew how lame that was. Marriage was no substitute for knowing anyone. *Well, he was my dreamfeeder for a while at J. Walter. As you know.*

I know. He gave me a hard tug, trying to get me to catch up even with him. *How do you think it is, rifling through people's dreams, introducing elements and symbols and watching what happens to their minds.*

Cleaner than pathosfinding?

Different. Another hard tug. *Different from pathos-finding but no 'cleaner,' as you put it.* Tug, tug. *But you're as clean as you can be. Especially now. You do work clean, Allie. That's good. Remember that. You do work clean. But you are altering states of consciousness. And you have to live with the consequences.*

But I'm only supposed to alter a client's consciousness, not my own!

You can't alter anything without altering yourself. So you must alter yourself lucidly. Or you'll never get out of the dry-cleaner's. He was hauling me along so quickly now I was stumbling.

Wait—slow down—I can't—

No slowing down, Allie, nothing waits, not even your own mind.

Our hands parted. Pyotr Frankis went on a few steps and then turned to look at me. *It's all here, Allie. Everything you do, everything you've done. It all lives in you. It's everything you can't dry-clean out because it* is *you.* A hard wind suddenly sprang up and Pyotr Frankis lifted into the air like a kite, spreading his arms and legs. *XXXXXXXXXXXXXXXXXXXXXXXXXXXXXX!* he said.

What? I yelled over the wind. It was starting to carry him away.

I said, XXXXXXXXXXXXXXXXXXXXXXXXXXXXXX! he yelled back.

What? WHAT?! I still can't understand you!

Truth and information are not the same thing! he shouted, and he shot up into the sky instantaneously, shrinking to a tiny black dot that hung briefly in the air and then winked out.

I stood staring up at the spot where he had been. That wasn't what he'd been trying to tell me, that truth and information weren't the same thing. He'd been saying something else but I just hadn't been able to get it. *XXXXXXXXXXXXXXXXXXXXXXXXXXXXX.* I focused my concentration; there was a sizzling sound. It had been pressed into the sand in front of me in green glass symbols: *XXXXXXXXXXXXXXXXXXXXXXXXXXXXXX.* Okay, now I'd retain it and work on a translation later. Probably take me the rest of my life, I thought.

The desert began to fog over. Getting on time to wake up. I was letting myself go with it when, ever so faintly over the sound of the wind, I heard someone calling my name. At first, I couldn't tell what direction it was coming from; then I turned around and I saw him, far, far away. He was waving at me, and in spite of the distance and the fog, I could see the expression on his face, even the glimmer of his cat's-eyes, and I could feel the difference, the *pressure* of his presence, nothing like the way the image of Pyotr Frankis had felt. This wasn't a dream phantom, the way it had been in my dreams at J. Walter. A dream phantom could only appear, like a ghost; it couldn't take any action beyond that.

Still with you, Allie. I'm still here.

No. It had only been the eye trick. Just his eye, and the eye was locked in the cathedral. Not him. Not *him*. Only a living mind was a hologram.

It's really me. I'm still with you.

Couldn't be. You couldn't have someone else—*really else*—living in your mind. That was a fact.

It's really me, Allie.

Truth and information are not the same thing.

The desert faded.

"What I'm sure Pyotr Frankis was trying to tell you—
or rather, what you were trying to tell yourself—is
simply that you're an accumulation of events," said
Jascha. He sat on the couch with his arms spread out
along the back, more comfortable than he probably
should have been. I kept wanting to ask him if his wife
knew where he was; I honestly couldn't guess whether
she did or not. I felt like I both knew and no longer knew
him, and whether this was because he was a different
person now or I was, I couldn't tell, either. Sometimes it
felt one way, sometimes the other. Life as an either/or
experience.

I was knotted up on the chunky table Fandango had
talked me into putting in as a space-taker-upper right
after I'd finished with Kitta Wren. More furniture, she'd
kept saying over and over. You need more stuff to touch
and see and sit on. Later on, when you don't need it any
more, you can get rid of it. But see if it doesn't make you
feel better. Damned if she wasn't right about it, too.

"That sounds plausible enough," I said to Jascha,
before a silence could definitely fall between us. "Now
explain why you decided to drop in on me now, even
though I didn't call you."

"Because you *didn't* call," he said simply. "I gave it a
little while, and when you *still* didn't call, I figured I'd
better see what you'd gotten yourself into."

"You already knew what I'd gotten myself into. This
agency."

"You're still a smartass."

"And nobody still loves me."

Well, that did make a silence fall between us. I plowed
into it before it could get too thick. "What about the last
part of the dream? With McFloy."

"We've been over that. Like you said and I said.
Impossible. You can acquire bits and pieces like neuroses, or elements fed to you in dreams, and things that
rub off on you from other people—like the stuff with

Kitta Wren—but you can't hold an actual separate identity that isn't you in your mind. I promise you that's a fact."

"Truth and information aren't the same thing. I promise *you that's* a fact."

"So you told yourself. But you have to admit that they do coincide often enough to let us all get around in the world safely."

I shrugged.

"And you've been dry-cleaned. The program couldn't have missed it if it were there."

"It wasn't written to clean out a whole entity. Just pieces, characteristics."

"And we've just said you—as an entity—are an accumulation of events. Which are pieces and characteristics."

"But when it's a whole person, it becomes more than that. More than the sum of the parts."

Jascha shook his head, which was very lightly gilded now, so lightly you almost might not notice. "And a dry-cleaning program doesn't clean out the sum of the parts. It knows which parts belong to the sum and which don't. Just as you did with that stuff of Kitta Wren's."

I felt a chill. "If I hadn't had myself dry-cleaned quickly enough, it might have taken root. Become part of the sum."

"Maybe. And then again, maybe not."

I glared at him. "*That's* helpful."

"No, now really. Why do you turn out to be one kind of person and not another? Because one event fits the configuration that you are and another doesn't."

"Now you're talking like everyone's a composite like Pyotr Frankis."

"Pyotr Frankis is manufactured. He's an android, really—discorporate, but still reprogrammable. His configuration can be altered by the manufacturers in any way. Or, I should say, can be altered on the manufacturers' level. But not on *his* level, by him."

The incompleteness theorem. I didn't feel any warmer.

"On the other hand, you, like all human beings, are a composite on a different level than Pyotr Frankis—a higher level, we all fervently believe. It's not a matter of simple reprogramming. If your configuration were such that it allowed whatever rubbed off on you from Kitta Wren to become part of your—" He thought a moment. "—your pattern, then that's what would have happened and I doubt you would have been able to dry-clean it out so easily, if at all. Of course, your configuration—*you,* I mean, I'm tired of that word—might be able either to keep the stuff from Kitta Wren or slough it off equally in character." He shrugged. "I'd have to do a bottom-up analysis of your core personality to tell and I'm nowhere near qualified for that kind of thing. Nobody is. No one's been able to prove any of that stuff conclusively one way or the other—it's all just very strong theory." He laughed. "That's the thing about mindplay. The rules change when they change and everything is true unless it isn't."

I groaned. "I thought God didn't play dice with the universe."

"God doesn't play dice with the universe. He plays dice with you."

"Everywhere you go, smartasses. It's astounding that anyone ever loves anyone."

That shut us both up for a long moment. Then Jascha laughed again, a little nervously. "Well, just trust me when I tell you there's nobody in there. Except you, of course," he added quickly.

"Why *did* you come to see me, Jascha?" I asked, smiling at him.

His answering smile was studiously carefree. "I thought that by now you'd probably need a crazy dream explained to you. And I was right. I also wanted to ask how you like your eyes, now that you no longer have your own."

"They're fine. Great. I like them."

"Any particular reason you chose cat's-eye?"

I felt my smile fade a bit. "They seemed to be the right choice. I always did like them."

"They look fine. Very becoming. They don't look— they don't look bad at all." He seemed to be about to say something else and then changed his mind.

* * *

I wheedled two extra Restaurant-of-the-Month chits out of Nelson Nelson on the phone, making him extremely suspicious when I introduced Jascha through the screen. But he gave me the chits and we had a fine if strange dinner at a place called In The Raw. Which everything was, including us.

Okay. It wasn't a very nice thing to do. But it wasn't Jascha and his wife I was trying to put a wedge between.

"Didn't come home last night," Fandango said matter-of-factly.

"Sure didn't," I said, dialing up birch beers just for something to do. Then I changed my mind and ordered ginger beer, just for something else to do.

"It's good to have a life."

"Sure is."

"And you're not going to tell me about it."

"Sure won't. But have some birch beer."

She took the glass from me with a pouty look. "Thanks." She got halfway through the glass before she couldn't contain herself any more. "So at least tell me who he is, now that you've got yourself a life."

"Someone from a while back." I settled on the table with my back to her. "From a previous configuration. Somebody else's life."

WIRERAMMER AND WIRERAMMEE

The phone screen didn't light up. I tapped the side of the unit once gently and then a little harder. Still no video. I was about to tell whoever was calling that my monitor was out when words began scrolling up from the bottom.

NO VISUAL OR AUDIO TRANSMISSION AT THIS TIME. URGENT YOU COME TO THE FOLLOWING ADDRESS WITHIN THE NEXT 6 HOURS, NEXT 2 HOURS OPTIMUM. ACKNOWLEDGE FOR ADDRESS TRANSMISSION.

I watched the words float upward. WHAT FOR? I typed, knowing damned well what for.

CONFERENCE, came the answer. REFRESHMENTS PROVIDED. ADDRESS AS FOLLOWS . . .

I stared at the address for a long time before I took it down. What the hell. If I went out there now, maybe I'd be back before dawn, or at least before Fandango found out I'd spent another night somewhere else. Before I left, I packed a few bearer chips. Just in case.

It was nicely decorated for a vegetarian restaurant. I was always amazed at what you could do with vegetable fibers in the way of furnishings. Not to mention clothing—there was an old-fashioned host wearing a suit probably made out of hydroponic cornhusks. He seated me at a tiny table in an alcove that would have been away from the crowd if there'd been a crowd and left me with a vegetable-fiber menu that was probably edible in a pinch, if not particularly tasty. I glanced at it and then pretended great interest in the holo loop running in the wall next to me. It was an agricultural scene from perhaps three centuries ago, full of sweaty laborers in ragged clothing picking a crop. The crop they were picking happened to be cotton, but it was the thought that counted.

It ran one full time and had started over again when a

man sat down across from me. He was wearing a turban and two halves of two different pouch suits that were almost the same shade of brown, which was nowhere near as jarring as the plaztoid mask glued to his face. Plaztoid eventually melts into the flesh, permanently altering the appearance, and never for the better. It reminded me of ritual scarification, except most people didn't wear it by choice. Burn victim, I thought, and then corrected myself: uninsured burn victim. A moment later I corrected myself again: Jerry Wirerammer.

"Don't say that name," he said in a low voice as I opened my mouth. "I'm not *that person* any more. Legally, I mean. But I'm still . . . you-know-who in essence, unless or until they catch up with me."

I tried to look at him without seeing the plaztoid. "Who is it this time? Your two fans, the bootleggers, or Power People? Or someone else altogether?"

"The bootleggers. They—" He broke off. "Is there someone behind me?"

I glanced over his head at two women making their way through the main room toward the door. "Just a couple of people leaving."

"Tell me when they're gone."

I watched the women leave. From the way they looked at the host, I didn't think they'd be back. "All clear. Go on. The bootleggers."

"They finally bought out my contract with Power People. I stopped moving well for them and they were happy to give me up. The bootleggers didn't know my popularity had fallen off and they weren't too happy about the deal. And Power People wouldn't buy me back."

The idea that he might have spoiled his own market with bootlegs (and with bootlegs of bootlegs) probably hadn't occurred to Jerry.

"So they went to court. Filed against me claiming I'd cost them money. The court ruled I was liable for the loss."

"And you don't have the money."

"They wouldn't take it if I did. After Power People sold me off, my, uh, other business associates found out

I'd done a little business of my own on the side and now they want me."

"But they've got you."

"No, they want *me*. They're going to wipe me and part me out for salvage." He picked up the menu. "You hungry?"

"No."

He tossed the menu aside without looking at it. "Good. Let's go. I don't want to hold still for too long."

I let him herd me out of the restaurant onto the street. Three onionheads linked together on a short chain marched past me, two of them giving me a glare. The third one winked. Bored and hoping for trouble, apparently. I looked the other way quickly by way of declining. There was nothing that would ruin a night faster than getting stomped by a three-way onionhead marriage. Well, almost nothing.

The evening had suddenly grown chill; I bought a disposable jacket from the autovalet next to the restaurant while Jerry fished several bits of paper out of his various pouches and rifled through them hurriedly.

"Now what?" I asked him, pressing the jacket closed. It was a little too large, and the wavy line print was enough to give you a headache if you looked at it too long, but it was pretty warm for a street product.

"Five minutes," Jerry said, looking at one slip of paper and stuffing the rest into one of the chest pouches. "There's this mobile party we can pick up, if it's running on schedule."

"And if there are openings for both of us," I added.

"There should be." Jerry scratched at his plaztoid-covered cheek absently as he looked up and down the street, which was empty now except for the retreating figures of the onionheads. "I've hooked onto this party before. They've always got room for a couple more." He rubbed his arms against the cold.

Without thinking about it, I put an arm around his shoulders. "Listen, I'm not exactly in the mood to join a party, especially a mobile one. Why don't I just take you home?"

He shook his head without looking at me. "My place is

sealed off. They put a private security company on it.
They'd pick me up if I got within a hundred yards of the
front door."

"I meant my place."

He turned to stare at me in surprise. The plaztoid
didn't allow him much in the way of expression but I
could see it in his eyes. "*Your* place? You'd do that for
me?"

"The Nelson Nelson building is pretty impregnable,
as you pointed out to me once."

"Maybe not for them. You don't know. They could get
in just about anywhere." Jerry glanced down the street
again. "Even if they couldn't, I'd have to come out
sometime. And they'd jump on me immediately. Better
for me to stay out here in camouflage. No camouflage for
me at your place. I'd kind of stick out, don't you think?"

I had a brief, half-assed idea of passing him off as
Fandango's husband, but it was better not to drag her
into Jerry's problems. I knew from experience that once
you were in Jerry's problems, it was damned near
impossible to get away from them. Besides, there was no
guarantee that Fandango would go along with it. Even if
she did, NN would probably find out and evict him.

The mobile party's chartered airbus arrived, descending in a contained flurry of music, laughter, and general
noise. A purple androgyne in a gold-dust stocking thrust
his/her head out of one of the windows and whistled to
us. "Two more!" s/he called over his/her shoulder. The
front door slid down and became a ramp leading up to
the admission port. The bored navigator didn't even
bother looking at us.

"You want on, get on," she said, staring at her console.
"Otherwise don't hold us up, we're on a schedule."

"Room for two more?" Jerry asked, tugging me up the
ramp after him.

The navigator's diamond eyes glinted. "Two more,
eight more, twenty-four more. What's the difference?"

Jerry stopped short at the admission meter and turned
to me. "You got any money?" Giggle.

I handed him one of my chips. He held it in front of a
small screen. The navigator jerked a thumb over her

shoulder. "Step to the rear of the party, please, watch your step, no brawling, dueling, or acrobatics while the party is in motion. Next stop, the Boom-Boom Room high atop the scenic Glorioso Building in Commerce Canyon. Rest, refueling, lavabos, and first aid." The door slid up again, bumping my ass.

The main party area of the bus was a cross between a regular airbus and someone's living room. It was full of people lounging on benches, on the floor, holding onto handstraps as they ate or drank or talked, sometimes with someone else. The purple androgyne who had greeted us from the window threw him/herself on Jerry's shoulders like a long-lost relative, babbling something I couldn't make out. With an apologetic look over his shoulder, Jerry allowed himself to be drawn over to a built-in seat by one of the windows. I grabbed the nearest empty spot, wondering if I should cab home from Commerce Canyon or hang in for a few more stops to look after Jerry. A mobile party provided pretty good camouflage but it wasn't going to run forever. Maybe he was planning to go home with someone. Like the androgyne, who was now sitting on his lap listening intently to whatever Jerry was whispering into his/her ear.

Someone passed me a platter piled untidily with food and drugs. I handed it on without taking anything.

"First mobile party?" someone said close to my ear.

I turned around and looked into a gilded male face. His gilt wasn't genuine and had been poorly applied; hairline cracks threaded the golden areas along the cheekbones and temples, and the part on the bridge of his nose looked ready to flake off at any moment. The silvery biogems ruined the desired effect anyway.

"Yah," I said, pulling back a little against the acceleration of the bus. "First time ever."

(*But that's not true*, said a small voice in my mind. *You've been to mobile parties before. Lots of them.* Unbidden, a scene from the pool came to me, all of us in flight against an impossible jeweled sky over a blue-green earth while one figure soared higher than anyone, suddenly swooping down out of the sun, catching me and taking me down to a terrace outside a ballroom, where an eye sat on a small table—)

The window seat where Jerry had been sitting with the androgyne was now occupied by three women in diaphanous ragbags. I looked around and saw what might have been the back of Jerry's head disappearing into the small crowd at the rear of the bus.

"The facilities are back there," the badly-gilded man told me. "If you care to use them. I usually like to wait till I'm on the ground, myself. Just an idiosyncrasy." He pushed the platter of drugs and food at me again. I shook my head. He held it out to a passing man in a bright pink explosion of feathers, who took it and balanced it on his head as he went on.

Abruptly the music, which had stopped when the bus had let us on, started up again. It was Coor and Lam's *Transcontinental Elopement*, the third Urban Chase movement, full of lumpy, discordant percussion. I winced. As soon as we touched down on the Glorioso Building, I was going to sprint for a cab, with or without Jerry. There'd been no reason to come along with him and he'd never actually asked me to, just taking it for granted that I would. Why he wanted me with him when he was so concerned about being camouflaged was beyond me anyway. I got up, intending to ask the navigator how soon we'd reach the Glorioso Building, when my new friend caught my arm.

"On the other hand, if you'd like to try the facilities while we're in motion, I could be persuaded to experiment," he said, with a tentative smile. The bus hit a small air pocket and his near-jowls trembled.

I pulled away from him. "Body functions are things I prefer solo, thank you. I think."

"Body functions? Who said anything about peeing? The *facilities*. The *equipment*." He touched my arm lightly. "Swap memories. It's a great way to get to know each other."

I looked toward the rear of the party. The purple androgyne had reappeared alone, giggling to the man in the pink feathers.

"Goddammit," I muttered and threaded my way

hurriedly through the bus, which suddenly seemed more crowded, as though everyone on it had decided all at once to come to life and party harder. The bus itself seemed bigger, too, all of a sudden. I swam through it, dodging eager hands and the hyperactive arms of a woman dressed like a flamingo, who was either dancing or having an inner dialog with gestures.

At the rear of the bus was a small compartment with an opening near the floor just big enough for me to crawl through. Once I did, I almost backed out again—it wasn't much bigger than three of the pods from the pool at J. Walter put together, dimly lit by one small glowball.

Jerry and some other guy were lying on a tangle of blankets, on either side of a small mindplay unit I recognized as a memory-exchanger. They were already plugged in and the system was running. It didn't take long. They were finished before I could begin to feel seriously closed in.

The other guy disconnected and sat up first, groping for his optics in the half-tank hanging off his side of the exchanger. He popped his eyes in, blinked at me, and broke into a goofy grin. It didn't fit his carefully sculptured features.

"*I* know you," he said cheerfully. "You're . . . no, don't tell me, the name's on the tip of my brain. You used to . . ." He rubbed his forehead. "There was something you used to do . . . something crazy . . ." He struggled a moment longer and then shrugged, crinkling the gold braid on his shoulders. "It'll come to me later maybe." He glanced at Jerry's still form. "Did you want to be next? He's ready."

I moved away from the entrance hole so he could crawl out.

"This guy's a charge," the man said. "He's really full of it. I think I got the better end of the deal. All I gave him was my ex-wife and my ex-husband."

I crawled over to Jerry, who still hadn't made a move to get up and disconnect.

"Come out of there," I said in a low voice, putting my hand on his chest. "I'm not coming in after you."

Jerry sighed, his eyelids fluttering slightly against the connections snaking under them.

"I know you can hear me. Come *out*. This is Allie and you know I won't go in there with you." I paused. *"Jerry."*

That got him moving. He sat up quickly, fumbling the connections to the system as he removed them from his optic nerves. I was tempted to put his eyes in for him but I couldn't bring myself to touch them.

"What are you doing?" he said, his eyes watering profusely. "I figured you'd just get off at the Boom-Boom Room and be happy about it. And I told you not to use that name."

"What are *you* doing? Is this National Gangbang Jerry Wirerammer Night?"

"For chrissakes, don't use that name!" he said, looking worriedly at the entrance. "I'm getting more camouflage, what do you think I'm doing? I'm cloning my own memories and passing them out while I clone memories from other people and lay them over my own. That way, if they catch me and put in a probe, they'll find all these memories from other people and think I'm somebody else. And if *my* memories start showing up all over town, maybe they'll think someone else got me and parted me out." The plaztoid mask crinkled a little. "It's brilliant. They'd never suspect."

I tried to think under the clang-bash of the music. "It won't work," I said.

"Yah, it will." Pause. "Why wouldn't it?"

"Because underneath all the memories is your unmistakable configuration—your Jerry Wirerammer-ness."

"Will you stop using that name!" He gripped my arm roughly.

"All right, your you-know-who-ness. No matter how many memories you take in, they're still someone else's. You remember them as Jer—as you-know-who."

"Not if I layer on enough memories. I know how to do it—I've seen someone do it before. Just layer on enough of them and they'll dominate your mind. You start believing you're somebody else for real."

I stared at him. "Then you lose. Either way. Either the bootleggers get you or you smother yourself."

"I'll take the chance. Besides, you were just saying I couldn't obscure my basic you-know-who-ness."

"But you can dissolve it. I know. Because *I've* seen someone do *that* before." More than once, I added to myself.

"I'll *take* the *chance*, Allie. Now, do *you* want to contribute a memory or two to the cause or are you going to crawl out and give someone else a turn?"

I crawled out into a forest of gaudy legs and managed to stand up with some difficulty. The purple androgyne gave me a bright goofy grin and a wave. I looked away and headed for the front of the bus.

"Mind if I sit up front here on the floor?" I asked the navigator.

"Damned right I mind," she said without taking her eyes off the gridboard in her lap. Through the windshield, the lights of the city glittered while no one looked at them. "It's bad enough I have to fly around with a buncha urban booboes partying themselves into flat-line. I'm not going to have any of you cozying up to me, and plenty better than you have tried. Get back where you belong. Go take a drug."

I didn't have the energy to plead a case of mistaken identity with her. Instead, I stayed as close to the front of the party as I could so I'd be able to get out in a hurry. By the time we landed at the Glorioso Building, I'd counted a dozen people crawling in and out of Jerry's compartment. And those had only been the ones I could see clearly.

"Welcome to the Boom-Boom Room, foremost open-air rooftop nightateria in the state!" sang the woman with the gold birdcage enclosing her head.

"How do I get transportation out of here?" I asked her, waving aside the menu of delights she was trying to hand me.

"The aircab stand's on the west side," she said, missing a beat. "You can see the sign. Sure you don't want to stay a bit? The new holo display's up, you'll love it."

I brushed past her, looking for the sign through giant three-d phantoms of warriors in spiky armor and princesses in spiky armor and angels in spiky armor. Spiky armor was apparently the next phase.

"Looking for me?"

It was the man with the bad gilt-job. I shook my head.

"Oh. I'd kind of hoped . . . the facilities here are better, you know . . ."

I found the cabstand sign glowing hotly yellow through one of the spiky-armored angels, who was swinging its sword through a gaggle of touristy-looking types oohing and aahing at each pass. Another woman with a birdcage around her head offered me a tray of drinks as I headed for the stand; four people in a huddle called for me to join them. Canned music came up from somewhere and blared at the sky, cuing all the angels and warriors and princesses to dance. I was out of breath by the time I reached the stand and sank down on the empty bench. Pressing the call panel, I sat back and closed my eyes to wait.

Sometime later, a voice said tentatively, "Allie?"

The purple androgyne was standing over me, looking concerned.

"We're all worried about you. You don't look happy."

"Well, don't worry. I always look this way."

The androgyne sat on the edge of the bench next to me. I could see his/her eyebrows were actually tiny purple feathers. "But we all want you to have a good time."

"What do you mean, 'we'? Who's 'we'?"

The androgyne looked surprised. "All of us Jerry Wirerammers, of course. I remember all those crazy things you used to do, putting on madcaps and going nuts, and—"

I moved away slightly. "Get out of here. Go back to the party. With the rest of the Jerry Wirerammers. However many there are now."

"But you'd always try anything to light a fire in your brain, I remember—"

An aircab hummed overhead. I jumped up, diving into it as soon as it landed.

"Allie, wait! It's going to be a hell of a party, from here we're going on to the hallucination pits—" The closing door cut him/her off in midgiggle.

I gave the cab the agency's address. Only after it had lifted off was I able to sit back and un-tense a little.

Until it occurred to me that I hadn't seen Jerry before I'd left. The real Jerry, that was—if there was a real Jerry any more.

Sure there was. A person was more than just an accumulation of memories—

One thing after another and nothing relates much to anything else.

Yah. That was Jerry, all right. Distributing memories of me as I'd been back when he'd been bringing me drugs and madcaps and nothing further than that.

Some people aren't enough by themselves. They find ways to make themselves more. Some of them litter the world with themselves like confetti, said a quiet voice in my mind. *That's where the pieces go. Flying on the mental wind. Disintegrating in a dead brain. Drowning in a pool.*

The image of Pyotr Frankis's face rose up in my mind, except it wasn't completely him. He looked a little like Jascha and a little like Paolo Segretti and a little like—

The Snake revolved slowly in the pupil of the eye. Jerry's face appeared in the center, grinning goofily; the way it was in the holo portrait I'd found in my cathedral.

I'm locked out of your world and you've turned your back on the outer world.

But he'd still found a pool to drown himself in.

If Jerry Wirerammer did not exist, it would be necessary to invent him. And if he did exist, it would be necessary to liquidate him.

"Destination!" the cab said loudly and I realized it was the second time it had spoken to me. Sleepily, I waved a chip at the pay screen and got out.

VARIATION ON A MAN

Well, I should have seen it coming, especially after Jerry. But I'm convinced (still am) that the Pearl Necklace Episode caused Nelson Nelson to give me the Gladney case.

All mindplayers can pretty much count on getting Pearl Necklaced sooner or later, but messing around with the past the way I had, I'd brought it on myself. And it's a far more vivid experience for pathosfinders than it is for neurosis peddlers, say, or belljarrers, who don't spend as much time in direct mind-to-mind communication with their clients, or at least not in quite the same way.

My Pearl Necklace came during a routine reality affixing. Reality affixing was mandatory for mindplayers by federal law, and mandatory reality affixing still went against my grain as much as it had the day Paolo Segretti had told me I had to go through it with him. There was something about having to have my perceptions stamped *Acceptable Per Government Regulatory Standards* that still irritated me. On the other hand—or lobe, if you will—I'd brought that on myself, too. A mindplayer who insists on imposing her own meanings on everyone else's mentality is not someone you'd want running around loose with other people's minds.

At least it wasn't time-consuming. All I had to do was go back into the agency's system and let it probe me for ten minutes' real time, if that. NN told me I should go at it as a particularly intense session of meditation and as long as I was myself, I certainly had nothing to feel uneasy about.

As long as I was myself. Yah, I thought about that one. If McFloy was in there as a full separate entity, the system would help me find him, and if he were a delusion, it would help me neutralize him.

As long as I was myself. And so, given the circumstances, who else would I be? The system stimulated this particular question and up came the Pearl Necklace.

Infinitely long, every pearl holding a separate moment in the life of Deadpan Allie, it showed me a series of completely self-contained events, touching each other but not really connected. Suddenly, I couldn't see where the sum was greater than the parts and it hit me: *I have not always been as I am now*.

Nothing to it out in real reality—you take it for granted. But it's a terrifying realization when made purely within the confines of your own mind with no physical life-landmarks to refer to. *I have not always been as I am now*—and I couldn't remember being any different. Nor could I conceive of what I'd be like in the next moment.

The bottom dropped out and I felt as though I were falling toward disintegration.

And then I was fine again and the Pearl Necklace was gone. The foundation of everything I'd lived was under me. The system ran through the rest of the reality-affixing procedure and then disengaged. I put my eyes back in and went off to have a nap.

Naturally, the crisis was reported to Nelson Nelson. I knew it would be, but he never mentioned it. Instead, he called me into his office to give me an assignment.

"In your work with artists," he said, while I lay on the couch and tried not to be obvious about the rash the tacky upholstery was always giving me, "what would you say your primary objective as a pathosfinder is?"

I rested my cheek on my left hand and thought it over. "To assist in reaching a level where inward and outward perceptions balance well enough against each other so that—"

"*Allie*." He gave me a Look. "This is *me* you're talking to."

"Help them move past irrelevant and superficial mental trash to the real feeling, the real soul."

NN raised himself up on one elbow and actually shook his finger at me. "Never, never, *never* essay-answer me."

"Sorry."

His eyes narrowed. He had brand-new pink jade biogems and they made him look like a geriatric rabbit. "Don't be sorry. In spite of your initial choice of words, you're right. Would you also say that, in many cases, the pathosfinder is responsible for helping an artist locate the creative On button, as well as helping to enhance the soul in the work?"

For someone who didn't like essay answers, he was pretty fond of essay questions. "In many cases, sure."

Now he looked satisfied. "That's why I'd like to put you on the Gladney case."

"Rand Gladney? The composer? I thought he'd been sucked."

"He was. But he's out of full quarantine now and his new personality's grown into mature form. Of course, he's not really Gladney any more and never will be again."

"Have they told him who he used to be?"

"Oh, yah. Every detail. He wanted to know. Most victims of involuntary mindsuck do. They're all intensely curious about their former lives and the doctors figure honesty is the best policy. Better for them to hear about it in a sheltered environment where they can learn to deal with it. Anyway, I thought this would be a good opportunity for a pathosfinder to work with an adult who has no history whatsoever and help him become an artist."

Terrific, I thought. "What kind?"

"Good question."

I didn't groan. "Well," I said, "is there any indication that he has ability as a composer?"

NN gave me his that's-your-problem grin. "You'll know after you delve him."

I ran through the bare minimum of information on Gladney that NN had dumped into my dataline while my portable system was being overhauled. With some relief, I saw that Gladney's potential wasn't as vague as NN had made it out to be. Prior to having his mind stolen, Rand Gladney had been a composer of middle-high talent with a fair number of works that had settled into the cultural mainstream. At the time of his erasure, he'd been approaching a turning point in his career where he would have either ascended to greater ability and prominence or settled slowly into repetition and, eventually, semi-oblivion. In seven years, he'd peaked twice after his breakthrough. And that was just about all NN wanted me to know about the Gladney-that-had-been, other than his media notices.

The Gladney-that-was-now had been out of full quarantine for a month, though he was still hospitalized and his movements were restricted. I pored over all the background information on rehabilitating mindwipes just as though I were interested in it only for the sake of the case. It was a precarious business, like trying to stand with your hands both on and off someone at the same time. Personality regrowth began with the restoration of language, first by system and then by humans. If the humans didn't replace the system at precisely the right moment in regrowth, you ended up with a person unable to think in any mode but a mechanical one. People like that made great logicians but they were lousy on theory. Most often they resolved the conflict between the definite and the indefinite in their lives by suicide or voluntary mindwipe, which were pretty much the same thing. There were very few brains hardy enough to redevelop a mind after a second erasure; the myelin sheathing on the axons just wouldn't stand up to that kind of abuse.

I paused. Mechanical? Not McFloy. I searched the data to find out what happened to a mindwipe if the humans replaced the system too early in language resoration, but there was nothing about that in there. Maybe nothing was supposed to happen. Even when it did.

In any case, Gladney (who was apparently still going by that name for the sake of convenience) had passed all the critical points in redevelopment and become a person, again or for the first time, depending on your point of view. He was certainly not the same person— the man who had emerged from the blank brain was (probably?) reminiscent of his former self but no more that self than he was anyone else.

The extreme convolutedness of such a situation was easier to accept, I'd heard, if you had even more of a mystical bent than mindplayers usually did. Funny, I hadn't really thought of myself as being especially mystical—but if I wasn't mystical, what was I? Maybe someday I'd get one of those impossible bottom-up core personality analyses and we'd all find out I was just in this for the visuals.

I filed the idea away for later consideration and went over Gladney's aptitude tests. His new personality had grown in with a definite talent for music, and more—I was rather startled to find that he now had perfect pitch. The previous man had not. It made me wonder. Was perfect pitch something that had shown up due to some alteration in Gladney's brain chemistry brought about by mindsuck? Or was it just due to different brain organization? Or a brand-new configuration? And how important was it for me to know?

"Truth to tell," said the woman with the carnelian eyes and the too-short apple-red hair, "we ended up selecting you for your business name. Anyone operating as Deadpan Allie must have quite a lot of control over herself." She smiled brightly. Her name was Lind Jesl and she looked less like the chief doctor on the Gladney case than she did someone finishing up her own recovery. Except for the carnelian eyes and the hair, she was as plain as possible, her stout body concealed in a loose gray sacsuit. The office we were sitting in was even more austere, a cream-colored box with no decorations in the way of wall hangings or sculpture. Even the computer desk was all folded into a stark, bare block. The whole thing reminded me of the infamous White Room image from Marty Oren's mind. McFloy had come up in a place like this. I tried to keep the thought far away.

"Of course," she went on, "your self-control will be vital when you delve our boy. An involuntary wipe is supremely sensitive and impressionable, even at such an advanced stage of regeneration. Just the experience of you probing his mind is going to make quite a mark on him. Your flavor, as 'twere, will leave a bit of an aftertaste."

As 'twere. "I'm very careful."

"Yes, certainly you are." Her gaze snagged briefly on my equipment piled up beside me before she gave me her five-hundred-watt smile again. "And we wouldn't have hired you if we weren't as confident of his ability to think independently as we are of *your* ability to refrain from exerting too much influence."

She was putting a lot of emphasis on the very thing guaranteed by the fact that I was licensed to pathosfind in the first place. "What kind of results are you looking for?"

"Ah." Five hundred watts went to six hundred as she folded her pudgy hands and plunked them on her stomach. "We're hoping you'll help him learn how to combine the various elements that make up a composer into a whole that will be greater than the sum of the parts."

I blinked.

"We know that he has a musical *bent*. A definite leaning toward music, an affinity for playing instruments which tends to accompany perfect pitch. But as yet, these things are fragmented in him. He's having difficulty achieving a state where they all work together. In fact, I'd say he has yet to achieve it, even for a few moments."

"Isn't that just a matter of, well, practice? And experience?"

"Usually. But I know Gladney. *This* Gladney. There are signs of a definite barrier of some kind that he just can't or won't find his way around. We don't know for certain because we haven't delved him since the very early part of the regeneration. That was, oh, nine months ago, which goes back further than his memory. Delicate Plant Syndrome, you see—if you keep digging up a delicate plant to see how well the roots are taking, it dies." She sat forward, her hands disappearing into the voluminous cloth of the sacsuit. "We feel he's ready for mind-to-mind contact now, but with a pathosfinder rather than a doctor. We want him to feel less and less like an invalid and more and more like a person."

"How long has he been in quarantine altogether?"

"Altogether, it's been a few weeks over a year. He was delivered to us two hours after the mindsuckers got him.

We're hoping to release him completely in another six months at the most. Depending on how much progress he makes with you. It could even be sooner. Or later."

"Have you let him hear any of his old work? The previous Gladney's music, I mean?"

"Yes and no. Which is to say, he's heard it but he doesn't know who composed it. We've removed all identification from all the recordings we've given him, not just Gladney's."

"Does he react any differently to the Gladney compositions than he does to any of the others?"

"He reacts to all music rather guardedly. He puts them through a mental sorting procedure and he *can* tell whether or not different pieces of music were composed by the same person with an accuracy of close to ninety-eight percent, on the average. I suspect he might also be able to arrange a composer's works in the correct chronological order as well. He's *very* bright. But—" Jesl spread her hands. "Something inside isn't meshing. As 'twere."

As 'twere. Had I invented this woman? "Has he tried to compose?"

"Oh, yes. Some short things he won't play for us. We had to bug the synthesizer we gave him. According to our musical consultants, his work shows potential. There are moments when it *almost* breaks through, but it always stops short of achieving—well, fullness. As 'twere."

As 'twere, oh, god. I considered the possibility that the evaluation of the consultants might be faulty. Perhaps the musical direction he was taking was just different from the old Gladney's and what he wasn't achieving were their expectations. I'd just have to see for myself.

"When can I meet him?" I asked.

"Right now, if you like. We've fixed up a room for you not far from his so you'll be within easy reach of each other. I'll take you down there and then we'll visit our boy."

The room they'd given me was an improvised efficiency with a freestanding lavabo unit and jury-rigged meal dial. The bed was a hospital bed disguised as a civilian one—not very wide but, to my great relief, as hard as a rock.

I'd brought only a few personal things with me, which I didn't bother to unpack. I debated taking my equipment with me to Gladney's room and decided against it. He might feel too pressured if I appeared wheeling my system with me. I wanted some extra time myself, just to see what this twelve-month-old adult was like on the outside before I went inside. I hoped he wasn't a prodigy.

The man lying on the bed had once had the pampered good looks found in most people of celebrity status. Over the months he'd lost a good deal of it, the way an athlete or dancer will lose strength after a period of inactivity. He was still attractive but his appearance was changing, veering off in another direction. Typical of a regrown mindwipe, I'd read. In a few months, it was possible he would be so changed that no one from his previous life would recognize him.

He got up for Jesl's brief introduction, touching hands with me gingerly, as though he were afraid he might burn himself. Something like bewildered panic crossed his face as Jesl made a quick but unhurried exit, leaving us on our own. I wouldn't even have to think about reading his Emotional Index; he was all but thrusting it on me.

"So. You're my pathosfinder." He gestured at a small area arranged around an entertainment center, minus a dataline, with a few chairs and a space-taker-upper table. He'd probably set it up himself but I could tell he wasn't completely at home with it.

"Anything you'd like to ask me about?" I said, sitting down. The chair gave like soft clay under me and I realized I was in another one of those damned contour things. I wondered why they'd given him a contour and then remembered it was supposed to be a boon to the lonely. I was going to have a rough time being deadpan if it started any funny stuff with me. Fortunately, it seemed disposed to let me sit in peace so I decided to tough it out rather than change seats.

"I hardly ever use that one," Gladney said, watching as it molded itself to support my elbows. "I can't get used to it. But it's fascinating to watch when someone else is in it." He turned his attention to my face. "What are those gems—your eyes?"

"Cat's-eye."

"Everyone here at the hospital has biogems. Even some of the other wipes. Dr. Jesl says I can order some whenever I want to but I don't feel I can yet. *He* had biogems."

"Who?"

"Gladney. The original one, not me. After he was sucked, the hospital replaced them with standard browns." He smiled. "I remember how surprised I was when they told me almost everyone has their eyes replaced with artificial ones. It still amazes me a little. I mean, my eyes don't feel artificial. But then, I guess *I* wouldn't know the difference, would I?" His smile faded. "It's strange to think of you going into my brain that way. Through my eyes. It's strange to think of anyone else in there except me."

Sure was.

"And yet there have been a whole lot of people in there," he went on, rubbing his chest absently. "Mindplayers, for *him*. And then the mindsuckers. The hospital's system, the doctors. And now you."

"Actually, that isn't the way it is," I said. "We'll be in mind-to-mind contact in the system but I won't really be *in* your mind. There's only room for you in there—" I paused, suddenly overcome by déjà vu. I didn't need a memory enhancer to know that I had repeated nearly word for word what Paolo Segretti had told me four years ago just before my first mindplay experience. I'd even sounded like him.

"Anyway," I continued quickly, "mind-to-mind contact is a way of life. Not just mindplay but many forms of higher education. And people buy and sell various things. Neuroses. Memories—" Nice rolling, Deadpan, I thought. You had to bring it up.

"Yah, I know. People buy and sell." He lifted his chin with just a trace of defiance. "They steal, too. I made them tell me about it, and what they wouldn't tell me, I looked up. How Gladney's mind was stolen because there was some guy who admired his work so much that he wanted to *be* Gladney. So he had Gladney embedded in his own self, not just overlaid the way those franchises do." He paused. "Power People. What a concept. Anyway, he went crazy. Trying to be two people at once, while Gladney didn't want to be him." He slouched in his chair and rested his head on his right hand, digging his fingers into his wiry brown hair. "I asked them why they didn't just take Gladney out of him and put him back but they said they couldn't do that after he'd already been implanted. Even if they'd found the suckers before that, it would have been impossible because this brain"—he tapped his head with one finger—"had already begun developing a new mind. Which is me. Doesn't seem fair."

"Fair to whom?"

"Gladney. He just disintegrated. Evaporated when they cleaned him out of the other man. And here I am. Variation on a theme." His gaze drifted away from me to something over my left shoulder. I turned to look. He was staring at the synthesizer near the bed. It was a small one, taking up about twice as much space as my portable system did when assembled. The keyboard looked a little dusty.

"Use it much?" I asked.

"From time to time."

"I'd really like to hear something you've composed."

"Ah?" Panic. "You would?"

"To get acquainted with your music."

"So that after you get into my brain and find my music box, you'll know whether it's mine or not, huh?" He waved one hand. "Never mind. You don't go into my brain, I forgot. I've done nothing but short pieces and I don't think of any of them as complete. Not when I compare them to other things I've heard."

"I would still like to hear them."

He hesitated. "Would a recording be all right? I don't like to play in front of anyone. I'm not an entertainer. Not a performance entertainer."

I could hardly believe he was going along with it. "A recording would be fine."

He got up and puttered around with the entertainment center for a minute, keeping his back to me. Abruptly, music blared out of the speakers and he jumped to adjust the volume.

"Set it to repeat once," I told him.

He turned to me, ready to object, and then just shrugged and thumbed a shiny green square on the console before sitting down again. "Just a musical doodle, really," he said, apologizing for it before it could offend me.

In fact, it was a bit more than that, a dialogue between piano and clarinet, admirably synthesized, but even my ear could tell it was too tentative. And it wasn't complete at all. It was more like an excerpt from a longer piece that had yet to form. I was no musical authority, but on the second time through I could pick out spots where a surer composer would have punched up the counterpoint, let the two instruments answer each other more quickly. There might have been the makings of a canon in it. I toyed with the idea that he'd been misidentifying Bach as the old Gladney.

"How did you compose it?" I asked after it had played through again.

He frowned.

"Did you just sit down at the synthesizer and fool around until you found a sequence, or—"

"Oh." He laughed nervously. "That's a funny thing. I heard it in a dream, and when I woke up, I went to the synthesizer to play as much of it as I could before I forgot it. First I just played all the notes. Then I put them with the appropriate instruments."

"Was that how it was in the dream—piano and clarinet?"

"I don't remember. I just remember the music. Piano and clarinet seemed right."

I knew what the answer to my next question would be, but I asked it anyway. "What was the dream about?"

He was rubbing his chest again. "Gladney."

Jascha, thou shouldst be with me at this hour. Instead of the one who was with me.

I managed to talk him into playing a few more of his incomplete compositions. When his discomfort went from acute to excruciating, I gave him a reprieve and told him I was going to get some rest. His relief was so forceful I could have ridden it out of the room and halfway down the hall.

There was a message in my phone, an invitation from Dr. Jesl to have dinner with her and the other medicos working on Gladney's habilitation. I begged off and asked her if she could supply me with dupe recordings of Gladney's recent attempts at composition without his knowing it. Also some of the previous Gladney's work for comparison. She could and did and I spent most of the rest of the day and a good part of the evening in an audiohood.

Maybe if I'd known more about music—the real hardcore stuff, mathematics of progressions and so forth—I'd have been able to pick out more similarities (or differences) between the two Gladneys' work. I called for recordings by other composers he'd listened to and played portions of those as well. Our boy, as Jesl called him, hadn't been trying to crib from Bach or anyone else. He had avoided being derivative as much as possible, admirable in a beginning talent and also evident of already well-developed self-control, which is good only when it doesn't grow into inhibition. What he had borrowed from other composers was mostly technique—my ear was good enough to pick that up.

I listened to the piano-clarinet piece again and again. It wasn't a copy of the first Gladney's work, but compared to the first Gladney's other pieces, there was something terribly related-sounding about it—as though he was picking up where that man had left off. Or at least trying to.

He'd been unable to tell me exactly what had happened in the dream where he'd heard it, just that he'd known the dream involved the first Gladney. That was somewhat unsettling and would have been more so if he had composed all his music after dreaming about that former person, but he hadn't. I would have found that reassuring if the piano-clarinet piece hadn't been so obviously superior to all of his other attempts.

Variation on a theme, he'd called himself. It nagged at me.

I waited until he had been escorted off to some kind of day-to-day culture orientation workshop early the next afternoon and had Jesl let me into his room so I could set up for our first session. That way he wouldn't have to receive me as a guest with all the attendant awkwardness again.

The bed, I decided, was the best place to put him; he'd be more receptive lying down. Not that he wasn't terribly receptive, all things considered. I mentioned to Jesl how surprised I was that Gladney would be so cooperative with me immediately. She told me that was another characteristic of rehabbed wipes; they became accustomed to being probed in various ways.

I was assembling the system when the question I hadn't wanted to ask finally broke through and asked itself

Could I really do this job?

Sure. I'd been mind-to-mind with a wipe before. Valuable experience.

That wasn't all it was. Another mindwipe. What if he dissolved himself, too? What if I got in there and he pulled the image of Jerry Wirerammer out of me? *What if he tasted too much like McFloy?*

Calm suddenly washed over me. I sat down on Gladney's bed and did a little measured breathing. Gladney was not McFloy. It was just that simple. Gladney wanted to *be* and he wanted it on his own. McFloy had never gotten far enough to find his own life enough for him. And Jerry didn't even come into it, not like McFloy. All right. It would be all right. I would go in and do the job deadpan as hell. It would be like righting an imbalance, to do for him what I hadn't even had a chance to try to do for McFloy.

By the time Gladney returned, I had the system assembled, the compartmented tank for our eyes ready on the stand by the bed, the optic-nerve connections primed, and a relaxation program ready to run the moment he was hooked in.

He didn't seem surprised to see me, only a little resigned and nervous. "You're not going to want to hear any more music, are you?" he asked.

"No more recordings, no." I patted the bed. "Come get comfortable. We don't have to start right away."

He smiled, stripped off his overshirt and chaps (it never fails to amaze me what will come back into style) and flopped down on the bed in his secondskins.

Rather than play one of the usual preparatory games like *What Would You Do?* or *What Do You Hear?*, I eased him into chatting about his rehabilitation—or habilitation, looking at it from his point of view. I thought I'd learn more about his state of mind from simple conversation than from games. After all, what past experience did he have for a game? It would only oblige him to be inventive and pull his concentration from the situation at hand. Chitter-chat was the right approach. He had some rather astute observations on modern life, as any outsider would, and I hoped he wouldn't lose them when he became an insider.

Eventually, he began winding down. I let him get away with some delaying tactics, going to the bathroom, taking his vitamins—delaying tactics can be important personal preparation rituals, provided they don't go on for too long. When he began talking about having something to eat, I made him lie down and start breathing exercises.

He was a good breather, reaching a state of physical receptiveness more quickly than a lot of more experienced clients I'd had. When the time came, I removed his eyes for him; just pressed my thumbs on his closed lids and out they popped into my palms as smoothly as melon seeds. Gladney didn't even twitch. The connections to his optic nerves disengaged with an audible *kar-chunk*. Hospital eyes were always a little more mechanical than they had to be. After I placed them in the left side of the holding tank, I slipped the system connections under his flaccid eyelids. A tiny pulse in the wires told me when he was hooked into the mental fingerpainting exercise I'd selected for him. Mental fingerpainting was about the right amount of effort for someone on his level. The system supplied the colors. All he had to do was stir them around.

I breathed myself into a relaxed state in a matter of moments but I waited a full minute before popping my own eyes out and joining him in the system. I wanted to give him time to get acclimated. Some people experienced a disorientation not unlike sudden weightlessness and they needed a minute alone to right themselves before they have to get used to another presence.

My materialization was even more gradual than usual to spare him any trauma. I used Pyotr Frankis's old trick of coming in as another color, oozing in greenly and then revealing myself as a second consciousness. Bright lights flashed as he recognized me, some of them nightmare purple, but it wasn't me he was afraid of. There was a little fear from not having a body to feel but he was becoming accustomed to that. He was edgy about something else entirely—quick images of traps snapping shut, closet doors slamming. But there was a certain amount of exhilaration, too, at being in a realm where almost nothing is impossible.

The images began to flow more continuously from him, rolling over us in a tumbling series, gargantuan confetti. Most of them were portions of dreams, scenes from books he'd read; some were strange scenes he was visualizing in the heat of the moment, just to see if he could. I stabilized and moved with his attention, reminding him gently that I was still there. The image of my own face came, followed by a series of others that gradually became more bizarre. The undertones running out of him indicated this was how he imagined everyone else in the world to be—exotic, different, mysterious, alien, existing on a plane he had only the haziest conception of because he lacked a past.

I emphasized my presence before he could become so caught up with his grotesque faces as to get hysterical. He steadied, his energy level decreasing. I felt him adjust something and there was a sense of balance being established, as though two large masses floating in space were settling into orbit around each other. *Space* was a good word for it. The feeling of emptiness surrounding us was enormous and vivid enough to induce vertigo, if I'd suffered from it. Which I didn't.

This is me. So much nothingness to be filled. He was unaware that he'd said anything; it simply came out of him as everything else had. There was a brief image of the previous Gladney and he tensed at the thought. *Somewhere. In this big emptiness . . .*

The Gladney-that-had-been image drifted away from us and disintegrated. His thought remained incomplete. He was at a loss now, drifting nowhere, so I gave him a new image as a prod, a very simple one: the synthesizer. As soon as he saw it, he reflexively reran the music, the piano-clarinet piece. I could hear little extra things in it this time, notes and embellishments absent from the recording. He was on the verge of rolling with it, letting it come the way it had been meant to, when hard negation chopped down like a guillotine blade.

We were left in silence. If he could have withdrawn from me, he would have, but he didn't know how.

I waited, making my presence as unthreatening as possible while I took his Emotional Index. He registered in peculiar fragmented sensations of movement rather than in visuals, because everything was movement for him. I could see that now. The universe was movement, the movement of vibration. Like a tuning fork. Even he himself was a tuning fork and right now he was vibrating in the key of fear-sharp. One octave up, I could hear a whiny echo of guilt. The intensity of it ebbed and I turned the music on again. This time he didn't shut it down, just pulled back from it as far as possible and allowed it to replay as the original recording.

We'd get nowhere at this rate. I had to get into the music—*inside* the music. I slowed down my time sense and concentrated, tightening myself until I was small enough to slip in between the notes. At that level they thundered, no longer recognizable as music; my consciousness vibrated in sympathy. Concentrating a little more, I felt the thundering rumble of the notes become more ponderous and now I could detect something else within the vibrations, faint but present nonetheless. I would have to concentrate even harder to find out what it was, but to concentrate that forcefully is to alter your state of consciousness in such a way that you're not actually *conscious* in the sense of *awake*. I would not be able to monitor Gladney. From his perspective it would seem as though I'd gone from being real to being imaginary.

It came slowly. The notes swelled until I could perceive only one at a time and I let the nearest one swallow me up. It was a piano note, G, perfectly formed in perfect pitch, a universe created by the oscillation of a string in the air (that was how he saw it, not as synthesized but as the real thing). Each sweep of the string through space created the universe of the note anew, the string reaching the limit of its swing before the ghost of itself opposite had disappeared. And within the note—

He looked up with a smile of mild interest. The face was unmistakable in spite of all the changes he'd been through in the last year and a half.

Come closer, he said.

Gladney?

The same. The smile broadened. *Well, not quite the same.* Those pampered good looks in full flower; the well-tended skin, the sculptured jawline, the hair brushed straight back and falling nearly to his shoulders. His face was the most solid thing about him; the rest had been sketched in vaguely. I could get no undertones from him, no feelings, no images.

He locked me in here, he said. *So I won't get out and take—*

The note passed away and we were in another. Gladney was standing on a high hill in the middle of the day.

—what used to be mine. He looked around. In the distance the horizon ran wetly, melting upward into the sky. *I live in the music now. He can't come in unless I get out.*

It wasn't possible. If anything had been left of the old Gladney's mind after the suckers had finished cleaning out his brain, it would have shown up while he was still in quarantine. This had to be a delusion of the present Gladney, some kind of kinky survivor guilt. And besides, you couldn't hold a separate identity that wasn't you in your mind. Someone had promised me that was a fact, and truth and information weren't the same thing, but I couldn't think about that now, I had to be deadpan.

The outdoor scene disappeared as the note went on; now we were in a vague representation of the old Gladney's recording studio. He looked up from the piano he was sitting at.

Can you prove who you are? I asked him.

You see me as I was. Isn't that enough?

No. The Gladney-that-is has perfect pitch—that could easily translate to his being able to reproduce his old appearance. If you are really the Gladney-that-was, you can tell me something about yourself that the Gladney-that-is has no knowledge of.

The delusion spread his hands. *He's studied up on me thoroughly. They gave him access to newstapes, vid-magazines, performance spikes.*

There's still plenty he doesn't know, I said. *The private things. Certain memories, feelings. Tell me something only your family could confirm as true.*

His face took on a defiant look but there was no more feeling from him than there would have been from a holo transmission. That in itself would indicate he was a fabrication, I thought, but my merely telling Gladney that wasn't going to help him. His intellect might believe me but his emotions wouldn't.

Tell me something, I prodded again.

He rose and leaned on the top of the piano. *Don't you think a man with perfect pitch would be able to interpolate the private feelings of another man who had grown from the same brain?*

The studio was gone. He was leaning on a small table in a quick-eat while I stood just outside the entrance. I could hear the drumming of his fingers on the table.

Tell me a fact, then. Just one fact he couldn't possibly know.

He straightened up. *The mindsuckers damaged me. I remember only what he knows.*

A logical cover, I decided, but I was unsure what to do next. Arguing with a delusion would only strengthen its sense of presence. Even just acknowledging it was giving it something to feed on. Confronting it was Gladney's job, not mine. I was going to have to get him down in the music with me.

The note passed; we were in a bedroom now. Gladney lay crosswise on a futon with his arms folded behind his head. He was looking at me upside down and I could see how much better he was defined.

I'm residue, he said happily. The upside-down smile was grotesque. *I'm a myelin ghost. You can't get rid of me without physically damaging his brain.*

I hooked my feet under the futon and willed myself upward. His bizarre upside-down smile rushed away from me as I grew through the ceiling of the phantom room, up into the emptiness to the limit of the note. The piano string swung across a sky made of the present Gladney's face. My abrupt appearance gave him a surge of alarm that nearly dislodged me.

Where were you? he said, demanding.

You know. The piano string moved between us. I stretched out my arms. *Take my hands before that string comes back.*

No.

Why not? It's your music.

No!

From the corner of my eye, I saw the string return to view, slicing through space. *Please, Gladney. Don't let that string put another barrier between you and your own work.*

Panic at the idea of being cut off from his music made him grab my hands. Half a mental moment later panic at the idea of meeting his delusion head-on made him freeze. The piano string came closer; shortly it would pass through my wrists and fragment my concentration.

I can't pull you in, Gladney. You have to jump on your own.

I'm afraid!

Why? Say it!

I'm afraid because—

Say it!

He'll get me!

Who?

Gladney!

You are Gladney.

No!

Then, who are you?

There was no answer. The piano string had nearly reached us.

What are you? I asked. *Are you a composer?*

His affirmation was all he needed to send him under the string just before it would have severed my hands. He stared after it with both horror and elation and then we were rushing down into the music together in the push of his admission.

The delusional Gladney watched us descend. The real one made a soft landing on the bed beside it, still gripping my hands. Without thinking, he tried to pull me onto the bed between himself and the other.

The bedroom vanished. We were on an underground tube, the only three in the coach. I moved around behind Gladney and he had to let go of me. As soon as he did, the delusional image vanished. Gladney was startled, but not half as much as I was. He moved forward with his hands out in front of him, groping the air.

He's not here. Is he?

I didn't answer. I was still trying to figure out what had happened. Delusions didn't go away just like that. Nor did they have enough volition to come and go like consciousness.

Is he? Gladney half-turned toward me and I saw that his eyes were closed. Either he was making use of a fairly sophisticated mental maneuver, a sort of sneaking up on his own blind side, or he was faking it to stay blinded to the situation. I couldn't tell which; his undertones showed only confusion.

Suddenly his hands seized on something invisible. The delusion rematerialized, caught in Gladney's grasp. The air around them crackled with sparks from Gladney's terror.

I can't let go!

I'd expected that; I hadn't expected to be unable to tell which one of them had said it, though.

We went from the tube to a raft in the middle of the ocean, bright sun beating down on the water. Gladney still had hold of the delusion. His eyes were open now. A shadow passed over us; high-flying piano string.

High A-sharp, Gladney said, automatically identifying the note. All right, now I knew which one was talking. *We're getting close to the end of the melody.*

And then they both said, in unison, *What do I do with him then?*

You're asking me? It's yours. What do you do when the music's over?

We were in the lower branches of a large tree, then back to the tube very briefly (*B-flat grace note,* Gladney said), in the bedroom, on a windy rooftop several thousand feet above the ground. Gladney was forcing us more quickly toward the end of the song—well, one of them was. It had to be the right one; delusions couldn't act on their own, only in reaction. The images began to blend into each other, flickering and flapping. Gladney and his delusion flashed on and off in a variety of positions, Gladney still holding on, as though they were wrestling or dancing. Or both. The music went from slow-motion subsonic to recognizable melody, both Gladneys dancing-struggling in time to it. The delusion offered no resistance now but Gladney was too preoccupied to notice. The struggle became a tumbling, end over end over end over end. I saw Gladney's hospital room, the synthesizer, Gladney himself standing before it, staring it down as though it were an enemy. Dr. Jesl appeared briefly, carnelian eyes blind to the two figures tumbling past her through the entertainment center where Gladney sat studying a newstape of the Gladney-that-had-been on the holo screen. The tumblers rolled on, to the vision of a dimly remembered dream, that dream of Gladney, the old Gladney, lifting his head to the sight of three people, visible only from neck to thigh, rushing forward at him. The dream Gladney—the Gladney-that-had-been—cried out, fell back, and vanished, and then the tumbling men were beyond the original end of the melody. But still they went on and the music went on with them, piano and clarinet finally making contact, playing together and opposite each other in complement.

After some unmeasurable mental time, the tumbling began to slow with the music. And when it stopped, there was only one figure, not two. He drifted in emptiness, excited and drained all at once.

Enough. Before he could think of doing anything else, I cued another relaxation exercise and wrapped it around him. As soon as he was completely absorbed in mental fingerpainting, I broke the contact between us and withdrew.

It took a minute or so for his vitals to calm down. I changed the exercise from fingerpainting to simple abstract visuals. He was overstimulated, in need of a passive mode. After his pulse went down below eighty, I disconnected him from the system and put his eyes back in.

The moment he saw me, he broke into a sweat. "Don't try to talk," I told him, covering the system connections and slipping them into the drawer in the largest component.

"I *can* talk."

"Sure. I didn't want you to feel like you had to."

He turned his face away while I dismantled the system. His breathing was extremely loud in the room. Rhythmic. I let him be. The inexperienced were often overcome by an intense feeling of embarrassment after mindplay, particularly pathosfinding. It took some getting over.

"Listen," he said, after a bit, still not looking at me. "He was there. He was really there, alive in me. And I'd just come out of nowhere, a figment of my own imagination."

"You can't have his past," I said as gently as I could. "And there's no such thing as a ghost, myelin or otherwise. It's always just you."

He shook his head. "Not any more. Before, it was like that. But you took me down into the work—"

"You went on your own."

"Doesn't matter. You helped me go down and get him. Not get rid of him—I've *got* him."

Well, reintegrating a delusion would feel like that. If we prized our illusions, we were even that much more jealous of our delusions because they felt so much more real. *Really* real. A few more sessions and he would adjust to being exactly what he was, no more and no less, and he would accept his music as something that had always come from the desire to compose it, not at the behest of something beyond his control. I let myself out.

Dr. Jesl phoned me sometime later, rousing me from a doze. "Our boy has a supreme mad on for you," she said. "Thing is, I can't tell just what it's all about. I don't think he knows, either. Struggling with new emotions, as 'twere." She sounded more amused than worried.

As 'twere. I was too exhausted to explain about mindplay embarrassment compounded by the loss of a self-imposed handicap. "He'll get over it," I told her.

Which he did. Or seemed to. But it spooked me later on, when he correctly identified all of the old Gladney's music without anyone identifying it for him.

When he was stronger—when we were both stronger—I allowed myself an afternoon off. I left him at his synthesizer working on a new piece with difficulty but also with the determination of those who become real and stay real. I locked myself in the hospital room and cried for McFloy, for his not being able to overcome the survivor guilt, for being ultimately unable to fill his own empty cup, for all the stupid emotions that had gotten in his way, that wouldn't get in my way. They wouldn't call me Deadpan Allie for nothing, ever.

Deadpan Allie cried herself comatose. But just that once. I still had to finish taking care of Gladney.

And I didn't cry for Jerry Wirerammer.

L A S T   C A L L

I sat staring at the screen in mute amazement. The goofy grin, the let's-make-things-a-little-more-interesting tilt to the head, all intact, all just as I remembered them from a thousand years ago when I'd had an overdrawn kitchen and an urge to put on madcaps.

"Hello, Allie."

"Jerry . . . is it *really* you?" I said when I could speak.

He looked embarrassed. "Well, actually, it's not. I'm a Power Person. Sort of."

If someone could have died of the creeps, I would have right then.

"I'm, uh, a bootleg," he went on. "Kind of a bootleg, that is. I had one of the bootleg templates. Later I got hold of the original."

I didn't want to hear about it. "What do you want? Why are you calling me?"

Giggle. "Just to say hello, I guess. And let you know everything's really all right. I still exist, in a way. Here and there. I don't know about *there*, of course, but I'm *here*. Not totally, I mean. But sort of totally. It's a funny sort of existence but it works."

"What about . . . what about the original?"

He shrugged. "I'm not sure. My memory doesn't go that far. I know someone was after him and I imagine they got him, whoever they were. I'm not too clear on that. And it doesn't matter any more anyway." He paused. "That's all, I guess. I just had this urge to call you."

"Thanks," I said and pushed the disconnect pad.

He was going to haunt me no matter who he was. Some people wanted to be somebody, some people didn't want to be anybody, some people wanted to be everybody, and some people wanted everybody to be them. Hell of a thing, I thought, and called Fandango over to drink birch beer with me so I wouldn't have to think any more about it for a while.

WE ARE NOT AMUSED

"Great minds," said Jascha, "think alike."

"Sure. Also not-so-great minds."

It wasn't a big bed and it wasn't even as firm as I'd have liked, but it was a bed and it wasn't at the agency and Jascha was in it with me, so all was right with the world. For the moment. Through the open double doors opposite the bed, the sun was just starting to come up over the bay, which was only lightly misty this morning.

"Want me to close them?" Jascha asked, reaching for the remote on the nightstand.

"Nah. Leave the doors open. I don't mind." We had settled into an innocent cuddle, if any cuddle can be innocent when the people in question are naked. Jascha pulled the sheet up a little higher against the morning coolness.

"You tired? Or still all wound up?"

"Neither. Just sort of calmly alert."

Jascha breathed a theatrical sigh of relief. "Of course, that's assuming I'm not being premature," he added.

"If you're tired, Jascha, go to sleep."

"I'm just kidding, Allie. Jesus, what's happened to your sense of humor? You do remember kidding, don't you? You used to be awfully good at it."

I turned my head away from the hard red sunlight and closed my eyes.

"Anyone's capable of developing delusions under the right conditions."

"He correctly identified all of the old Gladney's music on his own. Not guessing. Which has to mean that was the old Gladney in there. Not a delusion. Which has to put the lie to your contention and everyone else's that you can't accommodate a completely separate mind in your own mind."

"No, it doesn't," Jascha said firmly. "The fact that he correctly identified all of the old Gladney's music means that great minds think alike. The new mind was born in the same brain. It had to have—" he floundered for a moment, "*resonated* somehow with the creations of the old mind. Sympathetic vibration. Kinship. Perfect pitch. He used a fantasy of the old Gladney to deal with the survivor guilt and it became a delusion."

Resonated. Oh, yah. "That's one way to explain it."

"That *does* explain it." Pause. "Sure you don't want me to close those doors?"

"I'm sure. I want to look at the bay."

"And how can you do that with your eyes closed?"

"All right, I want the doors open so I can look at the bay if I want to."

Silence fell for such a long time that I thought Jascha had gone to sleep. I was half-dozing myself when he said, "The best system in the world won't reach into your fantasy life unless you offer it up. You don't do that."

"Ridiculous. I do, too. I live a good portion of my life in fantasy. Remember? I lead a very mental life. They told me that way back when I was a mind criminal. It's far truer now than it ever was. Jascha, you weren't there in mind-to-mind contact with him. You don't know."

"True. I only know what you've told me. Including how you helped him resolve things."

"And what about Jerry Wirerammer?"

"I don't know. He doesn't seem to be part of this very mental life you lead."

"Sometimes I feel as though he almost straddles it— the outer and the inner. Someone else's inner; I never went mind-to-mind with him. He said I'd turned my back on the world he had to live in."

Jascha slipped his arm out from around me and sat up, rubbing his shoulder. He'd left off having himself gilded again; natural silver was starting to appear in his hair. Otherwise he looked about the same as he always had. "Well, my divorce is final," he said after a bit.

"It is?"

"As of a few minutes ago. It must be after 6:30. I think they said sunrise would be about 6:41 this morning."

I pulled the sheet up to my chin. "Do I say I'm sorry? For my part in it, anyway."

"Don't be ridiculous." He leaned his chin on his knees and stared out at the bay. The light mist was burning off rapidly. "It was one of those interim relationships, bound to come to an end."

"Then, why'd you get married?"

"I needed the permanence."

"Excuse me?"

"All right, I needed the feeling of permanence so I could have had it if I'd wanted to." He looked at me sideways, smiling.

"Oh. Well, why didn't you say so? That's something I can understand."

Jascha cuffed me lightly and got up to use the lavabo. It was big enough for two if you didn't mind getting your elbows tangled up all the time. I stayed in bed, squinting at the sun and its reflection over the water. I'd come to Oakland alone after finishing up with Gladney, but on the second day, I'd returned to my hotel room to find Jascha sitting on the balcony and his grip in the autovalet. What the hell. If he'd gone to all the trouble of tracking me down, I could let him stay. It wasn't until later that I realized I was relieved to see him. Not just a friendly face, but him, Jascha. And maybe much later, I'd think more about what all that meant, but not now.

I slumped down on the pillow and closed my eyes again. I'd wrapped up Gladney's case in four sessions total, including the first one. Once we'd excised his myelin ghost—or integrated his delusion, depending on your point of view—everything had broken for him. Perfect pitch tends to take on a life of its own. My personal feeling was that the present Gladney was better than the previous, but that could have been a matter of taste. Anyway, his career had begun reviving—or taking off—when I'd left the hospital. It was my own career I had some doubts about.

Of course, I could probably quit now. It had been four years since Paolo Segretti had given me the choice and I'd fulfilled my end. I could walk away from the agency, from mindplay, from everything, even go live in an enclave if I wanted to. (Maybe look up Marty Oren and Sudella. Not that they'd understand why I was there.)

Only that wouldn't take care of the problem. It would

only give me even less control over it—if I really had any control over it now.

I opened my eyes as Jascha stepped out of the lavabo, freshly washed and massaged, his hair and beard still slightly damp. "Next?" he said.

"Nah. I think I'll just lie here in my own sweat and grit until Nelson Nelson calls me back for another assignment, or until hell freezes over, whichever happens second."

Jascha threw himself down crosswise on the bed. "Quite a self-pity showcase you're running here."

"What would you do?" I sat up a little. "Honestly, now."

"I'd forget it, Allie."

"It was just supposed to be his eye. Just the eye trick. But he's there. *Him.* Maybe it was just the eye at first. And then he re-formed around it as an integral part of my mind."

Jascha looked puzzled. "Then, what's the problem? We've been over this. If it's an integral part of you, then it can't be anyone else."

"I don't *think* it can be that simple. He was—I was—" I stopped. XXXXXXXXXXXXXXXXXXXXXXXXXXXXXXXX. No, not quite. But I almost had it.

Jascha got up and slipped into a pair of light trousers and a white shirt rich with delicate blood-red embroidery. "Let's go out. Walk around. Be in the world. That's your problem more than anything." He reached over and yanked me across the mattress. "You're always talking about the world this and the world that and this reality, that reality, and real reality, but it isn't real to you." He pointed at the bay. "*That's* the shade, as far as you're concerned. *That's* your fantasy. You can dream lucidly now but you've forgotten how to *live* lucidly."

"Yah, I think I already mentioned that myself, leading a very mental life and all that. I can also refer you to Jerry Wirerammer, whoever he is now, if you want further testimony." I got up and went to the lavabo. "I do know what my problem is, Jascha," I said, punching the controls on the door for a hard needle shower and even harder massage. "It's what makes me such a good

pathosfinder. And I know how to cure it, but I'm not sure
I'd like living in an enclave."

"It doesn't have to be that extreme," he said.

"Maybe not for you." I stepped into the lavabo.

Living lucidly. We took a slow open-seated caravan
through the hills, gawking with the other tourists at the
houses jammed into the hillsides. Ancestral homes, most
of them; they were just about impossible to buy. About
the only way to acquire one these days was to be born
into it. Jascha and I didn't talk much, except to point out
some miraculous architectural feat showing through the
trees.

The caravan paused for lunch at the summit of one of
the hills, overlooking more of the bay. The restaurant
was picnic-style—one of those on Nelson Nelson's Restaurant-of-the-Month Club brochures, I noted. I tried to
picture NN reclining on a blanket on the grass gnawing
on spiced chicken wings; the image moved me to
laughter, which amused the other tourists and alarmed
Jascha when I wouldn't tell him what I was laughing
about. I didn't want to tell him I'd lapsed back into
mental living. Living lucidly was all right but not very
much happened. (If you were lucky . . . but then no
one would have called what Jerry Wirerammer had been
doing living lucidly.) I decided to wait and be disturbed
about my attitude later.

On the way down the other side of the hills, the
caravan passed an enclave. We'd have missed it if the
tour guide hadn't pointed it out. There wasn't much to
see, just a wire fence mostly hidden by trees. I stared
after it anyway, wondering if there was some way I could
get a closer look at it before I had to go back to the
agency.

Enclaves were such odd things. You could conceivably
live on the outside, never engaging in mindplay, and
maybe just seem a little odd to everyone else. I knew
that well enough. I also knew it was like deciding to be a
hermit in the middle of a city. You'd be out of touch, out
of step. Eventually, you'd want to be with people who
weren't having their dreams fed regularly or weren't

having a thrillseeker delve them for new and better forms of excitement.

Only . . . I looked around at the other people in the caravan. Unless we were all in the pool or hooked in together through a mindplay system, I was as separate from them as the people in the enclave were from me. We were all enclaves, really. Maybe the difference in an enclave society was really just perceived, in spite of what NN had said back when I'd done my first job with his son-in-law. So why bother to shut yourself away? Might as well stay out here; who knew the difference?

And then again, maybe it was something about the culture, I thought. Something about being surrounded with people who make mind-to-mind contact would eventually bring you in to be one of them or drive you away completely—

The leaves behind the enclave fence parted and I saw the face looking out at me. Just for a moment; then the caravan rounded a bend and the face disappeared behind a tree. I twisted around, crawling half out of my seat trying to get a last look.

"What is it?" asked Jascha, mildly irritated.

I looked at him. Was it possible to lie, *really* lie, to a person who has actually touched your mind? "Just trying to live lucidly, Jascha," I said. "Trying to get a better look at the scenery."

"You've got to look while it's happening," he said. "Otherwise you miss seeing it the way it should be seen."

I settled back into my seat. "My mistake. Thanks for the tip."

The expression on the face behind the fence had been sadly wistful. For the brief moment I'd seen it, I'd actually been unable to decide whose face it had been— Jerry Wirerammer's, or McFloy's—when it couldn't have been either. Just a trick of the light. And the mind.

Be alert, said a small voice in my head.

I ended up cutting the vacation short by a day. I left Jascha a note. It was easier than arguing with him. I also paid the bill on the room, though I knew that wouldn't make it up to him.

He left his own note on my phone back at the agency. *Did I mention that living lucidly includes loving lucidly? And if you won't marry me again, will you at least try to see that you have something of mine even though we never did the eye trick? It's just as real, though. And just as unreal, come to that.*

But we were too divorced.

"There's divorce and there's divorce," said Nelson Nelson. "You ever been divorced, Deadpan?"

I lit a cigarette, using the time to decide if NN was asking me an honest question or just gassing. I had no doubt the old fox could have wormed his way into my personal data; most employers can. And he was a great one for gassing questions he already knew the answers to. He'd told me once he did it because he was interested in other people's realities. I could have given him the long course on that one.

"No," I said after a bit. I don't know whether he knew enough to believe me or not, but he looked satisfied.

"Certain philosophers say real divorce is rare because few people ever make truly solid connections with each other."

"Philosophers?" I tapped my cigarette over the suckhole in the desk. "There's a philosophy of divorce?" You hear all kinds of things in the mindplay business.

Nelson Nelson laughed. "If the human race lasts long enough, there'll be a philosophy for blinking your eyes."

"And we'll know the new Messiah by the way she walks on bullshit."

"Now, now, woman. Bullshit has its uses as a lubricant. You'll come to realize that by the time you're my age."

That depended on what you were trying to lubricate, but I didn't tell him that. I shifted around uncomfortably on my couch. NN's practice of conducting business in a reclining position was getting tiresome and that damned vulgar upholstery was making me itch worse than ever. "So who are these philosophers of divorce?"

NN looked wise. "The other members of my Restaurant-of-the-Month Club, actually. We suppered in the jet stream last night and the subject came up with the cranberry soufflé."

"You discussed a case?"

NN's forehead puckered. His eyebrows were nonexistent these days, which made a frown one of his more peculiar expressions. "Allie, I didn't get to be one of the biggest mindplay agencies in the hemisphere through indiscretion. Someone else brought the subject up. I listened."

Manipulated the conversation and then picked someone's brain was more like it. "Did you hear anything that would help me?"

"Hard to say. I'm old enough to have seen several swings of the togetherness pendulum. For a few years, sometimes even as long as a decade, everyone's getting Two'd and Three'd and Gang'd. Then suddenly everyone's an island again and nobody wants to be committed to anyone else. But regardless of what people want, or think they want, they clump. They can't help it. Even self-proclaimed social outcasts align themselves in some way with other outcasts. No one ever wants to be totally outside the system."

I scratched some more and didn't say anything.

"Take an extreme case of clumping gone to bond," he went on in his listen-to-this-you-could-learn-something voice. "You remember the LadyBugs from a few years back?"

I nodded, still scratching away. "They were big news when I was at J. Walter Tech."

NN smiled with half his mouth. "They were big news everywhere in the mindplay business."

"Don't tell me," I said, sitting up. "The LadyBugs have split up, one of them wants to be a ballet dancer, and I'm supposed to pathosfind her."

NN gave me one of his Looks. "You get some funny ideas, Deadpan. The LadyBugs are still happy as sandbags and loony as Klein bottles. You follow contemporary composers?"

I shrugged. "Why?"

For answer, he thumbed a button on his couch frame. Music came up out of the walls and floated down from the ceiling and I damn near fell off the couch.

"Allie?"

"That's the Poconos Movement from *Transcontinental*

Elopement. Jord Coor and Revien Lam. Their work is unmistakable."

NN looked satisfied. We listened for a bit while I got over the creeps. The Poconos Movement was one of the more favored doses of the whole piece, all frisky piccolos and galloping guitars. You wouldn't have thought piccolos could describe the Poconos so well, but they did.

"Still with me, Deadpan?"

"Oh, sure." I squirmed into another position, scratching my left calf with my right foot and clawing at my ribs. "I always liked Coor and Lam."

NN turned the volume down a little. "Likewise. It has great spirit, isn't it so? Coor and Lam produced a fine body of work together, right up until a year ago, when they went their separate ways."

"Yah. Which one hired me?"

"Coor." NN raised himself up on one elbow. "And if you don't stop that scratching, I'm going to have you flayed alive to save you the trouble. What in *hell* is wrong with you?"

"I'm allergic to this goddamn gold lamé." I stood up, trying to scratch everywhere at once. My overblouse clung to me, snapping with static when I pulled it away from my slight if perennial potbelly that I could never seem to exercise off. Fusion power we licked; static cling has us on the ropes. It's a funny world.

"Here." Nelson Nelson produced a small tube and tossed it to me. "Suddenly everyone's allergic to gold lamé. I had Lindbloom in here about a thrillseeking and she could barely hold still."

Well, that sounded like Lindbloom, gold lamé or no gold lamé.

"Better?" NN asked as I swabbed cool blue jelly on my arms.

"Much. What is this stuff?"

"Home remedy. Take it with you."

"Maybe I ought to leave it here. For next time." I glanced at the couch.

"Deadpan, I'm hurt. You're sneering at the future I looked forward to in the dear, departed days of my youth."

"Excuse me?"

"Gold lamé. Back when I was a kid, they promised us a clean, glorious future where positively everything would be covered with gold lamé. Gold lamé curtains, gold lamé furniture, gold lamé clothes. They stopped making the stuff fifty years ago and now I have to have it specially manufactured. But I figure I'm entitled."

I pulled up one loose pantleg and smeared his home remedy on my thigh. "Tell me about Jord Coor. And I wasn't sneering."

"There's not much for *me* to tell you; I put all the information in your dataline and you were too sneering. Coor's trying to put himself together for a solo career and having a bad time of it. The six-month hiatus he took after the split has stretched into a year and he's feeling desperate."

"He waited another six months before hiring a pathos-finder?"

"Some people have to take the long way home just so they know they've been somewhere."

"Is he really ready to try it alone?"

"*He* says. That's something you'll have to determine. As always."

"What about his ex-partner?"

"Out of sight but traceable. Part of their separation agreement was a clause promising a certain amount of cooperation in any future individual endeavors, musical or otherwise."

"Was their split really that amicable?"

"Who knows? Divorce is a funny thing."

Sure was. "But they weren't married. Or were they? I don't keep up on celebrity statistics."

NN would have raised his eyebrows if he'd had any. I couldn't wait for them to grow back. NN did some odd things and I had yet to figure what it was he was acting out. His dear, departed future, maybe. "Well, not in the conventional sense. But they worked mind-to-mind for ten years. What do you think that means but marriage? *More* than marriage. Follow?"

I nodded.

"So if you should have to look up Revien Lam for some

reason, don't hook in with both of them. Don't put them in a composing situation together."

"But they don't want to compose together."

"Who said so?" NN snapped. "Did I say so?" He shook his head. "Deadpan, the thing you gotta remember about divorced people is when they have a real crisis, they think about jumping right back into the old situation, even if that's the worst thing they could do, and it usually is. But it's a known quantity and people clump. Don't clump them, Allie. The whole music world would love to see them back together again and they don't really want to be back together. Which, paradoxically, gives them common ground and pushes them closer together. Follow that?"

"Yah." I finished applying jelly to my other leg. "And I didn't sneer. They don't call me Deadpan Allie and lie."

"You sneered. Inside if not outside. I could tell." He cut off the music and put the Bolshoi Ballet on the ceiling holo by way of dismissing me and having the last word. "It's a mutually wished-for and consummated divorce, Deadpan. Leave it that way."

Fandango sneaked up behind me and propped her chin on my shoulder. "Hi. I'm your two-headed transplant."

I kept staring at the readout screen. "I'm not going to encourage you."

She tickled me under the chin with one of her dreadlocks. The damnedest things come back into style. "Why are you researching the LadyBugs?"

"I'm looking at a case of extreme togetherness that worked. Or has yet to fail, I'm not sure which." I pushed back from my desk and went down the three steps into the living room to flop on the couch. Fandango tagged after me, pausing at the bar to dial up a couple of birch beers.

"You think there's a difference?" she said, handing me a glass before she climbed into the pouch chair across from me. "Between something that works and something that has yet to fail?"

"Glad you asked." I waved at the coffee table. *Full*

Day, another Coor and Lam piece, came on softly. This one was only twenty-four hours long, looped for continuous play. "According to something I read by one of the leading experts on human relationships—who happens to be a member of NN's chapter of the Restaurant-of-the-Month Club, by the way—there are three main theories on the patterns that two-person bondings of any type follow."

Fandango turned her bloodstone eyes on me. The bloodstones were new. With the dreadlocks, they made her look like a cross between a werewolf and a witch doctor. I didn't mention that to her. She'd have just gone and added fangs for effect. "Let's hear it. I know you're itching to tell me."

"Don't use that expression. One theory says that a two-way partnership lasting until the death of one or both partners never reached its ultimate peak and thus never got the chance to deteriorate. Another theory says that all partnerships end before the actual split. In the last stage of the relationship, there are really just two sets of elements thrown together behind a facade of unity." I put my birch beer down on the coffee table. If I was going to lose this potbelly, I couldn't be pouring birch beer into it. "The third theory states that all partnerships are illusions. One personality dominates and absorbs the other. I guess the LadyBugs would be a rather extreme example, in a way."

"The LadyBugs are loono and have licenses to prove it," Fandango said, with not a little disdain.

"Then there are all the variations on those theories. The most interesting one postulates that whatever happens between two people, a third entity is created which can, in some cases, attain such definition and strength as to be a completely different person."

Fandango finished her birch beer and hung out of the chair to set the glass on the coffee table. "And what does all this tell you?"

Several things, none of which I wanted to think about at the moment. "It tells me experts probably work alone and not in partnership." I stared at the meditation mandala on the ceiling. Researching the LadyBugs, I decided, was the wrong approach. They weren't partners, not the way Coor and Lam had been. I thought of the Twins—I hadn't thought of them in such a long time. They weren't it, either. Congruence wasn't necessarily complement.

"Turn up the music, will you?" Fandango said, sinking down a little more in the chair. "It just entered my circadian peak."

I obliged her. Only her head was visible in the pouch chair. I'd never cared for the idea of being swallowed by a piece of furniture, no matter how comfortable it was supposed to be, but then, it wasn't my chair anyway. Fandango had dragged it over to my apartment from her place. That was the advantage of living at the agency— you could get out of your apartment and take it with you.

The LadyBugs were still grinning from the console in my work area above the living room. I abandoned the mandala and wandered back to my desk to punch for Jord Coor's entry. He was an emphatically plain man with a wide face and long, straight black hair. His eyes were the same flat black. Onyx biogems, according to his data. The overall effect was *blah*, as though his life's ambition was to pass unnoticed. Not the acter-outer type, which probably meant there was more than the usual amount of energy pent up behind that broad forehead. If he ran to form at all, he was prone to what I called the creative tantrum, as well as to bursts of creativity alternating with blocks. His being half a partnership had probably masked a lot of that.

After a while, I punched for Revien Lam's picture. The screen swallowed Coor and delivered his ex-partner's image with an electronic burp. Time for another tune-up. Revien Lam seemed to have tried to make himself as different from Coor as possible. He'd had a bleach-out, hair and all. Against his color, or lack of it, the sapphire eyes were startling. His features were pointy where Coor's were blunted, the face almost an inverted triangle. Only the knobs of his jawbone kept him from looking too pixieish.

Just for the hell of it, I shrank Lam's picture and

recalled Coor's, putting them side by side. They stared at me and I stared back.

Art makes strange mindfellows.

It was hard to imagine the two of them hooked in together, Coor through the left eye and Lam through the right, like a variation on the eye trick, I thought uncomfortably, working both in real time and the eternal Now of mind time. A rather trippy experience.

And a very long trip at that. Ten years of such continual mind-to-mind contact was a lot more intimate than two people should have been with each other, as far as I was concerned. They had to be a couple of pretty rugged individualists to have kept themselves sorted out.

"Rugged individualist," I said aloud.

"What?" asked Fandango, coming out of her musical trance.

I looked over my shoulder at her. "I said, 'Rugged individualist.'"

She waved at the coffee table and the music lowered. "Who?"

"Just a thought. Go back to your rhapsody and forget I said anything." I turned back to the screen and stared at the ex-collaborators some more.

If you stare at something long enough, sometimes it will begin to look wrong. Lam's picture was on the right and Coor's was on the left and the arrangement was making me uncomfortable to the point of irritation. I tried looking at them with my right eye covered and then my left. Feeding an image into one hemisphere of the brain alone can sometimes give you a different perspective on something, but I'd never been that good at isolating my visual fields without mechanical help. All I was getting out of the effort was more uncomfortable.

When I switched the pictures around, I felt a lot better, even with both eyes open. Aesthetically, the new arrangement was more pleasing, though I was damned if I could have said why. I sat back and put my heels up on the desk, gazing at the pictures through the V-frame of my legs. The system had placed Lam's picture on the right when I'd called for Coor's. Maybe if I'd made the placement myself, I'd have liked it better? I shook my head. That wasn't it and I knew it. I rested my gaze on the dividing line between the pictures for several seconds and then nearly fell out of the chair.

The resemblance between them was so marked I felt like an ass for not having seen it immediately. It wasn't exactly a physical resemblance and yet it was. The similarity lay in their expressions, especially in the eye and mouth areas—the same things that make the long-married look alike. I had the screen enlarge those portions and remove the distinguishing coloration.

I marveled. It was almost possible to forget which features belonged to which man. Just for the hell of it, I patched Coor's eyes and mouth into Lam's face and vice versa. The old eye-and-mouth trick. My system wasn't programmed for fine-detail graphics and the result was crude, but not unreasonable.

"And what does that tell you, Dr. Frankenstein?" Fandango said, hanging over my shoulder again. I patted her wiry hair.

"Take a nap and stop sneaking up on me." I punched for pictures of Coor and Lam as they had been prior to their becoming collaborators, careful to keep Lam on the left and Coor on the right.

The youthfulness of their faces startled me. I checked the dates. The pictures were fourteen years old, which made it something close to two years before they'd met. At twenty, Coor had that I'm-an-adult-I-know-things look to him while the seventeen-year-old Lam appeared to be the sort of twink you could sell a perpetual-motion machine to.

I made more enlargements of their features and side-by-sided them one at a time. There was a definite similarity of expression around their eyes even then, as though they might have been looking at things in the same way, literally as well as figuratively.

I punched up pictures from three years later. A year into the partnership, Lam had dyed himself black with red accents. The struggle for differentiation had already begun.

Forward another three years. The haunted look of

Lam's opal eyes was reflected by Coor's. I went to my auxiliary screen and called up a list of their compositions from that time. *The Freak Parade*. *Persimmon Dances*. *The Abstruse Pillow*. I listened to short excerpts from each one on the phones. It was easy to hear the conflict, but they'd conflicted so well together.

I jumped ahead to their last full year together. Coor looked weary and Lam looked crazed. By then it must have required incredible effort to keep from merging. Lam had been in the first stage of his bleach job, and it struck me that his decision to be bleached this time instead of dyed was probably a strong statement of his perception of what was happening between himself and his partner. And there was Coor, looking the same as always, making a statement by making no statement.

I leaned my elbows on the desk and looked from one face to the other. If I'd been shown all the pictures and then been asked to guess which man had hired me, I'd have probably picked Lam, not Coor.

And what about Lam? I punched for any available data. There wasn't much—some vital statistics, a facsimile of the separation agreement, and his last known address, two years out of date. Probably safe to assume he'd given up music entirely. Considering how he'd been pulling away even from the beginning, it was in character—another and final way to differentiate himself from Coor, a pattern of behavior he was locked into for good.

"And what does all *this* tell you?" said a voice in my ear. Fandango was still lingering behind me.

"It tells me some people gain freedom by trading one form of bondage for another."

"Yah? You don't have to tell *me* that. I'm a neurosis peddler, remember?"

"Well, you asked." I frowned at the screen. "I think my basic problem here is just training someone to be a unit after being half a team for ten years."

Fandango crouched beside me and wagged her dreadlocks. "Ah, they never should have broken up."

"That's a matter of opinion," I said, amused. "An

opinion that my client's been struggling against. Maybe Lam, too, for all I know."

"Sorry. I guess I can say it because I won't be doing the dirty work. But speaking as a member of the listening audience . . ." She made a face, which, considering the way she looked, was quite an accomplishment. "Maybe I don't know what I'm talking about. All I do is make people wash their hands a lot and associate sex with the color orange. But maybe it's better to be half of something wonderful than a whole nothing at all."

I couldn't answer right away, and when I did, my voice sounded just a little sharp. "It hasn't been determined that Jord Coor is nothing on his own yet. If it had, I wouldn't be on this job."

Fandango stared at me with mild surprise. "'Scuse me, but did I just Say Something?" She waved a hand carelessly. "Oh, never mind. Pardon my nose. And mouth, too. All I meant to say was that this kind of mindplay only postpones having to admit something like the truth, huh?" She got up and bounced back to the pouch chair, dreadlocks flying, and hopped in.

"Thanks for the moral support," I said.

"Anytime." She turned the music up again.

"This part of Massachusetts used to be such a mess that they put a two-hundred-year ban on external construction even after they cleaned it up. It'll be another eighty-four years before you see anything but naked landscape. If then." Jord Coor's square face was impassive in the near twilight. I wasn't sure that I hadn't met someone even more deadpan than I was. He pointed to the horizon. "Those low hills are called monadnocks, according to the locals. About half of them are occupied, hollowed out, like this one." He tapped his foot on the soft dirt.

"Pretty," I said.

He almost smiled. "For over a century, nobody knew that. It was all defaced with factories, ugly little industrial towns. Poison all over the place, in everything. I've seen footage." A small wind pushed a strand of hair over the lower half of his face and he tossed his head to shake it away. The motion put us unexpectedly eye to eye. The onyxes were like two bottomless holes.

"I thought this would be the ideal place to hide out, weather the first of the separation. Really go underground, in a place that was also coming back into its own."

I pretended to study one of the few tall evergreens around us while I sight-read his Emotional Index peripherally. His analysis sounded a bit simple to me but the set of his body said he was sticking with it, as though his partnership with Lam had been something imposed on him rather than something he'd entered into voluntarily. The no-longer-wished-for bond was now perceived as bondage or indenture. Human beings have a tendency to rewrite reality. *I don't love you anymore* would become *I never loved you to begin with;* it's no good now so that means it never was. I wondered if I'd be able to get him past that. I would have wondered plenty else but I refused to let myself dwell on any of it. They didn't call me Deadpan Allie for nothing.

A chill crept into the air as the sun slid closer to the lumpy line of monadnocks. Jord gestured at the manhole we'd climbed out of earlier and I nodded. The hole led down to an uncomfortably small elevator that took us back into the big empty chamber at the top of the stacked rooms he persisted in calling a house.

We went down to the living room, which was five times larger than it had to be, considering what he used it for, which was very little. A designer who apparently went to a lot of parties had shaped it so that it was punctuated with conversation areas and gathering spots, all around an off-center bar. It had an untouched, still-not-broken-in look. Jord just wasn't ready to make himself at home. Not a good sign.

He wasn't ready to begin work, either; he was treating me like a guest, or maybe an insurance agent, anything but a pathosfinder. Well, the first meeting was always uncomfortable, but Jord Coor's avoidance beat even Gladney's. He sat me in one of the nooks around the bar and dispensed Moxie and chitchat until I was bloated and more knowledgeable about north-central Massachusetts than I could ever have wanted to be. I let him run. He could run but he couldn't hide. Eventually he was going to blurt out something having to do with the reason I was there, and that would give both of us the momentum to go to work. Best for him to make the first move. Better to jump than be pushed.

When it came, it came without preamble. He looked up at me from his fourth glass of Moxie and said, "I just want it back."

"It?"

"Whatever it was I had before I met Revien. Sometimes I can almost feel it. It's almost there. But it's like stepping forward and finding the floor is suddenly gone. Nothing there, just emptiness. And I realize all those years with Revien—I've come away half an artist." He set his glass on a small shelf by his elbow. "That's how it feels, anyway. I've been changed."

"Did you expect that you wouldn't be?"

"Changed, certainly." His face hardened even more. "Changed but not diminished. Not shortchanged. As it were."

As it were, indeed. I nodded for him to go on.

"Apparently what we added to the partnership we subtracted from ourselves. Or what I added to the partnership *I* subtracted from *my* self. I don't know about Revien." He gave a short, humorless laugh. "And you'd think I *would* know, wouldn't you. Ten years in and out of each other's heads, you'd think we had no secrets." He stared past me. "But we were only half hooked in. That was close enough. Early on, we went all the way, hooked in both eyes, just to try it. Only twice, though. It was too much. Felt so strange, as though we were asleep, dreaming, and discovered there was someone else dreaming the same dream." His gaze slid over to me. "Have you ever felt that way with a client?"

I was proud of the fact that I didn't hesitate. "Mindplayers are specially trained not to get loose and runny around the borders, though most people don't have problems keeping self divided from non-self. It sounds like an effect, uh, peculiar to your relationship."

"Perhaps it was." He nodded slowly, staring at something past my right shoulder.

"Who first brought up the idea of separating?"

He took a deep, uncomfortable breath. "I don't know if it's a matter of an idea that came up. More like a sub-theme that was always there and evolved into being the main melody. We were always pulling apart as much as pulling toward each other." He frowned, wobbling between a hasty retreat from the subject and a headlong plunge into the problem.

What the hell, I thought; sometimes you can't jump without a little tiny nudge. "This might be a good time for the first session," I said casually. "While it's at the top of your mind."

He licked his lips, preparing an objection.

"It doesn't get any easier," I added.

His smile was sudden and unexpectedly warm. "No, I don't suppose it does, does it?"

He hadn't exactly cooled by the time we got up to his studio but I could tell by the jittery way he kept wiggling his fingers he was trying to build up some kind of resistance. The studio wouldn't let him.

It was a strange room, windowless and just big enough to keep a claustrophobe from stampeding. The acoustical walls and ceiling caught every little sound and seemed to focus on it, making each noise into something significant before it was gone. In the center of the room, a marvelously restored barrelhouse piano stood back to back with a techno-crazy chunk of synthesizer bristling with wires and stepladdered with keyboards, as though inviting comparison and choice.

"A synthesizer won't always do the job," Jord said as I touched the rich old wood of the piano. "Sometimes there's no substitute for the real instrument." One hand hovered over the yellowed keys, his fingers automatically falling into position for a chord. Instead of playing it, he looked up at me. "What made you choose cat's-eye biogems?"

"I found them interesting."

"Look toward the light." He lifted my chin and studied my eyes. "Revien would like eyes like those. They shimmer. The same way he does."

I pulled away from him gently. "Revien shimmers?"

"It's hard to explain."

"Then, don't explain. Show me." I went over to my system stacked by the far wall and began putting the components together. I could feel him watching, unspoken objections and excuses piling up between us, thickening the air.

"This is smaller than most of the systems I've seen," he said suddenly, from just behind me. I had presence enough not to jump. After you've been pathosfinding a while, you get to where you can not only sense an Emotional Index without looking but also judge a client's physical position relative to yourself. I hadn't thought a client could come up behind me without my knowing.

"My agency developed this model," I told him, keeping busy with the connections so he wouldn't know he'd startled me. "This one's only for pathosfinding and memory enhancement, which is why there's so little to it. Your last pathosfinder probably had a standard, multipurpose system."

"Revien and I used a composing box. It wasn't a lot bigger than this. Are you sure it'll do the job?"

I was grinning on the inside. "Back at the agency, we've got a system the size of a small canyon. You have to let it eat your head to use it. It does a job and a half, just about anything by way of mindplay, but it wouldn't do anything more for us than this does. Which is to provide a medium for the meeting of our minds. It works, but only as well as we do. You know how it is with machines."

He moved around to my right, frowning at the assembly. "Revien used to call our composing box the lunatic bridge."

"Why?" I asked, pulling some pictures out of a drawer.

"We'd send a piece of ourselves down the wire into the box and the two pieces would fuse into the lunatic that composed the music."

I didn't raise my eyebrows. "Interesting. Did you—do you—see it that way?"

"A lunatic on a bridge?" He wouldn't let the smile come. Attempting to out-deadpan me, maybe. "I tried not to. Try not to." He glanced at the sheaf of pictures I was holding.

"This is something my agency developed strictly for musicians. Some are flat photos, some are still holos, other are repros of old paintings. You take a good look at them, and tell me what you hear. Are you more comfortable lying down or sitting up?"

"Lying down. I'll get some mats out of the storeroom."

"Just one mat. I'll sit up, if that's all right with you."

I pushed the chair at the synthesizer over while he fetched a mat and went about molding into a contour for himself.

He almost froze on the first picture, but we'd built up too much momentum and it carried him into the exercise whether he liked it or not. But he took his time with the holo of a man and a woman in the middle of a glitzy blowout. The woman was Lindbloom, several years younger, before she'd started dyeing her skin. Even in plain flesh-tone, she was striking, which may have contributed to his stalling. People liked to stare at Lindbloom.

"A lot of laughter and chatter around these two," he said at last. "An old Coor and Lam piece playing in the background—*Transcontinental Elopement*. The man's caught between nostalgia and looking ahead, mainly to possibilities with the woman. But she doesn't think in terms of past or future, it's all a big Now to her. When she gets far enough from one experience, it's like it happened to someone else. She's timeless and that's her strength. He isn't, and that's his weakness."

For someone who had been slow to begin, he was making a strong showing. I went on to the next picture, a low aerial view of some half-aboveground homes in Colorado, with Pike's Peak taking up the background.

"Wind," he said after a bit. "Rustling. The air is colder than usual for the season. No birds singing. There's a faraway machine noise; no one could identify it even if they could hear it. They're all dug in, hiding, and they don't make a sound."

He barely hesitated on the third picture, a repro of the Magritte of a man with an apple obscuring his face. "He's trying to talk but the fruit muffles him. All that comes out are these '*mmf-mmf*' sounds."

The Magritte was the real breaker; he went quickly through the other nine pictures. By the time he finished, he was agitated and antsy, ready either to get started or to beg off for the night. I pulled the connections out of the system and untangled the wires.

"Eyes," I said, kneeling down beside him. Obediently, he popped them into my cupped hand. I put the system connections at his empty eyelids and let them crawl in to engage the optic nerves. I had programmed a tonal exercise for him instead of the usual color or pattern-building. Judging from the way he sagged on the mat, I'd chosen well.

I took half a minute to examine his eyes. Brand new and well taken care of. I put them in the left-hand compartment of the solution jar, consciously choosing that side, breathed myself into near-trance, and then popped out my own eyes.

I had intended to let him feel my presence gradually to avoid contact shock, but he seemed to have been waiting for me. At the first taste of contact, he drew me in with a smoothness born of years of working mind-to-mind with someone else. I hadn't expected him to receive me so easily. Old responses live long, die hard, and frequently leave a troublesome corpse.

But that was normal next to what I found, or what I didn't find. There were no visuals—absolutely none. My mind translated the lack into the dark of eyelessness. The urge to visualize was almost overpowering but I managed to check it.

The tonal exercise was still running and that was my next surprise. Most people seem to hear bell-like sounds when you hook them into a tonal. Jord Coor's reaction was something completely new to me.

He heard seagulls. Very musical seagulls—their cries complemented and harmonized the way they never did in outside reality. It wasn't unpleasant, but in the sightless night of his perspective it was rather spooky. I prodded gently, thinking that perhaps he'd been waiting for a sign from me before he turned on the pictures.

Sea? I asked. Actually, I wasn't sure whether I'd said *sea* or *see*.

A secret sea, he answered, without disturbing the gulls. I caught undertones of surf, a whispering rhythm and the not-quite-voice of the wind fading in and out. A perfect sound-picture, waiting for someone to add sight.

Do you never visualize? I asked. Carefully.

It's the sound that matters. Or is it just pretty pictures you want, holo? The last word came out more like *hollow.*

It's a matter of what you want, I told him. The cries of the seagulls died away as the exercise came to an end. We let it go. His presence grew stronger, becoming a pressure in the darkness, filling all the space around my own self. New sounds began, all the pleasurable sounds he could remember, footsteps on a hard surface, people's voices humming, the sharp musical clang of metal on metal, whispers, whistles, whales. His mental ear had remixed them into a harmoniousness not present when he'd first heard them.

Some would say all this is music in itself, he said. *But it isn't. It needs translation. Interpretation.*

A tumble of conventional music drowned out the sounds. Shreds and snatches of various things, including old Coor and Lam compositions, passed through me, as though he was trying to find the frequency at which I'd vibrate.

I felt for his Emotional Index. He was in a sort of performance mode. I let him go on throwing music while I did a gradual spread, sliding around him and into his terrain. It was exceedingly strange without visuals, but not unpleasant. Texture began to mix with sound and I had a sudden, vivid physical impression of him standing with his eyes closed, listening. What he was listening for, I couldn't quite tell—the music within that would be sparked by the sounds without, or perhaps the elusive music of the unconscious spheres. I couldn't make out whether this was a memory or the image he held of himself in the act of composing. His mind was stew, everything melting into and flavoring everything else, much more so than I'd found in many of my other clients.

Stew is a wonderful thing, free of the overcompartmentalization and learned behavior that can (and does) cripple some artists. But stew could be too thick and formless, a mass in which ideas lost definition and coherence and ultimately dissolved, leaving behind only a hint of what they might have once been, just old seasonings boiled out and gone dead. Jord Coor had not yet achieved this state, much to my relief.

I kept coming across abrupt, intense concepts and ideas sticking up like barbs—barbs and bait combined. The temptation to supply the missing visual element was nearly overwhelming. Trying to move around the barbs rather than directly into them was impossible; I'd come to depend on visualization the same way I depended on my physical sight. I sank down deeper into his terrain, careful not to probe too hard, looking for some sign of suppression.

It was like sinking blindfolded into a sensory-stimulation tank. Very sensual man, this Jord Coor. The undertones said he'd just never been terribly taken by the visual experience. He was not an habitual admirer of sunsets or scenery, his earlier bit of showing me the Massachusetts countryside notwithstanding. Most of his concentration had always been on the auditory and, after that, the tactile.

He answered my question before I asked it. *Revien. He liked pictures. Always Revien. He supplied the pictures, if that's what you're looking for.*

I was still troubled. There should have been pictorial memories stashed about here and there, pictures of Revien's pictures, but I couldn't find them. Either Jord had buried them that deeply or—highly unlikely—Revien Lam had taken them with him, in a kind of mindwipe. (And if so, had the mindwipe been forcible, or submitted to? Or, even more disturbingly, had Jord forced them on his partner? Expulsion? It was too much to think about at the moment.)

Sinking deeper now. Not much effort needed, he was drawing me down in a movement that felt like an embrace. The sensations became more intense, taking on a sort of insistence. Sensory offering, all fragments wanting completion. I began to get that besieged feeling I always got when a client was trying too hard.

Easy, I told him.

Mild wave of surprise from him. *But it's always this way.*

You're coming and going in all directions. Do you have a focus?

His mind went immediately to Revien Lam. I felt it instead of seeing it, but the thought was unmistakable. A memory of what it had been to share his presence, intense but dreamlike, something that might have happened only in his own imagination. And now a sensation of stretching out, reaching across a distance that might have been the span of a table or the emptiness of a universe, reaching for con

fall

fall

falling plummeting down a long tunnel and nothing nothing nothing

tact.

In the distortion of mind time, it was over before it had begun. I might have lost consciousness. It seemed that way. I found myself at rest far above the terrain, in the upper, superficial layers of his sense-memory. His energy level was markedly diminished.

Always, he said. *Always like that. Without him.*

I reached down into him again but his mind was drifting now. It was like pushing into layer after layer of silk streamers floating in midair, and about as substantial. I could receive no clear impression of anything except fatigue. Quitting time.

Just before I withdrew, it came to me, a wisp from a wisp, an actual visual that lasted for half a thought-beat, if that long.

Revien Lam, at last, of course. With a wire winding out from one eyelid like the trail of a dark tear.

Jord Coor was more than happy to have me leave him alone. I wheeled my equipment down to the big, emptyish guest room (taking the ramps instead of that box of an elevator) and plugged into the long-term eidetic fixer. Reviewing a session so quickly—or, rather, reliving it—wasn't always the wisest thing to do in terms of wear and tear on the psyche, but I had to study this one.

It didn't take long for hindsight to kick in and show me what had been wrong with the whole session in the first place.

He had drawn me in so quickly on first contact that I hadn't consciously noticed—there had been no personality-identity barriers to pass through, not even so much as a mild mental fence.

Why hadn't I noticed, I wondered. Had I just assumed they'd been there the way they were in every other mind?

My professional reflexes spoke up, maddeningly in the voice of Nelson Nelson.

Think about it, Allie. Those barriers would have proved an inconvenience to him and Lam. My brain helpfully provided the image of his office, picturing him in working recline behind his desk. I began to get a psychosomatic itch. Gold lamé *And maybe that's your key, Deadpan. Help him build up his barriers again— help him by helping him resist your help.*

I'd never gone mind-to-mind with the old fox so it was rather unsettling to find I'd given him a position in my mind as a persona for self-dialog. But then, there was no one else. No one else appropriate, anyway.

Which just goes to show you, he/I went on, *that the most affecting contact isn't always mind-to-mind. Is it, kid?*

I disengaged in a hurry, itching to get away from him.

I let a day go by before the next session, hoping the breathing space would allow us both to regroup. But when we hooked in again, it was more of the same, more stew, more chaos, that long reach toward something followed by the fall and the weightless, drifty mind-state of exhausted semiconsciousness, or quasiconsciousness, or something.

"The blank spot," Jord said after we unhooked. He was lying on the mat in the studio, blinking at the ceiling. "The place where I used to compose. Nothing there any more."

I had no intention of accepting that, but after three more sessions, I began to think I was licked. It was astounding just how little information I was getting from him. Most people's minds teem with associations, memories, and all the rest of the mental furniture that accrues during a lifetime. Stew notwithstanding, his seemed to be all put away or suppressed—I could receive only the briefest of impressions concerning episodes in his past that didn't involve Revien Lam. Did he really expect me to believe that for ten years there had been nothing in his life but composing with his partner?

In another few sessions, he might have convinced us both. Except that would have meant Big Obsession and there was none of that unmistakable, dangerous flavor in his mind.

Still, the only visual I could get from him was that same image of Revien Lam. Sometimes it was as static as the flat pictures I had showed him. Other times it was alive, the movements barely discernible, dreamlike but still there.

It was the lone visual that gave me the idea. Nelson Nelson would have advised against it, and five days before, I wouldn't have considered it myself. But we were falling into a feedback loop. If I could not shift him away from the idea of Revien Lam as a missing part of himself, then perhaps Lam—the Lam in his mind—could serve to trigger new reactions.

"Just one eye this time," I said, when we began the fifth session.

He looked up at me from the mat. That studied expressionlessness left his face like a mask melting away, leaving behind naked panic.

"Why?"

"It could be helpful to use a method you're accustomed to."

He almost flinched from the wire I held out to him; for a moment, I thought he would refuse. Then he took the connection, removed his left eye himself, and handed it to me.

I'd known doing a variation on the eye trick with him would result in a very different type of session, but even so, I wasn't prepared for the bizarreness of it. It was something like being awake and asleep at the same time, only much more so. More like being only partially in existence. I had to adjust my concentration radically and I wasn't sure that I hadn't asked too much of my mind. I might not have managed at all if it hadn't been for Jord Coor himself.

He fell easily into our configuration, his mind coming alive—*really* coming alive. He had no problem at all with the mix of textures. Mind and outer reality spilled over into each other for him, each one feeding the other. Now he could generate visuals, picking up little bits from his right eye. I saw myself as he saw me, a sort of professional mechanism sitting in a chair, steady, composed. The visual of Revien Lam oozed over into outer reality and shimmered in and out of being around me, a cross between a hallucination and a ghost. Sometimes it faded out on its own; sometimes Coor blotted it out. But the feel of him was always there, or rather, the feel that was the lack of him.

There was never any point of stability or equilibrium; he teetered back and forth between perceiving first the outside world and then the inside of his mind as dominant. The remaining eye remmed occasionally with dreams cannibalized both from actual vision and the mind. A keyboard that seemed to be a hybrid of the piano and the synthesizer spread out before us, a hallucinatory horizon. The keys sank as ghost hands danced on them. I couldn't tell whose hands they were; the music itself was inaudible.

Something new? I asked.

You can't hear it either? The right eye fixed on me

momentarily. *I think it might be something Revien and I were working on before he . . . went.*

Can you turn up the volume?

But the keyboard was already gone. There was a sensation of movement forward, acceleration, and then outside reality paled. An image of Jord Coor appeared with his back to me, walking away.

Jord?

He paused and turned toward me slightly.

Where are we going?

The corner of his mouth twitched so realistically I almost forgot I was seeing a mental image. Very briefly, I had a glimpse of his face in the outer world, duplicating the movement.

Jord?

He began walking again. I traveled along in his wake, undecided as to whether I wanted to catch up with him. He kept glancing over his shoulder at me, always the left shoulder, his eye hard and too bright. We were moving through a landscape that I couldn't quite make out, except that it felt bleak and barren, a wasteland or badland, an old dream.

Eventually, I felt us descending. The landscape darkened and rose up canyonlike. No stew here; everything was locked away behind rock. Nothing grew here. You could wander around in it for the rest of your life with empty hands.

The landscape leveled off after a while and I could discern a lighter area ahead. The end of the wasteland, I thought. So basic and literal. I should have expected it in this man.

And then Jord himself was gone—or at least, his mental image of himself was missing, though a good portion of his concentration remained, urging me forward wordlessly. I didn't like the feel of it, but I went. There was no firm reason to pull back and I was curious. The undertones barely registered, as though he had managed to vanish and remain at the same time.

Abruptly, I was standing at the edge of an abyss. I waited. There was light coming up from somewhere.

Jord?

Far away, I caught a slight movement. Jord Coor and I faced each other across the chasm. His head was a blur. I looked around, trying to find something to cross the gap with.

Then the light grew brighter and I saw he was walking toward me on empty air.

No, not air; a bridge that formed itself under him with each step. Lunatic bridge.

Halfway across, he stopped. There was a long, frozen moment when nothing happened and it seemed as though nothing would. I leaned forward and saw him clearly for the first time.

The right side of his body was blank.

With no more thought than anyone would have given to inhaling, he yanked me to him.

It would have taken a lot more magnetism than he had to eat me alive but it was still a bumpy experience. Rather than pull back against him, I rushed down, through, and out the other side. His realized half brushed me like tentacles, not quick enough to latch on and incorporate me. A halfhearted disappointment followed in cold waves as I kept moving, going back up the wire to break the link.

"I *am* sorry," he said, for the fourth or fifth time.

"It's all right," I told him while I puttered around with the system. I still felt off-balance, with a psychosomatic brownout in my right eye. So much for the eye trick. But it hadn't really been such a close call; subconsciously, I'd probably been prepared for an attempt at absorption. Still, it's rattling to have someone try to merge with you, change you into part of them, even if you have no affinity for it. "You didn't hurt me."

Jord fisted his left eye in a childlike way. "I knew you weren't Revien, I really did. I knew it the whole time but I was going to take you anyhow." He drew his legs up and rested his elbows on his knees. "I guess I've been incomplete for so long, I'll take anyone." No more of that careful expressionlessness now; all masks were off for good. I'd seen that look before, on people who had just realized how alone they really were in their own heads.

And in people who had discovered their lives weren't enough.

"He's got it, you know," he said. "Revien. He's got the other half of me. He *is* the other half of me now."

We do indeed adore our delusions, I thought as I tested the connection he used. Still good. I didn't tell him he was mistaken. I could have talked at him for the rest of the day and most of the night and maybe have made him admit he might possibly be wrong, that he'd only atrophied and he really was complete, just unused to working alone. And the next time we hooked in, it would be the same thing all over again. I was going to have to get him to demonstrate things to himself.

But the only way I could do that was to get a different perspective on him and the old partnership. And that was something only Revien Lam could give me.

Nelson Nelson was grumpy about it. Or perhaps he was just irritated at having to interrupt his viewing of the Bolshoi to take my call. It amazed me that anyone could watch *Swan Lake* and *Coppélia* so often without tiring. Seeing him through his ceiling holo was unsettling; it felt like I was going to drop down on him and mash him into his itchy gold lamé.

"Sure, I can find Revien Lam for you. It'll take a little while, so you might want to use that time to work with your client a little more."

"NN, the man tried to *eat* me. He's close to pathological in his insistence that Revien Lam either has half of his ability or *is* half of his ability. I've got to feel it from Lam's point of view."

"Feel *what*?"

"The partnership. As it was. All I can get from Coor is an absence of something and he tried to fill the absence with me. Granted, it wasn't the strongest effort in the world—I'd probably be hospitalized or something if it had been—but he still tried."

"And you really think Revien Lam can help you, even indirectly?"

"It's more information than I can get from Coor and that's *got* to be helpful."

NN actually harrumphed. "Seems to me any pathosfinder worth her neurons ought to be able to delve someone skillfully enough to get all the information she needs. Or is it that you believe him?"

Apparently no one had ever tried to eat NN. Well, who would have wanted to actually *be* that old fox anyway? "Any pathosfinder worth her neurons also knows when to back off from her client and find her data elsewhere," I said evenly. "My man's on the defensive. The only way I can reach him effectively is to show him I've got the information he's hiding from himself. And the only way I can get it is from Revien Lam."

We stared at each other through our respective screens. To be fair, I think I had the upper hand, literally—it's hard to stare someone down when you're lying flat on your back.

"I'll have Lam's location for you in a couple of hours. But I still think you're wrong. And what are you going to tell Coor?"

"I'll think of something. The truth is always good." I switched off before he could object.

Actually, I had no intention of telling Coor the truth, or at least not the whole truth. A lie would have been pointless and cruel, since he'd have felt Lam's impression when we hooked in again. I could hide plenty from him, but he knew what Lam's mind felt like firsthand.

I ended up telling him I was giving us both a couple days' thinking space. There was a certain amount of truth in that. He surprised me by being disappointed and apprehensive rather than relieved. I'd thought he would have appreciated the respite.

It wasn't until I was on my way to upstate New York that I realized he'd just gotten used to having me around. Sometimes it didn't do a lonely person any good to keep him company. Another entry to the list of things I should have known.

That Revien Lam had chosen to alight in an area not terribly far from his ex-collaborator wasn't so surprising. It would figure that they'd prefer similar geographical areas, in spite of Lam's continuing struggle for differentiation. But where Jord Coor was living completely alone in an underground enclosure, Lam had opted for the Park.

I'd heard of the Park, though I'd never been there before. It was a sort of continuously running circus/ picnic/freakshow/camp for those who didn't want the party to end. The Park population, which varied from week to week, roamed freely over a few hundred acres of weather-shielded countryside, eating, sleeping, and playing as the spirit moved them. There were no clocks, no calendars, few rules. Violence was punishable by immediate, permanent expulsion, but other than that, the Park people did as they pleased. It was probably the best way to lose all touch with reality short of buying a psychosis.

A lot of people tried to lose themselves in the Park for just that reason. Some could and some couldn't; the rest, the hard-core Park People, would have been lost anywhere. The Park just kept them from cluttering up the rest of the world.

I wondered what Revien Lam's motivation had been for signing himself into the land of silk and funny. Whatever it was, I was willing to bet it had something to do with wanting superficial contact with lots of people. Ten years of extreme intimacy was the sort of thing that could give a person a real appreciation for the superficial.

My first glimpse of the Park was shortly before sunset from the air, in the back seat of a flyer while the pilot snored behind the stick. Tents and pavilions dotted the rolling green landscape while people streamed among them like currents of confetti. The Park wasn't an easy place to find someone, but NN's office had contacted a guide for me, to help me find Revien Lam. I wondered how I was supposed to find the guide.

The pilot snored through the landing, leaving me to unload my own equipment at the front gates of the Park. People accumulated along the flimsy fence to watch me, drifting over like colorful bits of cloth blown by an idle wind. It was an amazingly quiet audience—no chatter, no laughter, hardly a whisper. Maybe, I thought, they'd all just gotten up. Or had yet to go to bed. Or sleep, anyway. The faces, mostly dyed or polished or both, weren't solemn. A few of them looked apprehensive, some even envious (of what, I wondered). Most of them had what I could already identify as a "Park Look," as distinct as the sound of a regional accent in a voice. Had Revien Lam traded in his likeness to Jord Coor for a facial uniform worn by a multitude?

I wheeled my equipment up to an ornate little kiosk at the entrance. There was no one inside, no bell to ring for service, and no indication that I should either wait for someone to take charge of me or just go in by myself.

I looked left and right at my audience lining the fence. They stared back, unmoved. I thought of cows. Finally, a man with a stiff fringe of apple-red hair detached himself from the group on my right and ambled over. He almost stopped, his gold starburst eyes looking me and my equipment over critically. Somehow, I had failed to measure up as anything sufficiently interesting to make him stop.

"Excuse me," I called after him.

He turned in slow motion without actually ceasing to wander away.

"How do I go about finding someone in here?"

His expression said I was sixteen different kinds of fool. "You look around." He moved into a loose gaggle of men and women on their way to a tall green tent.

No one else along the fence showed any inclination to come forward and offer any hints, suggestions, or hellos. I moved my equipment further inside the entrance, trying not to feel overly conspicuous. A laughing group of people playing some kind of game with big balloons materialized and surrounded me, allowing me to be part of their playing field briefly before they gamboled away, shedding one of the balloons. It bounced gently at my feet and I picked it up.

"That was an invitation," said a female voice behind me. I turned around.

You see it all, eventually; all the ways people play with their bodies. Dye-jobs, bleach-jobs, certain kinds of transplants, alterations that border on mutilation. You see people displaying just about anything of themselves, but this was something that could have been an image straight out of someone's troubled head, come down the wires of a mindplay system and into outer reality to be made flesh. Sort of flesh.

She let me stare at her. From a distance, I might have thought she was wearing a very close-fitting helmet that ended a few inches above her eyebrows, with her long hair hanging out from underneath. But up close, it was too easy to see her skull was made of glass.

Well, not real glass, of course, but something transparent. It was nauseating and fascinating all at once. There are certain kinds of minds a pathosfinder should refuse to enter; I was fairly sure this was one of them.

"I was a pathosfinder once," she said.

Surprise number two. "You must be my guide." It would be hard not to choke NN for this when I saw him again.

"I'd have known you were a pathosfinder anyway. Just by that look on your face. All pathosfinders get that look. Even the ones named Deadpan Allie."

"What look is that?"

"Like you're trying to see through solid objects." She caressed her transparent skull with her fingers. "Watch out. This is what you're headed for." Her young-old face showed a peculiar mix of remembrance and mild aversion. "It's what you're really after, you know. Letting everyone dip into your head, dipping into everyone else's. What makes you think anyone'll have need or desire for you in here?"

"I thought my office explained."

"They did."

I could have sworn her brain changed color, flushed. "Then, you do know where I can find Revien Lam."

"In a way. Once we get to him, you'll have to figure out how to find him on your own."

I nodded, thinking she must have been a pretty lousy pathosfinder.

Her lips stretched in a hard smile. "Only because of the telepathy. Mindplaying activated it, since you didn't ask." She patted her skull again delicately, the way other people smoothed their hair. "I'm used to receiving thoughts. It's made me a different person. Many different people." Her right lobe swelled slightly. "Do you know how many different people you are? Or have you stopped counting?" She frowned. "Well. Never mind. I'll take you to Revien Lam. He's one of the tent people. It's a long walk."

An hour later, I knew for certain she hadn't been gassing about that. I plodded after her, struggling with my system. You want to feel really awkward, push eight components of a supposedly portable mindplay system on a dolly through a free-form gathering like the Park, where the most anyone has in the way of encumbrance is a toy or something to eat. I took to reading Emotional Indices at random, including some of the balloonatics, who reappeared twice more to make an invitation.

There were a lot of anxious people in the Park, just from what I could tell by sight. It was catching; I could feel it beginning to chew at me around the edges. Glass-Skull (I realized belatedly she'd never told me her name) seemed unaffected by it, for all of her telepathy. She marched through groups lounging on the grass or milling around aimlessly or spilling in and out of the carnival-colored tents which apparently dispensed food, toys, and other kinds of amusements, just for the asking. The daily charge for living in the Park had to be fairly high. You just never think there are that many rich people in the world.

My guide didn't slow down until we reached the shore of a small lake in the center of a lightly wooded area. On the other side, I saw a collection of the standard multicolored tents with the standard multicolored people passing in and out of them in the eternal quest for diversion. Glass-Skull gazed at them across the quiet water while I shifted from one tired foot to the other.

"Would you like me to tell you what you're thinking?" she asked without looking at me.

I shrugged.

She laughed and led me along a dirt path around the pond, pausing again at the outskirts of the tent grouping.

"Which one is he in?" I asked, since she didn't seem disposed to go any farther.

"The largest one," she said, pointing to a red tent trimmed with gold braid and tassels. "It's a sort of dormitory, so you won't have any privacy. Except, of course, in your own mind. A luxury some of us wouldn't be able to stand even if we were capable of having it." She put her hand on my arm as I was about to wheel my equipment forward. The contact was electric; I felt my mind jump in response. Being touched by a telepath is always a jolt.

"You can go on by yourself." She let go and stepped back, and I was relieved to have her pressure fade from my brain.

The tent wasn't exactly crowded but there was an aroma of healthy bodies, or a healthy aroma of bodies, that made the air heavy and close. It reminded me less of a dormitory than it did of some kind of ward that had been abandoned by its keepers. I left my equipment just inside the entrance and took a walk around, stepping over the people strewn about. Two men and a woman invited me to join what seemed to be a complicated game of marbles—played, I noticed undelightedly, with biogem eyes—and burst into high laughter when I declined. A baby-faced woman with wiry metallic hair and silver eyes pressed an orange into my hand. I dropped it surreptitiously on my other side and maneuvered between a man who was tattooing something upside-down on his naked chest and the woman who was dictating it to him.

I knew Lam immediately. His natural skin tone was just beginning to come back from the bleaching but his flesh still looked tight and stretched, too delicate for exposure to direct sunlight. He was lying on a scatter of pillows as though he'd been tossed there, head thrown back and eyes closed. I stood over him awkwardly.

"Revien Lam?" I had to say his name twice before he raised his head slowly and looked at me.

My first thought was that he'd had a stroke. The two sides of his face seemed to have little to do with each other. Each eye perceived me independently, traveling over my face in separate patterns. Then he covered his

right eye and said, "Do you know me?" The words came
out with an effort—*Do. You. Know. Me.*

"Not exactly. I know Jord Coor."

"Ah." He covered his left eye, surveyed me briefly
with the right again, and went back to looking at me with
his left. I knew, then. I moved up to crouch at his left
side and put my lips close to his ear.

"When did you have it cut?"

"*Cut.*" His mouth worked silently. I'd have to be more
specific.

"When did you have your corpus callosum severed?"

"Cut. *Cut.* Three months after Jord cut. After we cut.
Cut ourselves apart." The words came a little more
quickly now, as though he were getting back into the
practice of speaking out loud. His head turned and the
sapphire eye glittered at me. "You are—?"

"I'm a pathosfinder working for Jord Coor."

He turned his head all the way toward me and let his
right eye have a look. "Music," he said, and hummed a
little.

"You've had your visual fields rechanneled, too,
haven't you?"

He went back to looking with the left eye alone.
"Completely divided. Right up the middle. Complete
sep. Aration. Two brains from one. What the hell, it's
company."

"Company?"

"Company. Not so lonely in here with the two halves.
See, completely divided, *but.* One final cord. One *spinal*
cord, still. I can feel each other."

We're schizophrenic and so are we, as Jerry Wirerammer had said once, inaccurate but witty. "Is there
someplace we can go to talk?"

He waved one hand clumsily. "I live here. Nobody
cares."

"I'd like to delve you. If you'd give permission."

"Permission." He nodded. "But still can't go outside.
Skin. Even after dark. Wind hurts sometimes. But
really, nobody cares in here."

If those were my choices, those were my choices.
"Would you be willing to hook in with me?"

He frowned and went to his right eye. "Repeat?"

He must have been one of those people whose verbal and comprehension skills were spread over both hemispheres like birdshot. "Would you be willing to hook into my system with me—" I pointed to it over by the tent entrance, "meet me mind-to-mind?"

Back to the left eye. "Which mind did you want to meet?"

"Either. Both, if possible."

He gave me a funny little smile, a composite smile from two faces. "Do our best. Haven't been delved since the split, without Jord, eye to eye. To eye."

As it were. I went to get my system.

It must have been about the strangest place I'd ever set up, but nobody, including Revien Lam, paid much attention to me while I went about my business. He went back to daydreaming or dozing or whatever it was he did with his two hemispheres. As soon as I was ready to go, however, I found myself with a sudden dilemma. Did I hook in with him one eye at a time or both together? I considered asking him and then decided not to. Depending on which hemisphere took the question, the answer might be different. I went for the left eye first, removing it for him and plugging him into the same tonal exercise I'd used on Coor.

I put my hands up to my own eyes and paused. Now, what about me? Should I use both eyes or just one—and if only one, *which* one? I ended up removing both. Since I had no idea of what I was going to find in there, it was probably best to go at it with all my concentration.

The tones translated to this half of his brain as his own voice singing syllables—*la, la, la, da, da, da*. The visualization was weak and fuzzy but I could make out his image of himself as a creature with a big head and a negligible body. The head was stretched and distorted at the top, too wide, forcing the eyes to look in two different directions. The left eye was bigger than the right.

The syllables suddenly became words. *It got so lonely,* he sang. *I never knew it could be that lonely.* A peculiar thing. *The nature of attachment and disconnection.* The top of his head stretched wider. *One and one equal one, sooner or later. Couldn't let that happen, we knew it. Merge into one person and we'd never sort him from me. But so* lonely. *Now I feel the ghost of his essence—or the essence of his ghost.*

I cast around some but I couldn't feel it in all the fuzziness.

Other side, he said.

I unplugged just long enough to switch the connection to his right eye and give that side a minute with the tonal. Then I went back down the wires.

It really was like entering a different mind. The personality barrier here was thicker than the one I'd gone through when he'd been hooked in through his left eye.

The moment I pushed through, I heard them— seagulls. The same ones Jord Coor had had, singing the tones. I lost my equilibrium and found myself sprawled belly-down on sand, the damp grains rough against me. The sunlight was nearly blinding. A very well-realized wave grazed my fingers.

Revien?

The tonal faded away and the beach went with it. I pulled myself together just as the abyss formed. Lam had me floating disembodied over it, like a dream observer.

Whose abyss is this? I asked the empty air.

Ours, came the answer from below me.

The image was beyond absurdist, impossible. A chasm could not have just one side or a bridge that connected that side with itself. My inner eyes crossed, uncrossed, crossed again; the visual steadied down, translating into a Möbius strip. A composite of Coor and Lam was standing on it.

This is where I live now, the composite said, touching Coor's dark hair on the left side and pressing Lam's cheek on the right. *Hidden away like the bastard child I am. I'm even still composing music, but he can't get at it.* Just beyond the composite, a pale image of Revien Lam shimmered in and out of existence; Lam's awareness leaking through from the other side via the spinal cord (final cord).

Why can't he get at the music? I asked.

Other side. Have to send it to the other side for it to come out.

But if Coor's composing ability is really here, you should be able to express music using this side alone.

Not outwardly. The ability to express is not what he left here. Only the ability to compose.

And your own ability to compose? Is that here, too? There was no answer. *Lam's ability,* I clarified.

Yes. You can see that, can't you?

Then you're not two opposite halves rejoined. You're the same side, superimposed. You're congruent, not complemented.

The composite wavered. *Coor is the complement to Lam. The congruence is complement.*

No, I said reasonably, *if you were hooked in through opposite eyes—*

I stopped. I'd forgotten that in a normal, undivided brain, the optic nerves fed equally into both hemispheres, not right into right and left into left, the way they did in Lam's mutilated organ. The notion that maybe Coor wasn't deluded about Lam having a portion of himself crept up on me, and I wondered belatedly what would have happened if I'd hooked into Coor through his right eye rather than his composing eye.

I was moving forward to examine the composite more closely when the visual cracked like a whip. For something like an eternity or a thought-beat, everything was jumbled and whirling. Then it all came back into ultra-sharp focus and I was standing on the edge of the abyss, where I'd been in Jord Coor's mind. No more Möbius strip—there was a real bridge across the chasm with three figures on it: the composite, Revien Lam, and Jord Coor. The *real* Jord Coor, blank on the right side, not a delusory presence. He was right there with us, in the Park, in the tent, in Revien Lam's mind.

Why hadn't it occurred to me that he would follow me, that he would suspect what I'd been up to? That he might even have been hoping I'd do it, or even pushed me into it, just to sneak up on both of us mind-to-mind?

Withdrawal and disconnection would take too long. I rushed toward them but it was already happening. They each had hold of the composite and were pulling at it, stretching it like heat-softened rubber. The whole visual shuddered and bucked, pushing me back.

This is between us! Jord said hostilely, and I wasn't sure whom he was talking to.

You have no right! Lam hurled repulsion at him and somehow managed to draw him closer. *Mine now! Mine!*

You stole it!

You forced me to take it! You gave it up willingly!

I strained toward the bridge and they almost merged in their joint effort to knock me away. I backed off quickly.

You're part of me now, whether you wanted it or not, whether I wanted it or not! Lam said.

I have a right to be whole!

The composite between them was becoming a shapeless blob.

You refused to be whole, you gave away, said Lam.

Not gave. You just couldn't give back. You sucked it all without giving in return!

You wanted to be part of me, the better to love yourself!

Then, that's how it is, Jord said. *We've both been after the same thing all along—you want me and I want me.*

The composite suddenly swelled and enveloped both of them. A million images spewed from the bridge, scenes from their respective pasts, now juxtaposed, double exposures. I pulled back even further. There was just one figure on the bridge now; it kept shimmering and changing. Sometimes it was all Coor, then all Lam, then various mixtures of the two, Lam dominant, Coor dominant, both equal. Shimmer. Melt. Change.

I withdrew, put my eyes back in, and without looking at the two limp bodies still hooked into my system, went outside and vomited into the grass.

* * *

"I did warn you," Glass-Skull said. She wiped my face with something damp. "How many different people are you?"

I looked up at her, still trying to pull myself together enough to call NN and ask him if this meant my license had just been voided.

She smiled. "Go ahead. Think about it. Everything you've done. The institute. The pool. A little bit of one mind here, a little of another there."

McFloy on the beach. McFloy doing the eye trick.

"It's more than being modified," Glass-Skull said. "You're transformed. You're polluted, stained, dyed, altered. And you will never be the same." She rubbed her head gently. I swear I saw her brain writhe in its transparent case.

I leaned forward and vomited again.

ALERTED SNAKES OF
CONSEQUENCE

I had no memory of being taken from the Park. My mind spliced outer reality to my very mental life without segue, just like a scene-change. Freeze on our heroine; ten years later, we pick up her story.

But it wasn't ten years, not that I knew the difference at the time. I didn't know anything at all, outer, inner, or in between. Eventually, or something, I found myself looking at a familiar face.

Are you lucid yet?

Forget it, I told Jascha. *Lucid dreaming, lucid living— forget it, just forget all of it.*

I was sitting on the techno-bed in his office, watching the sun come up over the bay. He was standing near the lavabo, looking at a monitor.

Every time you think you're doing it, something else comes up on you and changes everything. It's like old Glass-Skull said. You get changed, altered. Polluted. That's a good word, polluted. Jerry Wirerammer, now there was an idea. He was one of the polluters as well as a pollutee, but he was more of a polluter. Not like me. And he never got me. But you did. Every time you fed my dreams, Jascha, you fed me a little of yourself. I can prove it.

He tilted his gilded head to the side. Jascha was the only person I knew who could really wear gilt without looking overdressed and overpriced.

I can prove it because you're in here. I think, therefore you are. You think, therefore I am.

Something moved on the bed; a Snake rose up to attention like a cobra, but it wasn't a cobra.

Alerted Snake of Consequence. I said it right this time, didn't I, Pyotr Frankis? I looked over at him, sitting behind his desk, nodding at me with a funny little smile. *But where are the rest of them? All the Alerted*

Snakes Of Consequence, they should all be here now. It's time. Good thing we're not Freudians, isn't it?

The Snake moved a little closer without having moved. Or maybe it was my perspective that had shifted. *Deadpan Allie*, the Snake said. *But not terribly, I'd say.* The Snake bore a resemblance to Paolo Segretti. *Not terribly deadpan right now.*

It's my state of existence, I'll take a break if I want to. I looked down over the right side of the bed. There was a Snake on the floor next to the futon, not coiled but in a Snakey impression of a person lying on his side resting on one elbow with one knee drawn up. They were talented, these Snakes, but then, they'd have to be.

You're taking all this so hard, said the Snake. *What's the problem? What's the real problem?*

The real problem, I began emphatically, *the real problem is* . . .

Some kind of immense time went by, something long enough for dinosaurs to live and die in. The Pearl Necklace went by with it, the pearls passing like compartments on a nonstop northbound tube.

We've already covered that, Jascha said reasonably. *You're the accumulation of everything you've done. No problem there.*

No, now wait a minute here, I said.

Where?

Here, dammit, here!

Oh, you mean here.

I was looking around my old efficiency at J. Walter. The LadyBugs were on the dataline, looking vibrant and identical. Except they also looked a little like Snakes, too. *We're just fighting for our right to be different by being identical*, said the one on the right. *What are you fighting for?* asked the one on the left.

I'm fighting for my right to be not interfered with.

The LadyBugs were replaced on the screen with the Twins, Dolby and Dolan, Tweedledoo and Tweedledah. Tweedledoodah. *Aren't you compatible with yourself?*

Depends on who you ask, hey, Allie? said Pyotr Frankis, standing next to me.

Well, don't ask me, I said. The Twins gave way to Jerry Wirerammer.

Heya, Allie.

I turned away from the dataline and found myself facing the desert where Pyotr Frankis and I had walked together after I'd had Kitta Wren dry-cleaned out of me. *That was the turning point,* I said. *Kitta Wren. Up until her, I wasn't having any trouble. The punchy holographer, the Dancing Barbanos, the performance artist—none of them got to me. Got into me, I mean.*

No?

The Dancing Barbanos were performing an airy dance just above the horizon like a mirage. It seemed to be a Virginia reel in demishawn.

Not the way she did.

But it's gone. Dry-cleaned out, said Jascha.

But he isn't.

Why can't you just say your love for him isn't? Why can't you just admit that and be done with it?

Because he did the eye trick. It was the eye trick, not love.

A phantom beach, ghost waves moving over the dry desert sand. *I love your life, Allie. I love you.* The beach was gone; all the Snakes were lined up in front of me like limber sticks.

Alerted Snakes Of Consequence, one of them said.

You've got to watch out for us, said another.

When you love somebody—

Don't, I said.

Why not? It isn't trivial.

You bet it's not. Because that's right where he is. I locked it up in the cathedral, and if you say it, it gets out, and if it gets out, he gets out, and I can't have that. They're not supposed to call me Deadpan Allie for nothing.

Just like that, I was standing in front of the cathedral. The carving on the front door was a portrait of Fandango. *You know what a mindplayer is without a personal life?* she said. The portrait melted and changed into Jerry Wirerammer. *How about a personal life with no mindplayer?*

And then I was inside, leaning against the door. Pyotr Frankis waved to me from an open panel at the bottom of one of the stained-glass windows. The window design showed a woman lying on a futon looking at a row of pills and spansules and other things. The window next to it was a depiction of the same woman with the top half of her head covered by a madcap, as a man with a goofy smile looked on. The bottom panel popped open and Paolo Segretti's round face beamed at me. *There's only room for you in here*, he said.

That's what you think, I told him. *The rules change when they change and everything is true unless it isn't.*

Truth and information are not the same thing, said my great-grandmother's portrait.

I looked at the table below the portrait. The eye struck sparks of light like small fireworks. If it gets out, he gets out—

But he'd gotten out once. After I'd dry-cleaned out the last of Kitta Wren, when I'd been in the desert with Pyotr Frankis. Not just part of myself, somebody else. The entity McFloy, along for the ride because his own life hadn't been enough. All he'd been interested in was my mind.

If you try to cast it out, you'll end up crippling yourself.

All right, then, so I don't cast it out. I lock it up for good. Except once in a while, it gets out by itself. *He* gets out by *himself*.

I love your life, Allie. I love you.

So who asked him to? He'd come to me with the eye, I hadn't gone looking for him.

What's so bad about that? asked the Snake, tracing the pattern of the meditation mandala on the floor in front of me. *Maybe it's better to be half of something wonderful than a whole nothing at all.*

Half or nothing shouldn't be the only choices! It wasn't fair! They had a chance to live apart, to learn to be separate again but he followed me, Coor followed me to the Park and he barged in and Lam didn't have a chance after that . . .

Jascha shook his head. *Then, it fits their configuration*

to be one instead of two. For shame, Allie. Is that why you wanted them to be apart? Were you pathosfinding them in terms of yourself? That's not very deadpan. That's not deadpan at all.

For a moment, I reeled with uncertainty and the whole cathedral swayed with me. Then I steadied. *No. I wasn't imposing myself on them. But I wanted to learn how to separate myself from him.*

Jascha picked the eye up and looked at it. *But it's part of you. How can you separate yourself from yourself?* And then, before I could think to stop him, he raised his hand and hurled the eye at me.

I fled, through the countryside I'd first come to with Segretti, through the big room where I'd sat with Pyotr Frankis, past the river where we'd walked, past the bench where McFloy had drowned himself, into the desert again where undecipherable green glass symbols were burned into the sand. The Snakes paced me, wriggling along faster than snakes should have been able to travel.

Are you going to use it? asked one of the Snakes.

It's not supposed to be possible, for someone else to be resident in your mind, I said as I ran. *Not for real.*

Real? In which reality did you mean?

This one. That one. Whatever one we may find ourselves in. I was beginning to tire but I kept slogging through the sand, not daring to look over my shoulder. *The state of my existence—*

It's your state of existence, the Snake said, *but it's my reality. And that's the truth.*

Truth and information are not the same thing! I said. *And neither are reality and state of existence!*

XXXXXXXXXXXXXXXXXXXXXXXXXXXXXXXX.

Green fireworks burst out over the sky. *Brava!* Pyotr Frankis from somewhere. *Olé! Revelation is beautiful, isn't it?*

My energy gave out. I fell to my knees in the sand. The green glass symbols were gone. Pyotr Frankis smiled down benignly from where he floated in the sky. *Do you see now?* he asked. *Do you see that even thoug'. you alter yourself, you alter as yourself?*

In my own way.

Who else's way could it be?

Choose: Half of something wonderful or a whole nothing at all.

Choose: A whole self, or just an accumulation of elements that soon wouldn't be more than the sum of their parts. Madness. Fragmentation. Jerry Wirerammer.

They came in a series of flashes, a thought-beat long and an eternity, framed by the graceful snakes: Marty and Sudella (she was applauding with her eyes closed); Kitta Wren, dissolving; Gladney-that-was and Gladney-that-had-been, fusing. And finally, the figure on the Lunatic Bridge, shimmering and changing as it displayed all the aspects of Coor and Lam together.

Realities. States of existence. They can coincide, but they can never truly meet. Reality fluctuates, but existence *is*. Or is *not*.

I turned around to face the eye. McFloy was standing there.

Still here, Allie. Still with you.

Which one of us, McFloy? Which one of us is which?

He smiled. *Yes.*

I wasn't sure who actually said it, but it didn't matter. The holo I'd kept of Jerry Wirerammer appeared briefly. *It's a strange existence, but it works.* And then there were just the Snakes, dancing in the air, cutting curlicues and Möbius strips with their perfect bodies.

You will go down into darkness before you die—

Light, I thought.

—but you won't go alone.

"Light!" I yelled.

NN visited me every day in the hospital. He always showed up at mealtimes, relentlessly cheerful, applying the nutrient patch to my arm himself and chattering away about only the most innocuous things. He didn't bring up what had happened until I reached the point where I could keep down somewhat substantial fluids, but he was very brisk and all business when he did.

I was about to have my noontime frappé when he lit on the edge of my bed and said, "You know, in a way, it's always been true that we're made of all the lives we've ever touched. Even before mindplay."

I set the frappé aside. "Thanks. Let me write that down somewhere. Or are you recording?"

"Now really, Allie, what's so alarming about that?"

I glowered at him. "I'm trying to adjust. It isn't easy on the gut level out here. Do I look like a boardinghouse to you?"

Nelson Nelson picked up the frappé and stirred it with the straw. "I don't understand. The readings said you were so happy at the very end there."

"What 'very end' where?"

"When you called for light. Very unusual, you know, for someone hooked into reality affixing to speak aloud. Almost impossible, they say."

"*That* was a reality affixing?"

"Don't look at me. It was your reality." NN offered me the frappé. I pushed it away. "*Allie*. Think straight for a minute. As a personal favor to me. What's so terrible about your reality?"

"We're not discussing my reality, we're talking about my state of existence. I *said*, do I look like a boarding-house to you?"

"Well." NN shrugged. "You're as Allie as you ever were. Maybe not so Deadpan at the moment, but we'll make allowances for trauma, and that's all it is, you know.

You saw something bizarre happen to a couple of weak people and you were in mind-to-mind contact with them when it happened and it triggered your own unresolved dilemma."

"That's not supposed to happen! I've been dry-cleaned, I've been reality affixed, I've been trained—"

"*Please*. The mind is a very capricious thing! You've begun talking about it as though it were a suit of clothes. You think you can have that much control over it? *Please*. You want to dry-clean out the most Allie parts of yourself? Affix your reality so the neurons line up like little soldiers?" NN looked down at the frappé and then set it aside. "*Please*. You're making me *sick*."

I looked down at my hands, which had fallen folded together on the sheet. "They aren't weak."

"Pardon?"

"Coor and Lam. They aren't weak people. The LadyBugs are weak people but not Coor and Lam."

"Oh." NN was mollified. "Well, you would know better than I. You delved them. Coor and Lam, I mean. But, uh, I would like to know how you came to that conclusion."

"The LadyBugs wanted to *be* changed. Coor and Lam *did* change. By their own actions. They tried to deny it for a while and then they *were* weak. But when they came together in the system—" I shrugged. "It's not really so surprising that Coor followed me to Lam. Maybe he didn't even really have to follow me. Maybe Lam was drawing him all along, and when I finally went to him Coor had to follow. Maybe they'd have gotten together sooner or later. I just made it sooner than it might have been otherwise. They're not suing us, are they?"

NN shook his head.

"Didn't think they would. Coor and Lam might have, but not Coor-and-Lam—" I stopped. The thought burst on me all at once. Coor and Lam. *Cœur et l'Âme*. They hadn't started out that way, but the potential had been there all along. Some people resonate. Whether they know it or not. Whether they believe it or not.

I sighed. Was I going to have to adjust on every level of reality?

Maybe. NN was right. I had been pretty happy toward the end of the reality affixing—who had done it, anyway? I concentrated, feeling for a trace in my mind. The agency's system, of course; it was the only one I'd ever worked with that didn't have a facade personality. Good thing, too. I hadn't needed one more character running around in the system with me, confusing things. There was just room enough for me and McFloy, and the other pieces of our life adding up to more than the sum of our parts.

It's hard to adjust to that, said a silent voice in my head. Taking the next step.

I remembered that figure on the misnamed Lunatic Bridge, the third person that was Coor-and-Lam.

It's no wonder you didn't want to take it. But you did. You're not the Allie you were. But you *are* Allie just the same. So, all things considered, you have a right to post-mindplay depression. Or is that postpartum?

That's funny, I thought, I don't feel like a mother. Or a child. Why am I lying here in bed talking to myself like I'm somebody else?

I looked over at NN and felt myself grinning. He leaned forward and frowned at me slightly. "What are you grinning about?"

Nothing I couldn't live with. The state of my existence. And sometimes it was real. "Just something someone gave me once. A point of view, as it were."

"'As it were.' Deadpan goes hysterical, then cryptic. You probably wouldn't even tell me the truth as to whether you've been divorced or not."

I would call Jascha as soon as the old fox left me in peace. It was nothing we couldn't live with.

"I've never been divorced," I said. "Never in my life."

"There's a good Deadpan." NN picked up the frappé and shoved the straw between my lips just as the door opened and Jascha walked in, *looking* gilded and worried and real.

Sometimes things happen that make people *start* resonating with each other. Thank you, McFloy.

"Now, suck," NN said, "take it all in." And I did.

Special Offer
Buy a Bantam Book
for only 50¢.

Now you can have Bantam's catalog filled with hundreds of titles plus take advantage of our unique and exciting bonus book offer. A special offer which gives you the opportunity to purchase a Bantam book for only 50¢. Here's how!

By ordering any five books at the regular price per order, you can also choose any other single book listed (up to a $4.95 value) for just 50¢. Some restrictions do apply, but for further details why not send for Bantam's catalog of titles today!

Just send us your name and address and we will send you a catalog!